THE SAFETY NET

Translated by Stephen Sartarelli

ANDREA CAMILLERI

ISIS

LARGE
PRINT

First published in Great Britain 2020
by
Mantle
an imprint of Pan Macmillan

First Isis Edition
published 2020
by arrangement with
Pan Macmillan

Originally published in Italian as *La rete di protezione* by
Sellerio Editore, Palermo

ISBN 978–1–78541–922–5

Published by
Ulverscroft Limited
Anstey, Leicestershire

Set by Words & Graphics Ltd.
Anstey, Leicestershire
Printed and bound in Great Britain by
TJ Books Limited, Padstow, Cornwall

This book is printed on acid-free paper

CHAPTER
ONE

The alarm clock started ringing wildly.

Eyes still closed, Montalbano reached out towards the bedside table with one hand and, feeling around, tried to turn it off, worried that the noise would wake Livia, who was sleeping beside him.

But his fingers knocked into a glass that tipped over and then fell to the floor.

He cursed the saints. Then he immediately heard Livia giggle. He turned towards her.

"Did the alarm —?"

"No, I'd been awake for a while."

"Really? What were you doing?"

"What do you mean what was I doing? I was waiting for dawn and watching you."

Montalbano thought that the back of his head must constitute a rather boring landscape.

"Did you know that lately you sometimes whistle in your sleep?" asked Livia.

Upon hearing this revelation, Montalbano, for some reason, got irritated.

"How could I know that if I'm asleep? Anyway, be more specific. What do I whistle, pop songs, opera, or what?"

"Calm down! Are you offended or something? All right, to be more precise, you sometimes emit a kind of whistling sound."

"Through my nose?"

"I don't know."

"Next time, pay attention to whether I whistle through my nose or my mouth, and let me know."

"Why, does it make a difference?"

"Yes, it makes a huge difference. I remember reading something once about a man whose nose made a whistling sound and it later turned out to be a symptom of a deadly disease."

"Oh, come on! And, by the way, I had a bad dream."

"Want to tell me about it?"

"I'm sitting and reading on a veranda exactly like ours, except that it gives onto the quay in the harbour. At some point I hear this big commotion of voices, and I see a man crying for help and being chased by another man ordering him to stop. The man running away has a scarf around his head, a bandana, something tied under his chin. The man giving chase is wearing a large belt with a lot of sharp knives tucked into it. After a while the man being chased finds himself up against the side of a scow. He has a moment of hesitation, and the pursuer takes advantage of this to throw one of his knives, which strikes the man in the nape of the neck, plunges all the way through, and comes out the front of his throat, nailing him to the wood of the scow. Just horrible. So the pursuer stops and starts throwing more knives at the victim, tracing the outline of his body

2

against the boat. Then he suddenly turns and takes a step towards me. But luckily at that point I woke up."

"We sort of overdid it last night with the baby octopus!" was Montalbano's comment.

"And did you dream anything?" Livia asked.

At that moment the alarm went off. But how was that possible? It had rung just five minutes earlier!

Head still numb with sleep, the inspector opened his eyes and immediately realized he was in bed. There was no Livia. She was at home, in Boccadasse. He'd dreamt the whole thing, including Livia's dream.

He got up, went into the kitchen, prepared his customary mug of coffee, then showered. Moments later, he was sitting on the veranda, smoking a cigarette while drinking his coffee. The day promised to be a fine one. Everything looked freshly painted, so bright were the colours.

He had no desire whatsoever to go into Vigàta, or into what at least had been Vigàta until a few days ago. Because in fact the town had put on a completely different face. It had been, well, thrown back in time, turned into the Vigàta of the 1950s.

This irked Montalbano no end, because it all seemed so fake, as if he was attending a masked ball at the carnival.

The whole business had begun some four or five months earlier, when Tele Vigàta invited its viewers to search their homes for old Super 8 movies, which had been so popular around the middle of the previous century, and to send whatever they found to the studio offices. The television station would later integrate them into a programme, a kind of "The Way We Were", about what the town was like in the 1950s.

For whatever reason, the initiative was a resounding success. Perhaps because the whole thing had become a kind of game for the townsfolk, who were having a ball seeing how time had transformed them or their children from toddlers who looked like beautiful little angels just descended from heaven into toothless, hairless, sickly OAPs, and women who'd once been the light of the town into grannies good mostly for knitting socks.

Then they discovered that all this to-do actually had a specific purpose: all the material gathered was to serve as a visual aid for a production crew that was coming to town to film what is commonly known as a TV movie.

Without fail, a short while later the crew's technicians arrived, half of them Swedish, half of them Italian.

Now the strange thing about all this was that the group of Swedish technicians included some breathtaking stunners, who did a variety of jobs: as assistant set designers, sound technicians, stagehands, and so on . . . Which left the townsfolk a bit flabbergasted to see such beautiful women having to work, and wondering what the actresses would look like when they finally arrived.

And indeed, when they actually did arrive, work in Vigàta came to a standstill.

With the flimsiest of excuses, people dropped whatever they were doing and ran to the movie set. Things got so bad that law enforcement was asked to

4

keep the rubber-neckers away. And law enforcement, in this case, naturally took the form of one Mimì Augello, who had been put in charge of the officers protecting the film crew, with special attention given to the actresses.

This, in short, reduced the staff at the station basically to three people: the inspector, Fazio, and Catarella. Luckily it was a period of calm and nothing was happening. The Vigàta townscape had changed. Gone were the TV antennas, the rubbish bins, the neon signs. And there was nothing remaining of the shops Montalbano knew so well.

The inspector had had someone tell him the plot of the TV movie. The story was set, naturally, in the 1950s and involved a Swedish girl working as a boatswain on a steamship from Kalmar who falls seriously ill during the voyage and is admitted to the hospital in Montelusa.

Once she recovers her health she goes to Vigàta, to be near the harbour, and is taken in by a fisherman while she waits for her ship to return.

Due to a series of setbacks her ship is delayed, and in the meantime the Swedish girl falls in love with a youth from Vigàta and creates a life for herself in town, while nevertheless maintaining, deep in her heart, a secret hope that her ship will come back for her one day.

And she keeps nourishing this hope even after she marries and has a child.

Finally the day comes when the ship returns to harbour, and the young woman decides to board in secret, unbeknownst to her family. She arranges for a sailor to take her to the ship in his boat, but at the last moment changes her mind and turns back, to her home in Vigàta.

When Montalbano heard this story, it sounded to him like a plagiarism of a beautiful story by Pirandello entitled "Far Away", in which the main character is not a girl boatswain but a Swedish sailor named Lars.

But he didn't say anything to anyone.

As he was drinking his second coffee on the veranda, the phone rang. He went to answer. It was Ingrid.

His Swedish friend had, for the occasion, become the official translator for the film crew.

"Hello, Salvo."

"What is it?"

Ingrid didn't appreciate the inspector's blunt greeting. "Are you angry?"

"I think the proper word would be 'irritated'."

"I'm sorry for you. Don't forget that you have to come to the town-twinning ceremony between Vigàta and Kalmar tonight. It's at eight o'clock sharp at the town hall."

"Thanks for the reminder. I'm well aware that my presence is required."

"All right, then. See you later."

Well, wouldn't you know that they would take advantage of the ongoing circus to make the two towns twins!

He heard his front door open and then close again. "Adelina! I'm still here!"

"*Matre santissima!* Wha'ss wrong, Isspector? You no feeling so good?" asked Adelina, who'd come running.

6

"No, no, I feel fine. Not a trace of fever, unfortunately. I wanted to ask you if my good suit has been ironed."

"Which one, sir? The rilly dark one that looks like a black seagull?"

"Yeah, that's the one."

"Iss ready."

"OK, thanks. And you needn't cook anything for me this evening. I'll be eating our."

He pulled up outside the station but couldn't go in because a truck was stopped right in front of the entrance. He could see Catarella waving his arms to get the driver to move it. But the driver, who was Swedish, pretended not to understand, all that vaunted Nordic civility be damned.

Montalbano likewise pretended nothing was happening, got out of his car, and headed straight for the Caffè Castiglione, which hadn't changed a bit since its foundation in 1890, where he ate a cannolo just to sweeten his morning. By the time he got back to the station, the truck was gone.

"Any news?" he asked Catarella upon entering.

"Da nooz is cummin 'ard an' fass, Chief! 'Ere was a truck parked ousside 'ere till jess a coupla minnits ago, an' 'ey wannit a change the sign 'at says Vigàta Police t' say Dance Hall."

Montalbano said nothing and headed for his office, with Catarella following behind.

"Chief, ya know I tink I know why 'ere's no more fights or killin's or rabberies in town."

"And why's that?"

"Cuz in my 'pinion e'en the crooks've stopped crookin' cuz 'ey're all busy watchin' the crew shootin' the film in town. E'en a big-time dealer like Toto Savatteri, I seen 'im all slicked up an' fancy, drivin' a carritch onna set."

The carriage was probably stuffed full of drugs, thought Montalbano, but he didn't want to burst Catarella's bubble.

After lounging around the office for three hours, the inspector decided it was time to eat.

The film crew had naturally also invaded Enzo's trattoria, and what irked Montalbano most was the tremendous, deafening chaos the combination of Swedes and Italians managed to make while eating. Which was intolerable to him, as silence was normally the condiment to his meals.

And so he made a deal with Enzo that his table should always be set in the little room adjacent to the main room. There were few other tables there, and Montalbano made him promise that nobody from the crews, either Italian or Swedish, would be allowed, for any reason, to set foot in that room.

Despite all the bother, his appetite luckily wasn't lacking, and he ate very well: antipasti, spaghetti with fresh tuna sauce, and a platter of mullet. After which he went back outside.

Luckily there was no sign of any filming activity on the jetty. And so he was able to have a pleasant stroll, tranquil and undisturbed. And quiet, above all. Sitting down on the flat rock, he realized that, if things continued along their present course, the best solution might be to take a few days' holiday and see Livia in Boccadasse.

The idea that he would have to meet strangers that evening, and even put on a good face and make conversation with people he found utterly insufferable, made him feel so agitated that he made a sudden decision.

When he got back to the station, he summoned Fazio. "Listen, I'm going home. If you should need me for anything, just call."

Once he got home he decided that the best thing to do would be to lie down for a bit, and so he undressed and lay in bed, hoping to doze for half an hour or so.

When he woke up, to his great surprise it was gone seven. And so he dashed into the bathroom, changed his shirt, took the good suit out of the wardrobe, put it on, added a tie, and looked at himself in the mirror.

Adelina was absolutely right. He looked just like a black seagull.

The town hall was a sea of lights. A number of burning torches had been placed across the facade, and two floodlights lit up the entire building. The Italian and Swedish flags were flying side by side on the balcony. The assembly celebrating the twinning of Vigàta with Kalmar would be held in the council chamber.

9

Meanwhile, the guests waited in the great hall, where the tables that would serve the buffet after the ceremony were already laid out with white tablecloths.

Montalbano got there a little late, and by that time the hall was already full of people. As soon as she saw him come in, Ingrid rushed up to him and, taking his arm, led him to a giant about six foot six, a sort of blond bear — if any had ever existed — who was introduced to him as the director of the TV movie.

Ingrid then immediately presented him to two of the three Swedish actresses, adding that the third had suffered a slight indisposition and would therefore not be attending the ceremony.

It took him one look round to ascertain that Mimi Augello wasn't present, either. Which was very odd. Might he be suffering from the same indisposition as the Swedish actress?

Then some people started saying that the guests should move into the council chamber and take their assigned places. And that was how Montalbano found himself sitting in the front row between the parish priest and the commander of the port authorities. Also in the front row was a carabinieri lieutenant, but he'd been diplomatically seated four places down from the inspector.

The wall behind the high-backed chairs of the mayor and his council was entirely covered with a large nineteenth-century tapestry depicting Vigàta and its harbour.

After a while, from the hall came the sound of a sort of light waltz that nobody had ever heard before. The mayor of Vigàta, Mr Pillitteri, gestured for everyone to stand, and they all obeyed. After the waltz ended, they were all about to sit back down when the national anthem began, and everyone rose again. As they were finally settling in, however, everyone noticed that the four Swedes present were still standing.

"Why are they still on their feet?" Pillitteri asked Ingrid.

Ingrid asked one of the men in her native language, the man answered, and she translated:

"He says they're waiting for the Swedish national anthem."

"But that's what we played first!" exclaimed Pillitteri.

Apparently the Vigàta municipal band had given such a personal interpretation to the anthem that the Swedes hadn't recognized it.

After the misunderstanding was cleared up, Pillitteri had his Swedish counterpart from Kalmar, a sixtyish man with glasses and sandy hair, sit down beside him. The other three Swedish representatives were sitting in places off to the side normally reserved for councillors.

The audience, however, was in its proper place. Pillitteri quickly ceded the floor to his Swedish counterpart, who was translated by Ingrid and immediately launched into the complete history of his town. Which everyone, moreover, already knew, since for the past week the two local TV stations had been doing nothing but telling the story of their new twin town, which looked out on the Baltic Sea.

The mere mention of the Baltic Sea got Montalbano's brain whirring. Were there mullet in the Baltic Sea? Were there *purpiteddri*, baby octopuses like the kind Enzo fed him, in the Baltic Sea? And, if so, what did they taste like? Surely they must have a different flavour, since he'd already noticed, for example, that the fish from the Adriatic Sea tasted slightly different from the fish in the Tyrrhenian. So one could only imagine the difference of flavour in a fish from so far north as Kalmar.

The peal of applause brought him back to reality. Luckily for everyone, the mayor of Vigàta spoke little, but in fact his speech was cut even shorter by an unexpected incident. Namely, the large tapestry hanging behind him suddenly came detached from the wall and folded over itself halfway, exposing the upper part of a fresco depicting Benito Mussolini astride a white horse, sabre drawn. The mayor trailed off, a few people started laughing, a few others applauded, and a few more got angry, because Pillitteri wrapped things up in a hurry and then invited everyone to go over to the buffet, which, he pointed out with a certain pride, consisted entirely of what he called, in heavily accented English, *finghirfud*.

Indeed the mayor's wife, Ersilia Pillitteri, a smart woman with progressive ideas, had decided to send for some Palermo caterers specializing in *finghirfud*: naturally, little titbits one could only eat with one's fingers. In fact, one saw neither hide nor hair of spoons or forks or knives on any of the serving tables. What there were instead were a great many little tubs and glasses full of coloured stuff not easily identified, and for this reason the puzzled Vigatese were loath to reach out and grab any *finghirfud*. The mayor's wife decided to set the example. Picking up a transparent glass, she explained that it contained a mousse of *baccalà* topped with myrtle berries and a bay leaf; and, using the leaf as a spoon, she started eating it. A few brave souls followed her example. Montalbano took one of the little tubs and studied it carefully. At first glance it seemed to contain a meatball with something white beside it, which could have passed for purée. Unconvinced, he picked up the little meatball with two fingers and bit into it. It wasn't meat, as he'd thought, but a sort of mishmash of raw broccoli and overcooked green beans pressed around a core of salmon, in an apparent tribute to the Swedish. He felt like spitting it back out, but this seemed unbecoming to him, and so he closed his eyes and swallowed. To get rid of the nasty taste in his mouth, he stuck two fingers into the whitish goo, but this proved even worse, as the goo turned out to be a sort of *stracchino* cheese gone bad, with a sickly sweet flavour of coconut.

Putting the little tub down, he realized there weren't any more paper napkins to clean his hands with. Cursing the saints, he pulled his handkerchief out of his pocket, staining his jacket, naturally, in the process, and, deciding he'd done his duty, he turned his back on the distinguished guests and headed for the door, determined to eat at Enzo's.

"Inspector Montalbano!"

He stopped, turned around, and saw coming towards him a man a few years over sixty, tall and well dressed. It was the town council's chief engineer, Ernesto Sabatello.

"Were you about to leave?"

"Yes."

"If you don't mind, I'll come with you."

As they started down the stairs, Sabatello opened the conversation.

"You know, I had promised myself I would pay a call on you at the station one of these days, but then . . ."

"Did you change your mind?"

"Not at all. It just didn't seem appropriate to me. Bothering you over an entirely personal matter, and a rather silly one at that . . ."

They were now outside the town hall.

"You could give me a few hints right now, if you like . . ." the inspector invited him.

Sabatello didn't wait to be asked twice.

"I'll steal just a few minutes of your time, and then, if you find the matter of interest to you . . . Anyway, I have to confess that, like everyone else, I let myself get caught up in the search for old Super 8 movies for Tele Vigàta. I remembered that we had a big chest in the attic full of home movies, all filmed by my father, who must have been a maniac . . . Luckily the projector was also in the chest, and it still works. Anyway, in short, I looked at all of them and sent the best ones to Tele Vigàta. On the other hand . . ."

"On the other hand?"

"As I said, I'm sure it's just something silly and of no importance whatsoever, but I still can't explain it, because it seems so crazy, so illogical . . ."

"Want to tell me what you're talking about?" asked Montalbano, who was beginning to lose patience.

"Well, among all those reels, which showed all the usual family doings — birthday parties, vacations by the sea, a variety of different landscapes — there were six that were . . . I don't quite know how to put it . . . that were entirely anomalous."

"What do you mean?"

"Well, they all showed the same scene."

Montalbano didn't find anything so unusual about this, and he said so to Sabatello.

"If the same scene is shot repeatedly from different angles, I really don't see what —"

"Wait," Sabatello cut him off. "The image is still, and is always shot from the same angle. On top of that — and this is perhaps the strangest part of it all — the six home movies were shot over the course of six years, from 1958 to 1963."

"How do you know that?"

"Every reel is wrapped in paper with the date in my father's handwriting. For six years in a row he made those films in the same month of the year, the same day, and at the same hour: on the twenty-seventh of March, at ten twenty-five in the morning."

"But what's on the screen? What did he film?"

Sabatello took a breath before answering. "Part of a wall. Always the same one."

Montalbano looked puzzled.

"Part of a wall?"

"That's right."

"But is there anything on that wall?"

"No, nothing. No writing, drawing, or anything else."

"And does the appearance of the wall change over the years?"

"Well, I suppose a few more cracks begin to appear in the plaster, but nothing more . . . at least as far as I can tell. Perhaps a fresh look with your eyes, which are trained to grasp every tiny detail . . ."

The inspector realized what the engineer was getting at. "If you like, you can lend me the films and the projector."

"I'll get everything to you by tomorrow morning," the engineer said, smiling.

They shook hands, and Montalbano dashed off to Enzo's, hoping that the film crew hadn't gobbled up the whole trattoria.

CHAPTER
TWO

He had an awful night, because, despite the fact that he'd eaten at Enzo's, the nasty taste of the fake meatball and the equally fake purée had stuck to his palate, forcing him to get up cursing two or three times during the night to go to the bathroom and rinse out his mouth, without actually achieving any result.

He didn't manage to get rid of it until the following morning, by making himself some coffee so dense and viscous it looked like petroleum. When he got into his car to go to work he was in a dark mood, prompted by the thought that it was going to be another chaotic day under the sign of the TV carnival.

And indeed, as though on cue, he found himself behind a car transporter full of fifties-model vehicles, headed to Vigàta at a snail's pace.

"Ahh, Chief, inna mornin' 'iss mornin' some jinnelman by the name o' Stampatello come by witta dillivery f' yiz 'at I'm asposta dilliver t' yiz poissonally in poisson."

Catarella bent down, picked up a parcel a little bigger than a shoebox, and, turning back to the inspector, said: "Ya c'n go on, Chief, I'll follow up behine yiz witta packitch."

Once they were inside his office, Catarella set it delicately down in the middle of the desk, saluted, and went back to his post.

Montalbano sat down and opened the package. It contained the six reels that Sabatello had mentioned, and the appropriate projector. There was also a letter addressed to him.

Dear Inspector Montalbano,

Thank you, first of all, for making yourself available.

I am sending herewith the materials I mentioned yesterday.

I am keen to inform you that the reel shot in 1963 was the only thing Papa filmed that year, because his illness had worsened considerably by then, forcing him to remain in bed most of the time. He died on 15 May of the same year, in the family villa, and therefore in order to film that last footage he had to summon all his remaining strength to get out of bed. This, in my opinion, means that these little home movies were extremely important to him. But why? That is where I hope you will be able to help me.

I remain at your disposal for any further information you may need.

I include here my mobile phone number. With best wishes,

Ernesto Sabatello

It was the phrase "the only thing Papa filmed that year" — the fact that a man on death's doorstep would make the effort to film a patch of wall — that really sparked Montalbano's curiosity. And, considering the fact that the situation at Vigàta Police was one of dead calm, he immediately decided he wanted to get to the bottom of this as quickly as possible.

He took the calendar off the wall — which featured a large photo of the full staff of Vigàta Police — rehung it from a free nail near the door, closed the window to make the room dark, then turned on the light and plugged in the projector's cable, which was equipped with a transformer.

A small white square appeared on the wall before him.

He picked up the first reel and immediately felt paralysed. From what side should he thread it? Through which sprockets was the film supposed to pass in order to be projected? Which button activated the projector?

No, this really wasn't his sort of thing.

To avoid wasting time, he called Catarella in for help. And in the twinkling of an eye the switchboard operator explained the whole arcanum, as well as the button for freezing the image.

Catarella left, and Montalbano started the projector. But at the first sound made by the film as it ran through the sprockets, he stopped the machine and sat there for a few minutes without moving.

Only God knew from what depths of his brain a scene from his childhood had surfaced in his mind, of his father projecting a Super 8 home movie in which the image of his mother appeared for only a second, from behind. It was the only image he had of her, and that was always the way she appeared, etched in his memory: from behind, with her long blonde hair swaying gently like wheat in the wind.

He got up, went to drink a glass of water, then sat down again. He closed his eyes as if to erase all prior imagery from his memory, then reopened them and restarted the projector. Sabatello was right. The patch of wall was framed so that one could not see the base or the top of the wall, and one saw nothing else for the three and a half minutes that the film lasted.

When the first reel was finished, he moved on to the second. It was identical to the first.

He went forward and back three or four times, sometimes stopping the frame to have a better look at a detail; then, looking at the two films again, one right after the other, he tried to commit to memory everything he saw.

There was no difference whatsoever between the two.

There was one new development in the third reel. Out of a crack in the plaster a few blades of stunted grass were now growing. They were already gone, however, in the reel that followed. It must have been a windy day, since the little plants all around were trembling. In the fifth film, what had been the crack had broadened so that a piece of plaster had fallen off, bringing to light the blocks of tufa stone that lay underneath. The final reel, the one from '63, was exactly the same as the one before it.

20

Montalbano turned the projector off, went over to open the window, lit a cigarette, and smoked it with his elbows resting on the windowsill.

If the previous evening Sabatello's words had merely aroused his curiosity, viewing the images had turned his curiosity into a pressing need to understand. At the same time, as he became aware of this need, he became convinced he would never be in any position to give any logical, concrete answer to either himself or Engineer Sabatello.

Because a story like that actually touched a very specific point of the inspector's character, which, though it might be drawn to certain juridical questions, was also, and perhaps above all, attracted to the intricate muddle that is a man's soul.

Sitting back down, he called Fazio in and told him the whole story.

Fazio sat down beside him, and Montalbano set the projector running again. When they'd finished, Fazio turned around and gave him a confused, questioning look, but said nothing.

By way of reply, Montalbano handed him Sabatello's letter.

"What do you think?" he then asked.

Poor Fazio could only shrug.

"Listen, Chief, the first thing I ask myself is whether or not this gentleman was all there in the head."

"That I can't tell you, but I believe he was fully conscious. Otherwise in his condition he would never have got out of bed."

"Another hypothesis," Fazio ventured blindly, "could be that there was something hidden inside that wall, and that these home movies bear witness to the fact that nobody has touched that patch of wall."

"Then in that case," said Montalbano, "I have to assume that the home movie was made not only for the man who shot it, but was also supposed to be seen by someone else. You know what I say? Before casting ourselves out on the open sea of hypotheses, which'll take us who knows where, I need Sabatello to tell me a few things."

"Whatever you say, Chief," said Fazio.

The office door then crashed open and into the wall, sending the poorly hung calendar with the police-force photo to the floor. In the doorway Catarella, naturally, apologized, saying his hand had slipped.

Then he announced that Mrs Sciosciostrom was there with two gentlemen and wanted to speak poissonally in poisson with the inspector.

"Show them in."

After re-hanging the calendar from the nail, Catarella vanished, and in his place Ingrid appeared, followed by the blond bear — the TV movie's director — and by one of the four Swedes Montalbano had seen during the twin-towns ceremony.

Ingrid introduced him as the representative producer of the film on the Swedish side. Montalbano did something of a double take, as he'd noticed that the bear actually seemed to be dancing like a bear, balancing his body weight first on one foot, then on the

22

other, all the while gnashing his teeth. He seemed quite angry.

"We'd like to speak to you alone," said Ingrid.

"Excuse me," said Fazio, and he got up and left the room, closing the door behind him.

"Please sit down," the inspector said to his visitors.

Ingrid spoke first. She was wearing a very serious face, but Montalbano, who knew her well, noticed a little twinkle of amusement in her eyes.

"It's a rather delicate matter, Salvo. I don't know if you know what happened last night after the ceremony at the town hall."

"No, I don't know anything."

"The second half of the twin-towns ceremony had planned for a small bottle of water from the Baltic Sea from Kalmar to be poured into the sea at Vigàta. And so, with the two mayors leading the way, a procession formed and marched all the way to the harbour. When they got there the mayor of Kalmar handed the flask to the mayor of Vigàta, who uncorked it and poured it out from the central quay. At this point we all saw a motorboat come up, driven by Mimì Augello, with the actress Maj Andreasson on board as well, and that was when the fireworks started."

Hearing mention of that name, the blond bear sprang to his feet, not only gnashing his teeth harder than ever but accompanying the snarl with some guttural yells that sounded more like a roaring lion than a bellowing bear. The Swedish producer promptly stood up, grabbed him by one arm, and, speaking softly to him in one ear, made him sit down again.

Ingrid resumed speaking.

"You should know that this girl is the same actress who called in sick yesterday, as well as our director's companion. It was clear to everyone that the two were returning from a little boating escapade. Gustav, as you probably noticed, didn't take it too well. They began to quarrel in front of everyone, putting the future of the project at risk. So at that point Mr Ergstrom, the film's producer, begged me to talk to you and ask you to remove Augello from duty on the police escort service."

Montalbano sat there pensive for a moment.

"Is that a problem?" Ingrid asked.

"Well, yes," said the inspector. "First of all, what proof do you have that their little spin in the motorboat was any more than a little spin in a motorboat? I always proceed only on the basis of evidence. What evidence have you got? What do you mean when you say 'it was clear to everyone'? That was merely your impression, but I don't take disciplinary measures based on impressions."

Bewildered by his unexpected defence of Augello, Ingrid was momentarily unable to translate the inspector's words. But she was saved by the ringing of the telephone.

Montalbano picked up the receiver. It was Mimi Augello.

"Salvo. Are you alone?"

"No."

"Can you talk?"

"No."

"Then I'll do all the talking."

"Yes."

"Do you know what happened last night?"

"Yes."

"I'm very sorry, but I can't leave the house, because Beba, who found out, scratched and battered my face."

"Yes."

"Look, if I don't find a way out of this business, Beba swore she's going to leave me."

"Yes."

"So do me a favour. Assign someone else to do the job."

"Yes," said Montalbano, and then he hung up. "Excuse the interruption," he said to those present. "Further militating against fulfilling the gentleman's courteous request is the fact that my second-in-command, Domenico Augello, wasn't even on duty at that hour, and therefore I cannot intervene in any way. These factors and my reservations notwithstanding, you can inform the Swedish producer that in homage to the fraternal spirit born of the brand-new twinning of our two towns, I am willing to grant his request and shall therefore relieve Inspector Augello of his duties."

Looking ever more bewildered, Ingrid managed to say two letters to the Swede.

"OK."

Leaping powerfully up, the blond bear flew through the air and landed beside Montalbano, who, in utter terror, shot to his feet, ending up straight in the bear's arms, whose stifling embrace was meant to express his gratitude.

Freeing himself from the bear hug, which he was afraid might leave him mauled, Montalbano held out his hand to the Swedish producer, gave Ingrid a kiss and a hug, and at last found himself alone in his office.

Fazio came in at once.

"Did you know what happened last night at the harbour?"

"The whole town knows, Chief. You're the only one who didn't. What did they want?"

"For me to get Mimì out of their hair."

"And what did you say?"

"I was about to refuse, but then Mimì called and asked to be taken off the assignment."

Fazio smiled. "I guess Beba got a little heavy-handed."

Montalbano stared at him.

"Why, have there been other times when Beba . . .?"

"Chief, a couple of years ago Beba decided to take a different approach with her husband. Last summer, when you were up north in Boccadasse, Inspector Augello had to be rushed to the hospital after taking a heavy glass ashtray in the middle of the forehead."

In his mind, Montalbano tipped his hat to Beba.

"So, do we want to talk about these home movies?" he then asked.

"At your service," Fazio said resignedly, sitting down opposite the inspector's desk.

"Considering that we should be going to have a look at that villa, what do you say we start trying to work out what kind of wall that is? Is it an outer wall? A wall of the house? A boundary wall? A dividing wall? You

26

conjectured that maybe there was something hidden inside that wall. But what if there was nothing at all?"

"Then what need would there be for . . . ?"

"Let me finish. If that patch of wall was really what he was trying to commit to memory every year, then why always on the same day and at the same hour?"

"But what's there to remember about a patch of wall?"

"Nothing, for you and for me, but for the man filming, that patch of wall might represent, I don't know, a place of the soul, of memory . . ."

"Could you explain a little better?"

"It's a symbol, a bit like when two young lovers carve their initials into a tree and then go back to look at them later."

Fazio remained doubtful.

"Not convinced?"

"Not really."

"Tell me why."

"I don't know. I'm sorry, Chief, but you said, before the Swedes got here, that it was best to meet Sabatello before venturing any hypotheses. Why did you change your mind?"

"You're right . . ."

"Meanwhile something occurred to me," Fazio continued. "If, as it seems, you intend to look at that bit of wall over and over, wouldn't it be better if I had all those short films copied onto a single DVD, in the order in which they were made? If I take them now, you'll have a disc ready by this afternoon."

"OK, you can take everything with you. And ask them to make at least three copies."

He pulled up outside Enzo's, and as he was about to go in, he had a moment of hesitation. In order to reach the little room with his personal table, he had to cross the big dining room full of noisy customers. What if he ran into the blond bear again? And the bear wanted to display his gratitude anew by forcing him to sit down at his table?

He ducked his head carefully inside the doorway and looked around. The blond bear wasn't there. So he decided to go in, greeting everyone with his arm raised, and then slipped into the little room.

He had the unpleasant surprise of finding all the tables taken, and so he stopped in the doorway. Enzo came running up.

"Inspector, you have to forgive me, but it was getting late and I had to seat all the new arrivals. But I left you a place at the table of Ragioniere Butera, who's a man of few words."

The ragioniere was a regular client nearly ninety years old, thin as a rake, and known as the living memory of the town and its inhabitants, having worked for many years at the town hall.

Montalbano approached the table.

"May I?"

"Mmm-hmm," he said.

Montalbano sat down.

The silence between the inspector and his table companion lasted until Enzo came to take their orders.

Then, just to be polite, and because something had occurred to him, Montalbano opened his mouth, violating the strict law of silence surrounding his meals.

"I beg your pardon, Ragioniere, but this afternoon I need to inspect the area where the old Sabatello villa used to be. Do you by any chance know where that is?"

"Of course," said Butera. But then he fell silent. Apparently to get the full response from the ragioniere you had to use computer logic, asking one specific question after another until you received the complete response.

"Could you tell me where it is?"

"Yes," he said, then paused.

Montalbano became worried that he'd formulated the question poorly, and so perhaps the computer might not reply. Luckily, however, Butera continued.

"It's in the Granata district," he said, then reverted to pause mode.

At this point Montalbano gave up, except that at that exact moment Enzo arrived, serving the inspector a plate of spaghetti with a sea-urchin sauce, and a broth of fish and angel-hair pasta to the ragioniere. And, for some mysterious, unknowable reason, Butera started speaking the moment he brought the first spoonful to his lips. He had a youthful voice that contrasted with his elderly appearance.

"But all that's left of the Sabatello house are some ruins. It was once a beautiful villa, with two storeys and a tall turret from which you could see the sea. But it's been more or less abandoned for at least fifty years. Ever since Engineer Ernesto's father, Francesco, passed away from a tumour at a young age. After that Mrs Sabatello, left alone with her son, moved in with her parents in Palermo. Ernesto studied there, got a degree in engineering, and then immediately left to work in Argentina, where he stayed for about ten years. In the meanwhile, the uninhabited villa, with no one to look after it, was left to its inexorable decline."

He stopped eating and speaking at the same moment. He resumed some ten minutes later, when he found a plate with steamed sole dressed in olive oil and lemon before him.

"Did you want to ask me anything else?"

"But didn't Francesco Sabatello have any brothers or sisters or other relatives who could have looked after the —"

"He had a twin brother, Emanuele, who'd had an unfortunate birth."

"In what sense?" asked Montalbano.

"In the sense that he couldn't speak, never went out, never communicated with other people. He was incapable of doing anything on his own. At the time there wasn't even a name for this sort of autism; nowadays, no matter how severe, it can usually be treated with excellent results. But back then these kinds of people were normally kept isolated. Francesco was bound to him not so much as to a twin brother but as a sort of protective, loving father. He always took him everywhere with him, and paid no mind to the difficulties. Among other things, Emanuele didn't understand others when they spoke to him; he only understood the things his brother said to him."

"So, what did he do, in the end?" asked Montalbano.

"The poor man! He killed himself."

"After his brother died?" Montalbano asked again.

"No, before," said Butera, finishing his sole and no longer opening his mouth. Except, in the end, to get up, say goodbye to the inspector with a slight nod of the head, and go out.

When Montalbano likewise left the trattoria and got into his car, before starting it, he paused for a moment to reflect. Then he said to himself: "Why not?"

And he pulled out his mobile phone. "Cat, do you know where Granata is?"

"I tink iss in Spain, Chief."

"Listen, do me a favour and get me Fazio."

After Fazio explained where the district was, the inspector started the car and drove off.

After crawling for a long time up a cattle track that was all ridges and potholes, he found himself on top of a small hill, from which, as Butera had said, he could see the remains of the villa below. He stopped and got out. He immediately recognized the Sabatello property at the foot of the hill, the ruins of a large house with a turret rising above the rest. The building had lost half of its roof, and all the window frames were gone. There must once have been a large park all around, as one could still glimpse some rubble from a former boundary wall amid the now wild vegetation. The landscape had become desolate.

When he'd first come to Vigàta, he made a point of knowing the whole area in which he would have to work, and for that reason he'd spent a good deal of time driving around in reconnaissance. The countryside now before his eyes had once been fertile, green, and full of life, because it was respected and cared for by man. It had now become practically a desert, the domain of snakes and yellow grass incapable of sprouting flowers. The land looked as if it had been touched by a biblical curse condemning it to sterility, and the houses, run-down as they were, seemed to have suffered the same fate.

CHAPTER
THREE

He got back in the car and drove downhill until he arrived in front of a big iron gate, one half dangling dangerously forward and held in place by a single hinge, the other completely hidden behind a cluster of climbing plants.

He got out of the car and took a step through the gate. From there he studied the villa's facade. The wall had almost no plaster left on it. The skeleton of a balcony, only the iron framework of which remained, looked like a toothless mouth. And the windows looked like blind eyes.

It made his heart ache. A sudden wave of melancholy swept over him. He would never manage to approach that ruin alone. He felt the same sense of uneasiness that always came over him when he found himself near a dying person.

He turned away from the villa, got back in his car, and returned to Vigàta.

"Did you manage to find the Granata district?" Fazio asked, coming into his office.

"No, I didn't go. I decided to take my usual walk along the jetty instead."

He'd been about to tell him the truth, but then he'd felt instinctively ashamed of it. Fazio put the box with the film reels down on the desk, then took an envelope out of his jacket pocket and handed it to the inspector.

"The DVDs are in there. I had three made. The reels were copied in the order in which they were shot."

Montalbano opened the envelope, took out one of the discs, and put it in his pocket.

"I'll have a look at this at home."

"There's also a DVD player in Inspector Augello's office," Fazio added.

"That's good to know," said Montalbano, putting the envelope in a drawer.

Only then did Fazio sit down. He was looking at Montalbano a bit awkwardly.

"What's wrong?"

"I did something on my own initiative. Sorry."

"Meaning?"

"Well, since you seemed pretty caught up in this affair . . . on my way here I ran into an old friend of my father's, Peppi Cannizzaro, who's a master builder. I thought he'd probably know a little more about walls than we do, and so . . . ."

"And so?"

"So I mentioned the mystery to him, and I asked him if he could give us a hand . . . He's in the waiting room right now, in fact."

The inspector didn't hesitate for a second.

"Well done, Fazio. Let's all go into Augello's office."

Cannizzaro was tall and fat, with a likeable face. He must have been a little over sixty years old, but he wore it well.

He watched the DVD in silence, and when it was over he said:

"Could I see that again?"

After the second viewing, he gave his opinion.

"If you ask me, that's probably not a boundary wall."

"How can you say that?" asked Montalbano, his curiosity aroused.

"The *tistette* are too big for a little wall like that."

"What are *tistette*?"

"Blocks of tufa."

"Could it be a wall dividing one room from another?"

"No, sir, also because of the *tistette.*"

"So that leaves only the outer wall of a residential building."

Cannizzaro twisted up his mouth.

"You don't agree?"

"Maybe of a sorry little shack . . ."

"Can you explain a little better?"

"It's very sloppy work. You can tell from the way the plaster fell off. No, if you ask me, that's the outside wall of a building, but not a house; something more like a warehouse or a garage . . . But that's about all I can tell you."

Montalbano had an idea.

"If we went to the place itself, would you be willing to come along?"

35

"Sure, anything to help."

"How about tomorrow morning?"

"I've got all the time in the world. Just give me a ring."

Fazio and Montalbano took down his home phone number — Cannizzaro didn't own a mobile phone. Then they said goodbye, and the master builder left.

"If you wont be needing me any longer . . ." said Fazio.

"Sure, you can go."

Left to himself, the inspector thought things over for a moment, then turned on the DVD player.

The quality of the images was actually better in the digital copies than in the original films, and this was why, as he was watching them with the master builder, he thought he'd noticed a few new details.

After half an hour of careful study, he became convinced of three things.

The first was that at the time of day in which those films were shot — that is, at half-past ten in the morning — the sun was not shining on the wall.

The second was that in five of the six reels, a kind of brighter frame appeared in the right-central part of the image, rather like the effect of some indirect light. But what kind of light would be turned on at ten-thirty in the morning? On second thoughts, maybe it was reflected sunlight. In fact, the brighter square didn't appear in the film shot on the windy day, when the sky was probably overcast . . .

The third and last thing was the fact that the sixth reel, the one shot as the person filming was practically dying, displayed not the slightest tremor in the hand. The image was stable, with no jerks or sudden movements, just as in the five reels filmed before it. Could the hands of a dying man possibly be so steady? No. All six times, the camera was surely resting on a flat, solid surface.

He had an idea, and didn't waste any time.

He rang his friend Nicolò Zito, editorial director of the Free Channel.

"Sorry to bother you, Nicolò."

"What's going on? Was somebody killed?" the newsman asked hopefully.

"No."

"Damn. I'm getting really sick of talking only about this stupid TV movie they've been inflicting on us! What do you need?"

"Do you know anyone who knows anything about those old Super 8 movie cameras?"

"Do I ever! And he's right here. Our lighting director collects the things!"

"And he's there in your offices?"

"Of course."

"I'll be there in half an hour, max."

He put the DVD in his pocket, grabbed the box with the reels and the projector, and headed off for Montelusa.

"The news director is on the air at the moment, but he's almost finished. You can wait for him in his office," said the Free Channel secretary as soon as the inspector arrived.

Montalbano went into the office and flopped into an armchair. On the TV screen beside the desk, Zito's big face signed off to the viewers until the next edition of the news and then disappeared, and in its place appeared the face of a young woman announcing the start of a cooking programme.

"Well, you are a sight for sore eyes!" Nicolò greeted him. They embraced.

"Sciuto will be right with us," said the newsman, sitting down behind the desk. "Why are you so interested in Super 8s?"

The inspector was about to reply when Sciuto poked his head around the door. He and Montalbano had known each other for a while.

"Here I am!"

The inspector explained briefly what he wanted to know and handed him the box. Sciuto gave it a quick glance and said they needed to project the films.

"You can do it right here," said Zito.

Sciuto diligently watched all six, with the other two looking on. A bewildered Zito then began to ask: "What on earth —?" But Montalbano interrupted him.

"Please don't ask any questions or we'll be here till morning. I'll ask the questions, OK?"

"What do you want to know?" asked Sciuto. "In the meantime I can tell you that they were filmed with a Paillard Bolex dating from before 1956."

"And in fact," said Montalbano, "the first film was made in 1958. What I want to know now is whether those cameras had a zoom at the time."

"Not yet," said Sciuto. "Focal length was controlled directly through the lens and couldn't be altered during the filming."

"In your opinion, how far away was the person filming from the wall being filmed?"

"I'd say about fifteen feet at the most."

"Were they using a tripod?"

"No. The cameras were handheld, using a special strap right on the device."

"So they couldn't be set down on a flat surface?"

"Some models could, yes. This one certainly was."

"One final question," said Montalbano. "Did you notice that in five of the reels, there's a little square that appears, brighter than the rest of the frame, off to the right?"

"Yes."

"How do you explain that? Could it be a defect in the cine camera itself?"

"No, Inspector. I'm almost certain that's just reflected sunlight."

"Can I assume the cine camera in all six reels is resting on a windowsill?"

"That seems the most likely explanation," said Sciuto.

"Thank you," said Montalbano. "For me that's enough," he added, standing up and taking the parcel.

"Oh, no, you don't," said Zito. "You can't just leave me here without the slightest explanation of any of this."

"I swear I'll explain it all in full detail in due course," said Montalbano, cutting the conversation short and leaving the room, thinking all the while that it was quite possible there would never be any explanation at all.

He went back to the station, put the box in a small cabinet, and then sat down, took the letter Sabatello had sent him, and dialled his mobile-phone number.

"Montalbano here, Mr Sabatello. Sorry to bother you, but —"

"Have you found something out already?" Sabatello asked excitedly.

"Not yet. But I need to talk to you."

"I'm happy to oblige. Unfortunately, I'm in Palermo at the moment and have to be here for another two days. I'll give you a ring as soon as I get back to Vigàta, all right?"

They said goodbye, and Montalbano headed home.

The first thing he did when he got home was to look in the fridge. Adelina had prepared a platter of finger-licking swordfish *involtini*, and there was also a small frying pan containing a vegetable dish he loved: *tinnirume*, baby courgettes boiled with their leaves.

He put the *involtini* in the oven to warm, set the pan of *tinnirume* over a lighted burner, and then went out to the veranda to lay the table, because the evening deserved it.

During the entire meal he didn't allow a single thought to stray from the subject of the fragrant delicacy of the *tinnirume* and the intense flavour of the swordfish, which certainly hadn't come from the Baltic Sea.

40

As he was smoking an after-dinner cigarette, the telephone rang.

It was Livia. Who immediately told him in great detail how, when she went shopping at the supermarket, Selene, her dog, had disappeared for two hours, only to reappear with the most innocent of faces and holding a box of spaghetti in her mouth.

Montalbano laughed heartily, because, despite his own more catlike personality, he really liked Selene and was grateful to her for giving comfort to Livia.

Then it was his turn to explain that nothing whatsoever was happening at the station, but he felt embarrassed to reveal that he was spending hours on end staring at identical films of a patch of wall.

At this point Livia asked the most logical question. "Well, if you've got nothing to do down there, why don't you come and see me?"

She's right, thought Montalbano. *Why not go and see her?*

Here I can't even talk to Engineer Sabatello at the moment.

"You know what? I think that's an excellent idea," he said.

"Do you really mean that?" asked Livia, incredulous.

"I'm serious. Tomorrow morning I'll drop in at the station and reserve a flight to Genoa. I'll let you know what time I get in."

"Are you really sure?" Livia asked again.

"Absolutely."

They spoke for another five minutes, then said good night.

Montalbano went and got a small suitcase and put what he would need for a two-day stay in it. Then he decided it would be best if he changed his suit. He took out everything he had in his pockets and put it down on the dining table. Since it was still too early to go to bed, he watched a documentary on maize cultivation to make himself sleepy. The documentary did the job, and he got up, brushed his teeth, and went to bed.

He slept deeply all night long.

When he woke up, after his ritual shower and mug of espresso he put on his travelling suit and went to have a look at what he could take among the things he'd left on the table the previous evening. In his hand he found a piece of paper with a telephone number that meant nothing whatsoever to him. He read it and reread it, and then finally remembered that it belonged to the master builder, Cannizzaro. He put the piece of paper in his pocket, along with his wallet and a number of other scraps with notes on them, got into the car, and headed off for Vigàta.

"Any news?" he asked when passing Catarella.

"Nah, nuttin', Chief."

"Listen, Cat. This afternoon I'm leaving for Genoa for two days. If you or anyone else here needs me, you know where to find me."

"Yessir, Chief."

42

He went into his office, sat down, and immediately dialled the phone number of Palermo Airport Police to reserve a flight.

"Montalbano here."

"So, Inspector, what do you say? Shall we do this inspection?"

Montalbano hesitated. What did he say? What inspection was he talking about?

"Hello!" said the voice at the other end of the line. "When do you want me to come to the station, Inspector?"

At last he understood. He'd dialled — or rather, his finger, independently of his will, had dialled — the wrong number, ringing the home of Cannizzaro the master builder. And now what? Now he must surrender to fate. This meant the inspection had to be done that very day.

He would inevitably have to make up some lie for Livia. "All right," he said. "You can come in to the station now, if you like."

And he headed towards Fazio's office. It was empty. So he went into the hallway and shouted to Catarella: "Find me Fazio and send him to me immediately!" And he went back into his office.

"'E ain't onna premisses, Chief," Catarella replied, appearing suddenly before him as if by magic.

Montalbano froze. "Where'd he go?"

"To the sit, Chief."

The sit? A sit-in?

"Is this some kind of political protest, Cat?"

"Nah, nuttin' pillitical, Chief. Ain't 'at wha' they call the place where they film a film? The sit?"

"It's called the set, Cat. And what did he go there to do?"

"Ahh, Chief, Chief! Alls o' 'eaven 'n' 'ell broke loose!"

"Meaning?"

"Alls I know izzat 'ey tol' 'im it was a 'mergency."

The inspector went into his office and sat down. He rang Fazio on his mobile phone and had to wait a long time for him to answer.

"I'm sorry, Chief, but at the moment I really can't talk," said Fazio, immediately hanging up.

What the hell was going on? Montalbano called back. "But is it going to take a while?"

"Chief, I won't see any daylight for at least another hour."

There was a knock at the door. It was Catarella. "Chief, 'ere'd a happen a be a Mr Accanizzaro presently onna premisses waitin' f 'yiz."

"Where?"

"'Ere. Jess ousside the front door."

The inspector went out.

"You'll have to excuse me, Mr Cannizzaro, but I had you come all the way here for nothing. Unfortunately, I won't be able to do that inspection this morning. Could we postpone it till ten o'clock tomorrow morning?"

"All right," said Cannizzaro.

They shook hands, and the master builder left.

Montalbano's mind was elsewhere. He could get no rest over the mystery of what was happening on the sit, as Catarella called it. He decided to go and have a look for himself.

"Do you know where they're filming?" he asked Catarella.

"Sure, Chief. Ya remember where there useta be the Sicilian Discount Bank where Gallo's mutter's auntie woiked? Well, iss not azackly right there innat buildin', but behine the buildin', in front."

"Good God, stop right there," said Montalbano, getting more and more confused. "How long's it take to get there?"

"You c'n go afoot, Chief. Iss jest a five-minnit walk. Ya jess take the second toin onna right anna toid onna left."

Montalbano set off.

"Do you think you're cleverer than everyone else?"

"In all honesty, no," replied Montalbano, looking up. Before him stood a carabinieri corporal with a malevolent glint in his eye.

"Then turn back," said the corporal.

Montalbano weighed his options and came to the conclusion that it was best not to reveal who he was. And so he turned around and saw that, without realizing, he'd cut in front of a group of some thirty people being kept at bay by three carabinieri, who were preventing everyone from turning the corner.

As he re-joined the group, he heard, from rather close by, a great deal of commotion — a confusion of shouts, yells, commands, and sirens from ambulances and carabinieri patrol cars.

"What's happening, anyway?" he asked someone.

"Looks like war has broken out."

"War?"

"Between Sweden and Vigàta."

"Why? What happened?"

A second person intervened.

"Apparently as they were filming the scene of the first kiss between the Swedish heroine and the Vigatese fisherman she falls in love with, someone in the crowd watching started yelling, 'With tongues, with tongues!' But, since they were filming live, the director became furious, stood up, and went and grabbed the guy who'd started shouting. And then some men from Vigàta came to his defence, so the Swedes felt obliged to come to the director's defence, and the whole thing went downhill from there."

"That's not at all how it went," said a well-dressed man with glasses and a stern air.

"Then please tell me what happened," Montalbano invited him.

"It was all a misunderstanding. The person who called out was actually saying, 'In the same tongue!' — meaning that they should all be reciting their lines in the same language, because the way it was going nobody could understand anything, since the Swedish girl was speaking Swedish and the Vigàta boy was speaking Italian."

"The truth of the matter," said a third, "is that up until they made our towns twin towns, everything went fine between the Swedes and the Vigatese, but after the twinning, things changed — we started seeing the kind of hostility that's typical between siblings . . ."

Someone else then started yelling.

"It's all the fault of the euro! They're trying to mix chickpeas and broad beans, apples and oranges. What could we possibly have in common with the Finns?"

"Leave Europe alone," said the well-dressed gentleman. "You're just kids and you have no idea what a miracle it is to be able to think that there won't be any more wars between us and the French, or us and the Germans, or us and . . ."

As they were all talking, some dense black smoke that was having trouble rising into the air turned the corner and poured into the street. Some started coughing. Seeing that the conversation had degenerated into politics, Montalbano began to walk ever so slowly, one step at a time, back to the police station.

The first thing he did in his office was to call Livia, and as soon as he said, "I'm sorry," she simply retorted, "I was expecting it," and hung up.

Montalbano decided to kill some time signing a few of his hated documents. Fazio returned about an hour later, looking dishevelled, with his tie crooked and one of his jacket pockets torn and hanging.

"There was a flare-up, Chief. Our guys had almost managed to calm things down when the carabinieri unfortunately intervened, and one of them saw fit to slap some cuffs on someone from Vigàta. Which got everything going again, even worse than before. And you want to know something? When the Swedes get pissed off, they're even worse than us!"

"Yes, I know," said Montalbano, thinking of the blond bear. And he asked: "Were there any injuries?"

"Yeah, six or seven people, but pretty minor stuff."

"Any arrests?"

"The carabinieri took four people away. Two Vigatese and two Swedes — just to keep things even, if you ask me — but the fact of the matter is that the set was damaged, and so tomorrow's shoot has been postponed."

"Excellent! That way, tomorrow morning at ten we can go and visit the Sabatello villa. I've already informed Cannizzaro."

Fazio smiled.

"What are you thinking?" asked Montalbano.

Fazio didn't answer. He was happy to work with a man who still had the time to feel passionate about staring at a wall.

CHAPTER
FOUR

It was time to eat. Before entering the trattoria, he noticed he couldn't hear any loud voices inside. In fact, there was total silence, as if the place was empty. He poked his head in cautiously to have a look. And indeed, all the tables were unoccupied. He went in just as Enzo was coming out of the kitchen.

"What's going on?"

"They're all at the carabinieri station, Inspector, protesting that the four men who were arrested should be set free."

"I don't think the carabinieri change their minds so easily."

"Apparently the mayor went and talked to the lieutenant. If you'd like to take advantage of the situation and sit down in here . . ."

"Not on your life," said the inspector. "What if they clear the whole thing up in the next ten minutes and then all come rushing in here hungry as wolves? It's much safer in the little room."

In it was only Ragioniere Butera, who was just finishing a dish of pasta.

"Good afternoon," Montalbano greeted him, sitting down at the table opposite his.

"Good afternoon," said Butera. "Did you go and look at the ruins?" He was speaking while eating, with his mouth open, and one could see little bits of chewed-up spaghetti sticking to his tongue and palate, or wedged between his dentures.

"I haven't had time," said the inspector.

"I remembered something," said Butera.

But, having swallowed his last forkful of pasta, he did not continue. Silence descended. Then Enzo arrived, served the ragioniere some boiled cod, and took the inspector's order. With his first bite of fish, Butera resumed speaking.

"In '45, when I was already working at the town hall, I went with Surveyor Sabatello to look at the damage sustained during the war. We inspected the villa from top to bottom. And I realized something odd. Francesco's bedroom was adjacent to his poor brother Emanuele's room. Nothing unusual about that, of course. But Francesco, just to be sure he could watch over — indeed, protect — his brother even during his sleep, had had a sliding door installed in the wall between the two rooms."

"It's possible Emanuele had sleep disturbances and his brother wanted to make it easier to give him sedatives in the middle of the night," said Montalbano. Then, taking advantage of the fact that Butera had brought another forkful to his lips, he asked: "Were they well-off?"

"They certainly didn't have any problems in that regard."

"Couldn't they have hired a nurse to look after Emanuele day and night?"

"Of course they could have. But at the time that sort of thing wasn't done. And at any rate I'm absolutely certain that Francesco would never have entrusted the care of his brother to another person."

Now that Butera had also finished his cod, he broke off all verbal communication, got up, nodded vaguely by way of goodbye, and went out.

Montalbano sat down on the flat rock and lit a cigarette. Having overcome a minor bout of remorse for having so readily failed to deliver on his promise to Livia, he started thinking back on what Butera had told him. Francesco's ideal situation probably would have been for him to have Emanuele sleeping on a camp bed right there in the master bedroom, though it's possible his wife would have been against it. That was no longer brotherly love taken to an extreme, but a different, mysterious sort of bond. They were twins, and maybe Francesco felt a sort of echo, in his flesh and in his head, of Emanuele's suffering.

And there, beside him, was the crab. It stood motionless in the middle of the rock next to the inspector's, and seemed to be staring at the shard of rock in front of it.

He's doing what I've been doing with that damn patch of wall, thought Montalbano.

Trying to provoke it, he bent down, picked up a pebble, and aimed it to the side of the animal. But his aim was off and the pebble struck one of the crab's legs, sending it scampering off contortedly. Montalbano felt bad for it, thinking he might have seriously injured it.

The word "injure" set off a string of free associations in his mind. He thought of Mimì Augello's face, scratched by Beba's fingernails.

With an excuse like that, Mimì was liable not to show up at work for a good month.

I've got half a mind to go and pay a little call on him, he thought, *just to see how things really stand.*

Then it occurred to him that it might be better, at least out of respect for Beba, to forewarn them of the visit by telephone.

But he didn't have his mobile in his pocket. Oh, well.

He would just show up unannounced. Meanwhile the crab had reappeared. "I'm sorry," the inspector said to it. And he headed off to Mimì's.

It was Beba who came to the door. Montalbano hadn't seen her for a while, and noticed that her eyes looked tired. Still, she was well-groomed, made up, and in fine working order.

A big, sincere smile lit up her face.

"Salvo! What a lovely surprise! Come in, come in."

The inspector went in, and Beba closed the door behind him.

"Sorry I didn't call before coming, but —"

"Oh, nonsense! You're one of the family here. Mimì's taking a little nap. Let me go and wake him up."

"No, wait," Montalbano said impulsively.

Beba gave him a confused look.

"Has something happened between you and Livia?"

"No, of course not. Is this not a good time?"

"What are you talking about? I was just in the kitchen reading the newspaper."

"Then let's go into the kitchen. That way you can make me some coffee."

Beba kept her house and kitchen splendidly clean. The inspector sat down at the table.

"Where's Salvuzzo?" he asked.

"He just went out. To a friend's house, to do their homework together."

"He's a studious boy, is he?"

"Yes, and the teachers have a lot of good things to say about him."

The coffee was ready. Beba filled Montalbano's demitasse and then poured her own and sat down.

"Did you come to find out how things were between Mimì and me?" she asked with a half-smile.

"Not exactly, but if you want to talk about it . . ."

"Salvo, after just one year of married life, I was already convinced that Mimì was incorrigible. I could leave him, but I still love him and he loves me, too. In his own way, but he does love me. I've accepted the situation, but he just won't acknowledge any limits, and so lately I've been losing it . . ."

"You were right to scratch his face," said the inspector.

Beba looked at him wide-eyed in surprise.

"Is that what he told you?"

"He called in to say he couldn't come to work because his face was all —"

"The stupid bastard! I gave him the tiniest little scratch under his left eye, and he started making like it was the end of the world and I'd ruined his face! The poor peacock!"

She ran a hand over her eyes and sighed. "Sorry for the rant," she said.

Montalbano reached out with one hand and stroked her face.

"The worst thing of all," Beba resumed, "is that he's got meaner with age. He doesn't give a damn about anything at home. I have to take care of everything. Let me give you an example. It's over a week now since he was supposed to go and talk to the head teacher of Salvuzzo's school, and he keeps putting it off from day to day. And it'll end up the way it always does: I'll have to go myself!"

"Why do you need to talk to the head teacher? Are there any problems?"

"Yes, but nothing to do with his studies."

"Then what's it about?"

"In Salvuzzo's class there are a few nasty toughs who have ganged up on one of their classmates and are putting him through the grinder. This boy, whose name is Luigi Sciarabba and who according to Salvuzzo is a computer wizard, is utterly unable to defend himself."

"But aren't the teachers aware of it?"

"No, because this stuff all happens outside of class."

"So what's Salvuzzo got to do with any of this?"

"Well, about ten days ago, he couldn't take it any more and came to Sciarabba's defence. And as a result he came home with a torn shirt and a black eye."

54

"Keep me posted on this," said Montalbano.

"I'll go and wake him now," said Beba, getting up.

Montalbano stopped her a second time.

"No, don't bother." He stood up. "Don't even tell him I came by."

"All right."

"Tell him I phoned and that, scratched face or no, I want him in his office tomorrow, because I have to go and do an on-site investigation."

"Get me Fazio," said Montalbano upon entering.

"'E in't onna premisses, Chief."

"And where is he?"

"Dunno, Chief, 'cuz 'e never came back afta lunch."

This meant that, to make the time pass, the inspector had no choice but to do the usual thing: sign more of those hated papers. This time he really gave it his all, to the point that the stack went from a height of about six unabridged *Webster's* to that of a mere *Roget's Thesaurus*.

"May I?" Fazio asked from the doorway.

"Come on in," said Montalbano, instinctively looking at his watch. It was six.

Fazio sat down opposite the desk, but on the edge of his chair, as he did when he felt uneasy.

Montalbano realized this, and asked, with enquiring eyes: "So, where've you been?"

Before answering, Fazio squirmed a little in his chair and swallowed twice.

"You have to forgive me, Chief, but I took another one of my own initiatives. Since you've been so keen on knowing as much as possible about that bit of wall, I remembered that my father used to collect a weekly newspaper that was published in Vigàta called *Libertàs*, which was an organ of the old Christian Democratic Party. And so I went to the library and looked at all the issues from the last week in March for the years 1958 to 1963. But I didn't find anything on the Sabatello family."

"You were wrong," said Montalbano.

"Why?"

"Because if the first film is from 1958 and was made to commemorate something, then that something must have happened before that year."

"Oh, my God!" said Fazio. "You're right."

"So go back to the library."

Fazio shot out like a pebble from a catapult.

Montalbano resumed signing papers, this time with a certain sense of satisfaction.

The ink was just drying on the last goddamned memo when Fazio returned, out of breath.

"Chief! Did you know that Engineer Sabatello's father had a brother?"

"Yes, a twin brother. And so?"

"I found five lines in the newspaper, Chief."

He put one hand in his pocket, pulled out a scrap of paper, and read:

Last Wednesday, Emanuele Sabatello, twin brother
of the respected surveyor Francesco Sabatello,

died in tragic circumstances. Unwell from birth but always supported by his family's loving care, Emanuele left this life amidst the comfort of his loved ones. The entire editorial staff sends the family their most heartfelt condolences.

"I wonder what those 'tragic circumstances' were," said Fazio.

"He killed himself," replied Montalbano.

"Really? And do you know what the date was that Wednesday?"

"The twenty-seventh of March 1957," said Montalbano.

"It really is no fun talking to you," said Fazio, leaving in a huff.

Back at home, Adelina had left a homage to Sweden in the fridge: a plate of cold pasta with salmon and passuluna olives. A perfect twinning.

He ate on the veranda, smoked his usual cigarette, drank two fingers of whisky, and, steeling himself, dialled Livia's number. There was no answer. He waited five minutes and then called again. With the same result. So he set his mind at rest and sat himself down in front of the TV. He watched a movie full of shoot-outs, and when even the protagonist got killed, he realized the story had reached the end, and he turned off the set and went to bed.

But he did not fall asleep right away. He realized that, thanks to Fazio, they'd actually established a solid fact. On every twenty-seventh day of March, Francesco Sabatello commemorated his brother's suicide, which presumably occurred at half-past ten in the morning. But why film a patch of wall to etch that date in one's memory? Engineer Sabatello would certainly be no help in answering the question. He was too small at the time to understand what was going on, or to have anyone explain it to him.

Therefore the only thing to do was to stop thinking about the wall and go to sleep.

And, in so doing, he dreamt of the wall.

At three o'clock in the morning he woke up from a nightmare, all in a sweat. He'd been trying to climb a smooth wall, over and over, dozens of times, using his fingernails and the tips of his toes, but he never managed to reach the top, because halfway up he always started sliding back down to the bottom.

They got out of the car. Cannizzaro headed straight for the piece of boundary wall that still held the dilapidated gate in place. He had his mason's hammer with him, but there was no need for it. He bent down near a part of the wall completely stripped of plaster and called to the inspector.

"Have a look. The boundary wall is made of building stones, so it's not the one we see in the film."

They went through the gate. At that point began a broad path that led to the main door of the house, but halfway there it branched off, and the second path went on around to the back of the house.

Cannizzaro started walking towards the front of the villa, and this time, too, there was no need for his mason's hammer. He pointed to the blocks of cement that had become exposed.

"As you can see, this isn't the wall, either."

"Let's go and see what there is behind the house," Montalbano suggested.

Once they'd rounded the corner, the first thing they saw was a garage with a caved-in roof. Here, too, Cannizzaro showed the inspector that the walls were made of hollow bricks. All that remained behind the villa was a ruin that stood about twenty feet from the house. It must originally have been some kind of tool shed or storage facility, about ten feet square. Now all that was left was a side wall, the one furthest from the house.

But the perimeter of the structure remained visible on the ground.

Cannizzaro went straight to the surviving wall, bent down, looked at the blocks of tufa, and said: "Inspector, the wall in the films is the same as this one."

Montalbano looked at it closely, then said:

"Excuse me for just a second."

"Where you going?" asked Cannizzaro.

"I want to go into the villa."

"Be careful. It might be unsafe."

Montalbano turned the corner, then made another turn, entering the villa through the opening that had once been the grand main door. The first thing that struck him was a terrible stench of rot, despite the fact that air circulated freely in the space. He took out his handkerchief and held it close to his nose the whole time.

The house had been stripped of everything, including the floor tiles, leaving a surface of beaten earth. The place looked like a veritable dump: empty cans, condoms, bottles, syringes, turds, even dead rats. The walls, which must have once been covered with fine wallpaper, now looked like one of those posters by the artist Mimmo Rotella, who amused himself showing the passage of time through the practice of *décollage*: unpeeling city walls to unveil old advertisements and various announcements from times past. Part of the ceiling had collapsed, the beams exposed and full of holes, now home to swallows and pigeons. The stairs leading to the first floor were clearly rickety and dangerous, and what was left, in spots, of the cast-iron banister looked like fragments of abandoned bones of prehistoric animals.

Commending his soul to God, Montalbano headed up the staircase and had a look at all the rooms, one after the other. There must have been a variety of bedrooms, studies, small sitting rooms, libraries. Nothing out of the ordinary.

Butera certainly hadn't been lying.

There were two rooms, one big and one smaller, whose windows gave onto the back of the house, linked by a sort of rectangle that must once have been the small sliding door between Francesco's and Emanuele's bedrooms.

Next to the master bedroom was a bathroom. Montalbano went in.

He looked out of the window. The view led in a straight line to the storage shed, but the home movie couldn't have been made from there, because the angle would have been from above.

He decided there was no point — especially because it was too dangerous — in going all the way up to the turret.

He went back downstairs.

In addition to the salon there was a big kitchen recognizable only by all the soot everywhere. The whole place had been ransacked.

Towards the back was another large bedroom with a bathroom beside it, directly under the one upstairs.

He looked out of the window.

And he became absolutely certain that all the film reels had been shot from that exact spot, with the camera resting on the windowsill.

As he was looking, the shed, as if by magic, became whole again before his eyes, and he saw before him the very same stretch of wall he'd seen so many times in the home movies.

"Find anything?" asked Fazio, who was chatting with the master builder nearby.

"Yes," replied Montalbano, in the tone of someone not wanting to be asked any more questions.

As they were heading back down the main path towards the exit, before their stunned eyes the heavy cast-iron gate, which had been dangling there for years and years, decided to give up the ghost. That is, emitting an iron-like wail, it came off the one hinge holding it in place and crashed with all the weight in the world against the bonnet of Fazio's car, caving it in.

Cursing the saints, Fazio started running towards his car, followed by the other two.

He managed to get into the driver's seat and tried to start the car, but the engine didn't respond.

It became clear that they had a rather thorny predicament on their hands. The first thing they would have to do was to lift the gate off the car; and the second, to have a look at the damage it had done to the engine.

From their initial attempts it became immediately clear that the three men would never succeed in moving the gate, which turned out to be heavier than they thought.

After half an hour of vain efforts, they gave up.

"So what are we going to do?" asked the master builder.

Fazio didn't answer, managing only to look over at the inspector with the eyes of a beaten dog.

"Give Catarella a ring and tell him to send some people to lend us a hand," said Montalbano. "They should also bring a long, strong cable."

It took Gallo forty-five minutes — a record — to get there. He brought two uniformed officers with him. Cannizzaro took the situation in hand. He got them to attach one end of the cable to the uppermost part of the gate, and the other end to the trailer hitch on Gallo's car. Then, as the gate came slowly off, the others pushed Fazio's car from behind until it was completely liberated. Cannizzaro had to use his mason's hammer to prise open the bonnet, and it was immediately clear the engine had been severely damaged and was not in working condition. And so Montalbano decided that Gallo's car should tow Fazio's into town.

They all got into the two cars and started on their way back, but of course they had to proceed very slowly.

"At this rate it'll take us till morning," Montalbano said in a huff.

Turning then to Gallo, he asked:

"How long do you think it'll take us to get to Vigàta?"

"A good two hours at the very least," Gallo replied gloomily, being accustomed to driving his car as if he was on the track at Indianapolis.

All of a sudden, without warning, a wolflike hunger came over Montalbano. Maybe because he'd spent the whole morning out in the open air?

At last, as they were beginning to see the town's first outlying houses in the distance, Montalbano spotted, on the left, a pole bearing a sign that said: TRATTORIA BONOCORE 150 m.

Yes, he thought. *I can manage to hold out for another hundred and fifty metres.*

Ten minutes later they were passing in front of the trattoria.

"Stop here!" Montalbano yelled.

Gallo slammed on the brakes, and Fazio's car nearly crashed into his from behind.

"What's going on?" asked Gallo.

"What's going on," said Montalbano, "is that we're going to stop here, get out of the cars, and all go and eat. You're my guests."

And so their morning inspection ended in a feast.

CHAPTER
FIVE

It was late when they came out of the trattoria all feeling a little heavier, so that the journey back to the station looked a lot like a funeral procession. Fazio got them to drop him off at the garage where he usually took his car to be serviced. Montalbano took advantage of this to get out of the car himself and continue on foot, in the hopes of jump-starting his digestive process. When he was outside the Caffè Castiglione, he heard a woman's voice call his name. He stopped. It was Ingrid.

"Salvo! It's so nice to see you! Have you got five minutes? Come on, I'll buy you a coffee."

They went inside and sat down. Ingrid stroked his hand. "You have no idea how much I miss those evenings we used to spend together . . . but lately this job's been taking up all my time. I haven't got a minute free."

"How's the filming going?"

"You couldn't really say it's going too well."

"Why not?"

"Because the director won't forgive Maj."

"They haven't made up yet?"

"Are you kidding! He mistreats her right there on the set, makes her do a scene six, seven times over, until she starts crying or has a nervous breakdown and the shooting has to be stopped . . . The producers are very worried and upset. At this rate it's all going to take twice as long as expected."

Upon hearing these words, Montalbano felt his heart sink. That meant that the carnival was going to drag on longer than scheduled, and he wouldn't be able to stand it. He would go crazy, being forced to live for a minute longer than necessary in a Vigàta that was no longer his town, but a Vigàta invented by television. No, those people had to get the hell out of there as quickly as possible. Then he had an idea. It seemed brilliant to him.

He didn't want to waste any time.

"Think you can manage to come out to dinner with me tonight?"

Ingrid looked at him as though stunned by the sudden invitation.

"Maybe. But . . ."

"And would you be so kind as to bring the director along?"

Ingrid's expression grew even more astonished. "But what have you got in mind, anyway?"

"I want to try to reassure him that nothing happened between his Maj and Mimì."

"And how will you do that?"

"I've already got an inkling how. And I'll just improvise the rest. With your help, of course."

"OK," said Ingrid. "I'll call you later, at the office, to tell you whether I've managed to work something out or not."

Fazio straggled back in about half an hour after the inspector. He looked crestfallen.

"What did the mechanic say?"

"What with fixing the engine and the bodywork, those repairs are going to eat up two months' salary, Chief."

"Can't you request a reimbursement?"

"How will I justify it? I wasn't out on an investigation, but merely accompanying you while you looked into some personal business about a wall."

"You're right," said the inspector. "I hadn't thought of that."

"And so, as you see . . ."

"I'll pay for the damages myself," said Montalbano.

Fazio sprang to his feet, turning pale.

"You're insulting me, sir. If you think I came in here to ask you for —"

"It's you who's insulting me, Fazio," the inspector replied harshly, "by assuming that I was thinking of something that was the furthest thing from my mind. Now sit back down."

Fazio obeyed.

"You're a man with a good head on your shoulders. So use it, then. Did you go to that villa on your own initiative, or because I, your commanding officer, asked you to?"

"Because you asked me."

"Therefore it's my responsibility. There's nothing more to discuss."

Fazio sat there pensively for a moment, then said: "Could we do it so that you pay for the engine and I pay for the bodywork?"

"No. You know that when I say something, that's it."

"All right," said Fazio.

"Let's talk about something else. Tonight, at ten o'clock sharp, I want you to call me on my mobile phone."

"What for?"

"Just call and start saying the first nonsense that comes into your head. And pay no mind to what I say. I'm going to put on a little tragic performance."

"But you'll explain it all to me afterwards?"

"Promise," said Montalbano.

There was a knock. It was Mimì Augello. He had a minuscule plaster on his face.

"Welcome back," said the inspector. "Come in and sit down."

"Sorry, Fazio, but I'd like to speak alone with the —"

"No problem," said Fazio, going out and closing the door behind him.

"I wanted to tell you about that damned boat ride."

"Mimì, I don't give a fuck what you did with the Swedish girl on that boat. You were not on duty, and she's a legal adult . . ."

"Nothing happened between Maj and me," Mimì said all in one breath.

Montalbano opened his eyes wide. "What do you mean, 'nothing'?"

"I mean nothing."

"Were you suddenly overcome by an urge to remain chaste?"

"No, no, but, for whatever reason, once we were on the boat, we both felt sort of strangely depressed. So we started talking. Maj's Italian is pretty good . . . At any rate, for that innocent little boat ride, Beba and I had a fight and Maj's now in trouble with her boyfriend. I would give anything to see Maj and her boyfriend make peace."

"So why are you telling me this?"

"Because I was thinking that you might in some way intervene . . ."

"How?"

"I don't know, maybe by letting them know through Ingrid . . ."

Montalbano felt like laughing. Mimì was suggesting that he do exactly what he'd already thought of doing and had set up.

"I'll see what can be done," said the inspector, cutting short the discussion.

Mimì thanked him and went out. Immediately the phone rang. It was Engineer Sabatello.

"I'm just now on my way back to Vigàta, Inspector. Shall we meet tomorrow?"

"Sure. Where?"

"I can come to the police station."

"We would be constantly interrupted."

"Then could I invite you to my place? Viale Libertà, 14. Shall we say for lunch?"

Montalbano shuddered. He ate only at the homes of people he knew were good cooks. He didn't feel up to risking it.

"Unfortunately I'm busy for lunch. I could stop by for a coffee, if that's all right. Shall we say three o'clock?"

"Sounds perfect."

As soon as they hung up, the phone rang again.

"It's all set," said Ingrid. "We get off at eight, but then I need to stop at my place."

"Is the director coming with you?"

"Without me he wouldn't know where to go."

"Do you remember the restaurant in Montereale?"

"The one with all the antipasti?"

"That's right. Let's meet there at nine."

"Don't you want me to come and get you at home?"

"No, Ingrid, I have an engagement and don't know when I'll be finished. I'd rather take my own car."

For what he had in mind, having his own car was essential.

Fazio came back in.

"Sorry to bother you, Chief, but we've got a hassle on our hands."

"Meaning?"

"Meaning we've got a squad of four men who follow the orders given on the set during the filming."

"I know that."

"But you don't know that three have requested reassignment. Only Gallo's not making any waves, but he's not married."

Montalbano felt confused.

"What the hell difference does it make whether he's married or not?"

"It makes a difference because the three wives, after they found out about Inspector Augello and the Swedish actress, started going nuts with jealousy and they keep making scenes with their husbands."

Montalbano sat there for a minute, thinking. Then he said:

"Since the blame for all this mess lies with Inspector Augello, why don't you go and tell *him* about it?!"

"And what should I tell him to do?"

"Tell him to write up a nice report for His Honour the commissioner. Given our limited means, we've been forced to acknowledge that we can no longer provide this service. Something along those lines. He can get the municipal police to do it."

"I'll go and talk to him right away," said Fazio.

When he got home, as he went into the kitchen to pour himself a glass of water, he stopped hesitantly in front of the fridge.

To open or not to open, that was the question.

Surely Adelina had cooked something good for him, which he would have to forgo. He decided that it was best not to know what he was missing, and so he didn't open the fridge.

He went into the bathroom and then changed his clothes, putting on a London-fog-coloured suit with accompanying waistcoat, which made him look somewhat like a cross between a cardinal in civvies and the president of an investment bank. Then he put on a tie that would have been fitting for a visit of condolence.

He needed to have a maximum air of authority and seriousness, to make the right impression on the Swedish director.

He glanced at his watch: half-past eight. If he left now, he would get there on time, and maybe even a bit early. But he actually wanted to arrive a little later than the others, so he could make a solemn entrance. And so he poured himself two fingers of whisky and sipped it neat, leaning against the jamb of the French windows.

Then he locked up the house and drove off.

As soon as he entered the restaurant, a waiter, who didn't know him, came up and greeted him respectfully.

"*Buonasera, commendatore.*"

He replied with a gesture halfway between a friendly hello and someone swatting away a fly. He immediately spotted Ingrid and the director, who'd chosen a table just a few yards from the water's edge. Good thing Ingrid knew the inspector's preferences. He pretended not to see them and kept looking around.

"Salvo! We're over here!"

He replied with a nod and made his way towards their table without smiling, walking with a slow, grave step. He shook the director's hand and kissed Ingrid's, then sat down between the two, sighing deeply. Then he cleared his throat, as if about to speak. But he said nothing.

"Are you all right?" asked Ingrid, a little worried about how the inspector was acting.

72

"Oh, I'm fine, fine," said Montalbano, looking her in the eye.

Ingrid smiled, relieved, having grasped from his glance that the play had begun.

The blond bear, face screwed up in a frown, kept his eyes fixed on the sea. Maybe he was thinking of his Maj.

"Ask your friend what he feels like eating."

Ingrid obeyed, then translated his reply. "He says he's not hungry."

Montalbano made a face halfway between severe and offended.

"Perhaps he doesn't like eating with me?"

As soon as she translated the question, the blond bear, talking all the while, held out an enormous paw to the inspector. Montalbano shook it, and very nearly came away with four fractured fingers.

"He says, no, on the contrary, he's very happy to be here with you, and that you're an admirable person. The only problem is, he's just not hungry," said Ingrid.

A waiter brought water, bread, and a carafe of wine, and asked whether they wanted antipasti and, if so, what kind, since they had a choice of sixteen different imaginative preparations.

"We'd like to try all sixteen," said Montalbano.

Meanwhile another waiter who moved like a ballet dancer poured some sparkling wine.

Taking his glass in hand, Montalbano stood up. Bewildered, Ingrid and the director did likewise.

"I propose a toast," the inspector said, in a tone befitting a grand occasion, "to the twinning of our two fine towns, and to the success of your film!"

He smiled at the Swede, smiled at Ingrid, drank his wine, and sat back down.

"*Prosit!*" said the other two, drinking and sitting down as well.

The blond bear seemed impressed with the brief ceremony and started speaking very fast. The gist of his speech, in Ingrid's translation, was that he was apologizing for not dressing up for their dinner, and for any inconvenience the filming may have caused the townsfolk. Montalbano granted him absolution with a half-smile, and at that moment the waiters began serving the antipasti.

"Explain to him that this is only the beginning. Afterwards there's going to be a first and second course," the inspector said to Ingrid.

Despite his prior declaration of not being hungry, the blond bear filled his plate.

At that exact moment the inspector's mobile phone started ringing in the breast pocket of his jacket.

Montalbano pretended not to hear it, and kept on eating.

"But isn't that your phone . . .?" asked Ingrid.

"Mine? . . . Ah, you're right. Excuse me for just a minute," he said, pulling it out and bringing it to his ear.

"Yes, Montalbano here."

Then, all at once, in a harsh tone:

74

"And I had also asked you not to disturb me for any reason whatsoever during —"

He stopped and listened.

"Very serious? What? Excuse me just a minute."

He turned to his table guests. "I'm very sorry."

And he brought the phone back to his ear. "So tell me how serious."

He sat there listening for a moment, then shouted loudly: "No! No!!!"

And he sprang to his feet with such violence that he knocked the chair he was sitting in to the floor.

The result was that all the customers turned around to look at him as he kept on shouting.

"But when did this happen? . . . How?! But is he in a serious condition? Did they pump his stomach? Has his wife been informed? Try to keep the reporters away . . . OK, OK, I'll be there in half an hour."

He bent down to pick up his chair, set it back on its feet with a crash, and sat down. After wiping his face with a handkerchief, he poured himself half a glass of wine and drank it. His hands were trembling slightly.

With a brusque movement, he pushed away the plate in front of him. He was frowning darkly.

The blond bear had turned into a statue. Only his eyes were moving, darting back and forth between Ingrid and Montalbano.

Under the table, the inspector knocked his knee against Ingrid's, to get her to intervene.

"But what happened?" she immediately asked.

The inspector sighed before speaking.

"It's an extremely delicate matter."

"Oh, come on, tell me! Please?"

"I'll tell you, but it has to remain between the two of us. OK?"

He looked her in the eye.

Ingrid translated his look: *As soon as I leave, tell the Swede everything.*

"OK."

"Mimì tried to kill himself."

Even though she knew perfectly well it was all a put-on, Ingrid's jaw dropped.

"Mimì?! Why?"

Montalbano looked around and began speaking in a soft voice, practically into Ingrid's ear.

"Less than a year ago, following a traumatic experience, Mimì realized he could no longer . . . well, he could no longer go with a woman. He tried every possible remedy, to no avail. Shortly before the film crews came to town, he went to Berlin to be examined by a famous specialist . . . And he just now received the answer on which he'd placed all his hopes. No dice. He'll never be the same as before. But now I have to go. You two should stay. Please give my apologies to the director."

He stood up, held out his hand to the Swede, who looked lost at sea, kissed Ingrid goodbye, and headed quickly for the door.

Just before exiting the establishment, he turned around to look.

Ingrid was talking excitedly with the director, who was listening attentively.

She was almost certainly telling him the whopping lie he'd made up about Mimì, and, sure as death, the guy was gobbling it up, hook, line, and sinker.

The first thing the inspector did when he got home was to take off his fancy suit and put on a pair of old jeans.

Then, since there was no reason to carry on with his Hamletic doubts, he opened the fridge.

Which proved woefully devoid of any sign of Adelina's arts. In a single bound he lurched towards the oven and opened it.

O wondrous sight! O scent of the sublime!

Before him sat a casserole of *pasta 'ncasciata*, enough for four hungry stomachs.

As the pasta was warming up, he laid the table on the veranda.

The phone rang. At that hour it could only be Livia. But it was Ingrid instead.

"Where are you?" the inspector asked her.

"In Vigàta. I just dropped the director off at his hotel."

"Did he buy it?"

"I'll say! But, you know what? You were great! You're a fantastic actor! I very nearly thought you were being serious!"

"Come on, tell me a little more."

"As soon as you left, I told him your little story about Mimì. He didn't even give me time to finish before he was already on his feet begging me to drive him back to his hotel so he could make up with Maj. He had me driving at two hundred!"

77

"Thanks for cooperating."

"Thanks be damned!"

"Why, what's wrong?"

"What's wrong is that I'm hungry as a wolf and the restaurant is closed now."

"There's a remedy for everything. Just come over to my place."

Ingrid couldn't believe it. "I'll be there in ten minutes."

She'd certainly earned a dish of *pasta 'ncasciata*, at the very least, thought the inspector, as he laid another place at the table.

An extra ten minutes in the oven might just ruin the pasta, so he went into the kitchen and turned it off.

Then he remembered that for the past two days Livia had been pouting and not answering his phone calls. True, he'd behaved badly, changing his mind about going to see her in Boccadasse. He'd been a complete idiot, in fact, but Livia was taking this too far, and the problem had to be resolved before it turned nasty.

On the other hand, if she answered, he had to be careful about what he said. It really wasn't advisable to tell her the truth; it would only make matters worse. Nor could he say it had anything to do with work at the station, since he'd already told her it was all quiet. Then he had an idea. Which he turned over and over in his mind. It seemed to hold up. And was as appropriate as could be.

He grabbed a chair, sat down, picked up the phone, dialled Livia's number. Ten rings, no answer. He called again. Livia answered on the ninth ring.

"What do you want?"

He wasn't discouraged. He had to disarm her at once by appealing to her maternal instincts and overwhelming her with lies.

"Livia, I beg you please to listen to me without interrupting, because I'm extremely tired, have a slight temperature, haven't had any dinner, and am already in bed."

"Go ahead."

Encouraging, no doubt about it. He boldly continued: "The other day I already had my ticket for Genoa when —"

Livia couldn't hold back.

"When something came up. And that's what I won't forgive you for, Salvo. You always give whatever comes up priority over me."

"You're wrong. It wasn't something that came up for me as a police inspector, but for me as a friend of Mimì Augello and Beba. In a terrible fit of jealousy, Beba attacked Mimì and sent him to the hospital."

"What?" asked Livia, stunned.

"Look, you have no idea what an effort I had to make to re-establish peace between those two . . . Beba even wanted to get a lawyer . . . I sweated through I don't know how many shirts and went crazy with the stress, but, in the end, I succeeded."

"But why didn't you tell me anything about this sooner?"

"You wouldn't answer the phone or return my calls!"

"That's true. I'm sorry, darling, it was really silly on my part."

"Here I am!" Ingrid shouted, coming in from the veranda. "Is dinner ready?"

The click of Livia hanging up in rage rang in Montalbano's ear like a rifle shot.

CHAPTER
SIX

He spent a useless morning at the station. He didn't even have anyone to chat with, since he'd sent Mimi Augello in his place to a pain-in-the-arse meeting at the commissioner's office, and Fazio had had to dash off to the fish market because of a brawl.

Somehow or other lunchtime arrived. He got to Enzo's early. The big room was empty; the crew was still at work. And it must also have been early for Ragioniere Butera, and so Montalbano ate slowly and blissfully alone in the back room.

He took his stroll along the jetty, smoked his customary cigarette while sitting on the flat rock, then turned back.

At three o'clock sharp, he rang the doorbell of Engineer Sabatello, carrying under his arm the box with the film reels and projector, which he'd brought with him from the station.

The door was opened by a tall woman of about sixty, well-groomed, whose face broke into a smile upon seeing him.

"Inspector Montalbano! What a pleasure! I'm Clara Sabatello. Please come in."

The inspector entered and heard a male voice call out:

"Is that the inspector, Clara?"

"Yes."

"Please bring him to me."

"Come," said the woman. "Unfortunately, he stumbled yesterday and got a bad sprain, and today he can hardly move."

They went into a study with a desk, a small drafting table, a sofa, and two armchairs. Sabatello was on the sofa, his left leg extended and resting on a footstool, the foot wrapped up. Beside him were two sturdy canes.

"You should have let me know," said Montalbano. "We could have easily postponed . . ."

"Postpone? For a trifle like this? I wouldn't hear of it! Please sit down, and you, Clara, please go and make us two nice cups of coffee."

"I brought you back the reels and the projector," said the inspector, taking the box and holding it out with both hands.

"You don't need them any more?" the engineer asked with a note of disappointment in his voice.

"I had them copied onto DVD."

"Please put the box on the desk and come and sit down."

Montalbano settled into the armchair nearest Sabatello.

Who smiled and said: "I'm all yours."

"Let me start by saying," the inspector began, "that the story you told me, and the reels I watched repeatedly, have piqued my curiosity more than you can imagine."

"I was sure they would," said Sabatello.

"And so I decided to go and have a look at the villa. Not knowing its exact location, I asked Ragioniere Butera, whom I believe you know, and who customarily eats at the same trattoria as I do. Butera in fact turned out to be a real gold mine of information on your family."

"I'm sure the man knows more about my family than I do," said Sabatello.

"So I can tell you, with absolute certainty, that the wall we see in the films is part of a small warehouse that used to stand about fifteen to twenty feet behind the villa, opposite the ground-floor bathroom window."

"The tool shed!" exclaimed Sabatello. "That's where Papa used to keep everything he needed for maintaining the garden and the fields . . ."

"I can also tell you," the inspector continued, "that all the reels your father filmed were shot by placing the camera on the bathroom windowsill."

"What you're saying is very interesting," said Sabatello. "But it doesn't answer the fundamental question: why?"

"You're right. Answering that question won't be easy. We need to know more. Butera mentioned to me the strong bond between your father and his twin brother, Emanuele. Do you remember anything about that?"

"I wasn't quite six years old when my uncle Emanuele . . . when Uncle Emanuele died, Inspector. But I still have some vivid memories of that time. For example, sometimes at the dinner table my uncle would refuse to eat. He would whimper, get all agitated, and push the plate away. And so Papa would then sit down between Mamma and his brother, put his arm around him, talk in his ear, bring the plate back in front of him, and, ever so slowly, my uncle would start eating. One day I got jealous and said I wasn't hungry, just to see what Papa's reaction would be."

"And how did he react?"

"He looked at me coldly and said that if I didn't eat the pasta at the very least, I was going to get a spanking."

"So Emanuele was entirely dependent on his brother?"

"Entirely, for everything. Would you do me a favour? Could you please hand me that green album that you see there on the desk?"

Montalbano got up, found the album, handed it to him, and returned to his chair. Sabatello thumbed through it, then handed it back to the inspector, open to a particular page.

"Have a look at the first photo. The man on the left is Papa, and the other man is Uncle Emanuele."

Their faces were the same, identical. Same hairline, same nose, same mouth. Both faces were serious and looking at each other. Francesco's eyes had an intense, warm, loving expression, whereas Emanuele had the eyes of a grateful dog happy just to be patted on the head by his master. The picture made a strong impression on Montalbano. He'd never seen that sort of look in a man's eyes before. He shut the album and set it down on an arm of his chair.

He didn't quite know what to say. Sabatello spoke first. "They were that way even as children, according to my mother, who'd been told by my grandmother. They were inseparable, to the point that in town they were nicknamed 'the Siamese Sabatellos'. And you know what else? Papa had always wanted to be buried alongside Emanuele. And since the niches in the family vault were arranged one on top of the other, the whole thing had to be restructured."

"Forgive me for prying," said Montalbano, "but your mother . . . She must have been a very generous woman . . . Didn't she ever rebel against her situation, which sort of pushed her into the background?"

"As far as I know, Mamma always accepted the situation. Which she must have already known about when they got engaged, actually. She herself told me, many years later, that she even quarrelled with her parents, who weren't terribly keen on the fact that Uncle Emanuele was living in what used to be their villa."

Signora Clara came in, served the coffee, and then discreetly withdrew.

"What do you remember about Emanuele's suicide?"

"Some vague, unfocused images. I'd gone off to nursery school. My mother'd taken me, since she knew how to drive . . . When Gasparino later came and picked me up, I —"

"I'm sorry, who's Gasparino?"

"Gasparino Sidoti. He was our handyman, and was about twenty years old at the time. He helped Papa in the yard, in the vegetable garden . . . Anyway, I remember the darkness, the shuttered windows, the drawn curtains, the contorted faces . . . Mamma hugged me and told me Uncle Emanuele was dead, and then took me upstairs, into the guest room, ordering me not to come back downstairs for any reason. When she left I started crying. I was confused and scared . . . Not because my uncle had died — what did I know about death? But because of all the mysterious bustle about the house, and being left alone in that room . . . Then the door opened and Papa came in. The moment I saw him I felt reassured."

"It's pretty normal," Montalbano observed, "for a small child, left alone —"

"No, I mean I felt reassured to see him looking untroubled. I remember that clearly."

"Do you mean resigned?"

"No, no, he seemed untroubled, serene. His face wasn't etched with terror like Mamma's. It was normal. As if nothing at all had happened. He sat down, took me onto his lap, and started speaking to me softly, the way he used to do with Uncle Emanuele. And this made me happy, because I thought that now that my uncle was gone, all his attention would be focused on me . . ."

"Do you remember what he said?"

"No. I vaguely recall a few words . . . the necessity of life and the necessity of death . . . I was too small to understand, and maybe he didn't even want to be understood . . . It was a kind of soliloquy . . ."

"When did you learn that your uncle had committed suicide?"

"Much later, when I was sixteen. I happened to overhear a conversation between my mother and a cousin of hers from Palermo . . ."

"What did she say?"

"That Papa, Uncle Emanuele, and Gasparino were at the villa that morning, and when Papa and Gasparino went to check on something in a field beside the villa, Uncle Emanuele, left momentarily alone, went and got the revolver Papa kept in the bedside table and shot himself."

"Did he shoot himself in the head, in the heart? Do you know?"

"I think I remember hearing them say he shot himself in the head."

"And, as far as you can recall, did he shoot himself inside the house?"

"No, he did it outside."

"Do you know where, exactly?"

"Not really, to be honest. Perhaps Gasparino could tell you."

"Is he still alive?"

"He's over eighty, but healthy as an ox."

"Could you tell me where he lives?"

"On Salita Papa Giovanni, but I don't recall the street number. Every so often I go and see him. But it's a short street. All you have to do is ask around."

Montalbano made a mental note of this. "You didn't have any servants?"

"I remember an old housekeeper, Lucia, who came only to clean, because Mamma would never give up her post at the stove to anyone."

"And was she there, that day?"

Sabatello thought about this for a moment. "I don't think she was."

"What makes you think that?"

"Because she was the person who used to take me to nursery school. She would put me on the donkey's back until we reached the edge of town. Then we'd continue on foot. But that morning it was Mamma who took me."

"Have you ever tried to find out what might have made him want to kill himself?" the inspector then asked.

"Yes. And I came up with a possible answer. Maybe, I thought, he unfortunately had a moment of what you might call lucidity, of normal consciousness, and he was able to see himself as he really was. I can't think of any other reason."

"When did your father become ill?"

"My mother told me that he was first diagnosed with a brain tumour in early 1957, in Rome."

"You don't know anything more precise than that?"

"No. Another medical luminary he went to in Milan not only confirmed the first diagnosis but gave him only a few months to live. But then a sort of miracle happened."

"And what was that?"

"The illness went into remission. But his last two years were terrible. The bedroom was moved to the ground floor, and when he wanted to sit in the garden for a few hours, Gasparino would carry him outside in his arms . . ."

"Tell me something. Why did you let the villa go to ruin?"

"Your question confirms to me that I turned to the right person, Inspector," said Sabatello, half grinning.

"Look, you're perfectly free not to —"

"No, no, I'm happy to answer your question. From age five to eleven, my life there became very sad. First, because of our grief for Uncle Emanuele, and later because of Papa's long illness and death . . . At first I lost my love of the place, but I finally ended up detesting it. But being far away had a lot to do with it, too. You see, after my mother died I went to work in Argentina . . . If anyone had asked me to sell them the villa, I probably would have accepted whatever offer they made. But nobody came forward, and so . . ."

He stopped and looked at Montalbano with a smile. "I haven't been much help to you, have I?" he asked.

"I wouldn't put it so drastically," said the inspector. "We were already in total darkness, so even a firefly creates a bit of light."

Congratulating himself on his poetic image, he stood up. "I'll be on my way, then," he said, holding his hand out to Sabatello. "And I thank you for giving me some of your time."

"Will you stay on the case?" Sabatello asked anxiously.

"I'll get in touch as soon as I have any news," the inspector replied, to reassure him.

As had already happened that morning, at the office he found only Catarella.

"Where's Inspector Augello?"

"'E called sayin' as how 'e's still at a meetin' atta c'mishner's, meetin' wit' peoples, ann' 'ey's not gonna finish meetin' afore eight a'clack."

"What about Fazio?"

"'E's on 'is way. 'E went to the garage t'see 'bout 'is car."

"Do you know how to play chess, Cat?"

It seemed like the only thing to do to make the time pass.

"Nah, Chief. I c'n play chickers but I don't got a chickerboard."

Montalbano went into his office, sat down, and the phone rang.

"Chief, Mrs Sciosciostrom'd be onna line f 'yiz."

"Put her through."

"Hello, Salvo. We're on a half-hour break, so I thought I'd give you a ring. Thanks to you, everything's going very smoothly now, and we're making up for lost time. But I wanted to ask you. Could I drop by at the station with Maj? We won't take up much of your time, I promise. If it's OK with you, we can be there in five minutes."

Montalbano hesitated. "With Maj? Why?"

"I dunno. She wanted to meet you."

"OK."

★ ★ ★

Just to be safe, he went to the toilets, had a look at himself in the mirror, combed his hair, and went back into his office and sat down. A split second later, Catarella knocked at the door. He was out of breath, as if he'd run a long way, and was holding one hand over his heart.

"*Matre santissima*, Chief!"

"What's wrong, Cat? Something happen?"

"Mrs Sciosciostrom's 'ere wit'a woman named Maj, an' alls I c'n say is my, my, my, oh my . . . Did I jess say 'woman'? Wha' I mean, Chief, is Venus in poisson, Chief! My oh my oh my . . ."

"OK, OK, knock it off, or you'll have a heart attack. Calm yourself down and then show her in."

Indeed Catarella was not mistaken.

On the other hand, unlike the Swedish model known around the world, she wasn't blonde but brunette, with skin white as snow, eyes blue as the heavens, and hair curly as the Greek gods'. Tall of stature, and designed with a compass that made perfect curves. Naturally provocative, but with an irresistibly likeable manner, she even had the inevitable kiss magnet, a beauty mark near her mouth, which Montalbano made a great effort not to kiss, extending his hand to her instead.

The two women sat down, and Ingrid began speaking. "We haven't got much time. I'm sorry, Maj, but I have to tell Salvo something first. I have some bad news for you. Starting tomorrow the production team will be shooting along the jetty for what they think will take two days. Along your jetty."

"So what you're saying is I won't be able to take my walks?"

"Unfortunately, yes."

Montalbano cursed the saints in his mind.

"OK, Maj, now you can say what you wanted to say to Salvo."

"I came here to thank you. Ingrid said you're a serious, honest man, and I can imagine the effort you had to make to tell a lie to get out of the situation that might become war."

Lie? What the hell did the Swedish girl mean by that? She might be referring to the show he put on at the restaurant. To be sure he wasn't mistaken, he replied:

"Well, in my line of work I sometimes have to force people's hands a little, like I did with the fake phone call at the restaurant, to make the truth come out. At any rate it was for the sake of justice, since Mimì told me about your long conversation on the boat . . ."

The Swedish woman looked at him questioningly, knotting her jet-black eyebrows for a second.

"That's what Mimì said to you?" she then asked.

"Yes, he said you talked for a long time . . ."

"Ahhh," said Maj. "If that's what he told you . . ."

She had an amused little glint in her blue eyes that did not escape Montalbano's notice. Suddenly he understood everything. And he didn't want to look like an idiot in front of the Swedish beauty. He smiled, though he was fuming inside.

"Don't think too much of the word 'talk' that Mimì used. He was a gentleman the whole time."

Maj returned his smile and looked over at Ingrid. They both stood up.

"I apologize, and I thank you again."

Montalbano kissed Ingrid goodbye, then held out his hand to Maj, but, as soon as he leaned forward, his lips, independently of his brain, went straight to the beauty mark and planted a kiss there.

"As soon as the two women had left," Montalbano stood up cursing and gave his desk a hard kick. What an utter bastard Mimì was! He'd gone there and told him the bald-faced lie that nothing had happened between him and Maj in the boat, just to tweak the inspector's sense of justice, knowing perfectly well that if he'd told him what had actually happened on the boat, he probably would have refused to have anything to do with it.

But as there was a God in heaven, he was going to make him pay for this. Immediately, and not later, by surprise. And it had to be something that wouldn't involve Beba. He had to think of something concerning work at the station. OK, but what, since not a fucking thing was happening at the station these days?

He sat there racking his brains until the ghost of an idea finally began to take shape in his head. Yes, that was it. He liked it so much he started laughing to himself.

Ten minutes later, there was a knock at the door, and Fazio came in.

"How are things with the car?"

"It's going to take a lot of work. Fortunately they gave me another car to use in the meantime."

"This afternoon," said the inspector, "I paid a visit to Engineer Sabatello."

"And what'd he say?"

The inspector told him everything, including about the strong impression made on him by the look exchanged by the two brothers in the photograph.

Fazio remained silent.

"What are you thinking?" asked the inspector.

"I'm thinking about something you just said to me."

"Feel like telling me right away, or will I have to wait thirty years to find out?"

"But . . . it's just speculation . . . nothing to back it up."

"Tell me anyway."

"If Francesco Sabatello was first told about the brain tumour in early 1957, isn't it possible he told Emanuele he was ill, and his brother shot himself because he knew he couldn't survive without his brother's continual help?"

"That's a plausible, logical hypothesis, but I'm not convinced. You see, Fazio, we know that Francesco was able to speak and communicate with his brother, but we don't know to what extent. In other words: to what degree did they understand each other? Was Emanuele, moreover, capable of distinguishing the notions of life and death? And, if so, wouldn't it have been cruel of Francesco to reveal his condition to him?"

"So, in conclusion, you favour Engineer Sabatello's hypothesis, that Emanuele had a moment of lucidity?"

94

"No. I honestly don't feel like taking a position one way or another. Because, on the scale of plausibility, both your argument and Sabatello's weigh exactly the same."

After a brief silence, Fazio resumed speaking.

"While you were telling me what Sabatello said to you, I remembered something that occurred to me when we were inspecting the old villa but later forgot to tell you after the gate fell on my car."

"OK, then tell me now."

"Do you remember when I asked you what it might mean to have filmed a wall, and you said that that wall was a symbol, a place of memory, like when young lovers carve their initials into a tree and then go back later to look at them, to keep the memory alive?"

"Yes. And so?"

"Couldn't it be that Emanuele shot himself while standing in front of that wall — or rather, leaning up against that wall?"

"Do you think that hasn't occurred to me? But think about it for a second. If somebody shoots himself — say, in the head — up against a wall, do you realize how blood-spattered that wall would get?"

"Sorry, Chief, but we're seeing a clean wall, one year later, in the 1958 reel."

"So, what's that supposed to mean?"

"It means the blood could easily have been washed away, say, by heavy rain."

"No. If any trace of his brother's blood had remained on that wall — it's his blood we're talking about, after all — if there'd been any left on that wall, I'm convinced Francesco would have preserved and protected that trace, perhaps by building a little canopy above it, or covering it with glass. He would never have let his brother's blood vanish into the void. Being able to keep looking at it might have been for him a way to keep his lost brother alive."

"What do you think you'll do?" asked Fazio.

"The only thing I can."

"And what's that?"

"Talk to Gasparino Sidoti. I'll do it tomorrow morning. Because I'm going home in a minute. Listen, Fazio, I want you to call Mimì and tell him to come to the station after his meeting, because I left an important piece of paper on his desk. So, goodbye for now. I'll see you tomorrow."

After Fazio went out, he found a pen and paper and starting writing a letter to Mimì, carefully weighing every word.

CHAPTER
SEVEN

Dear Mimi,

This letter must remain strictly confidential. I mean it. Nobody is to know about it. It must remain between us.

Late this afternoon, I received some absolutely reliable information, given the source, which I am not, at the moment, at liberty to reveal.

I will confess that as soon as I got the information, I remained undecided for a long time over whether or not to pass it on to the narcotics unit, as should have been my duty. In the end, I decided against it. The idea of beating those idiots at Narcotics made me feel a little better. I hope you will agree.

Here's the deal.

Tonight, sometime between midnight and five a.m. (the informer unfortunately couldn't be more specific), a small yellow van, with only the driver, will come down Via Lincoln. The driver will pull up outside number 54, Via Lincoln, get out, and deposit a medium-sized package outside the closed front door. After which he will get back in the van and drive away.

Moments later a car will arrive, probably an old green VW Polo, with two men inside. One of them will take the package, and the car will drive off to an unknown destination.

Your job will be:

To wait for the yellow van and try to get its number plate and any other information that might lead to identifying its owner;

To follow the car with the package to its final destination, which you will then duly note;

Not to take any action on your own, no matter what happens.

Dear Mimì, I understand how tired you must be after your endless meeting at the commissioner's, but I have no choice but to ask you to make this one final effort, because you're the only person I can trust to handle this.

See you tomorrow morning at nine. Break a leg.

Salvo

He reread the letter, thought it was good, found an envelope, put the letter inside, and then wrote on the envelope:

FOR INSPECTOR AUGELLO.
STRICTLY CONFIDENTIAL.

He stood up, went into Mimì's office, put the letter down on the desk, and headed home.

In the fridge he found an enormous seafood salad, fresh and fragrant. He laid the table on the veranda. The moon looked just like a ball of light, bright enough to illuminate his dinner.

The silence was so deep, you could cut it with a knife. It was interrupted only by the rhythmical rumble of a distant trawler, which sounded like the sea's own heartbeat.

He ate and drank slowly, savouring every forkful. Nobody was clamouring for him.

Then he cleared the table, went back out on the veranda, and sat down, this time with whisky and cigarettes. But he still didn't turn on the light. He spent an hour in this fashion, mind free of thoughts. Until, at last, a thought came into his head, strong and clear.

He had to put an end, as quickly as possible, to the unpleasantness that had developed between him and Livia.

There was no point in trying to call her. She wouldn't answer. Anyway, it wasn't the kind of thing you could clear up over the phone. They had to talk things over face-to-face, looking each other in the eye.

Why not, in fact, leave the following morning for Boccadasse?

Yes, the best thing would be to go and knock at Livia's door without warning. His surprise arrival would certainly help them to make up.

What the hell was he doing lolling about in Vigàta, anyway?

He wouldn't even be able to take his usual post-prandial strolls along the jetty for a few days, because of those morons and their TV movie . . .

And so, as if to avoid having any second thoughts, he stood up, closed the French windows, and started packing a suitcase, reckoning he would stay in Boccadasse for at least four days.

Afterwards, he spent half an hour in front of the television, channel-surfing, then went to bed.

His last thought was for Mimì Augello, staked out on Via Lincoln, waiting for a small yellow van that would never come.

He fell asleep with a smile on his lips.

The following morning he showed up at the station at eight thirty. He immediately rang the personnel office in Montelusa to tell them he wanted a week's leave. They were happy to grant it, since he had accumulated three whole months of holiday time he'd never taken. Then he summoned Fazio and told him to look up Gasparino Sidoti's telephone number. Fazio found it and gave it to him. Montalbano dialled it immediately.

"Whoozis?"

"This is Inspector Montalbano, police. Are you Gasparino Sidoti?"

"That's me. Is something wrong?"

"I would like to talk to you."

"To me? What about?"

"About Francesco Sabatello and his brother, Emanuele."

Sidoti remained silent for a moment, apparently puzzled by the inspector's words. Then he asked:

"Why do you want to go over such an old story?"

"Sabatello's son, the engineer, asked me to look into it. You can give him a ring to confirm, if you want."

"Do I have to come in to the station?"

"If it's no problem to you, I can come to you."

"When?"

"This morning."

Sidoti thought about this for a moment.

"This morning I have an eye doctor's appointment, but I should definitely be back by noon."

"All right then, I'll see you at noon."

As soon as he hung up, he rang the police station at Palermo Airport and had them book him a seat on the 6p.m. flight.

He didn't have time to put the receiver down before Mimi Augello came in, hollow-eyed from lack of sleep, unshaven, and looking enraged.

He closed the door and sat down.

"So, what have you got to tell me?" Montalbano asked, displaying great interest.

"That your top-secret informant told you a big fat whopper."

"What do you mean?"

"Salvo, I was lying there in wait from eleven-thirty to six o'clock in the morning, and I never saw any yellow van drive by."

Montalbano was having a ball. "But are you sure?"

"Sure as death."

"Are you sure you didn't nod off at some point?"

"Impossible. I drank four double espressos. And there's more. Not a single vehicle — not a bicycle, not a tricycle, not an HGV — stopped outside the door to number 54, Via Lincoln."

"How very odd!" commented the inspector, donning a bewildered look.

"Odd or not, the fact is that I lost a whole night's sleep," Augello said bitterly.

"What are you going to do, Mimì?" Montalbano said consolingly. "You have to be patient with these kinds of things. Just chalk it up as one of the many that didn't work out. You lost your chance to get a good night's sleep, you lost your chance with the Swedish girl on the boat . . ."

Upon hearing these last words, Mimì understood everything.

His face first turned pale, then red-violet, a bit like a dark bell pepper, then it veered towards lettuce green before, finally, regaining its normal colour.

"So you really wanted to make me pay for it, eh?"

"Mimì, you must never lie to me."

Augello stood up.

"So we're even?" he asked.

"We're even."

Mimì held out his hand, and Montalbano shook it. "Oh, Mimì: by the way, I'm leaving for Boccadasse this evening."

"For how long?"

"Four, five days."

"Say hi to Livia for me."

* * *

It was a residential street with buildings not more than three storeys high, modest but well maintained. Sidoti lived on the ground floor. The man who opened the door looked much younger than what must have been his age: he was properly dressed, on the short side, sported a mass of white hair, pink cheeks, and pale blue eyes behind his glasses. He had a pleasant smile.

"Hello, Inspector. Please come in."

At a glance Montalbano grasped that the apartment consisted of a rather large kitchen, a bathroom, a living-dining room — which they were in — and a bedroom. The old man sat him down in a chair at the table.

"Shall I make us some coffee? Or would you prefer some nice cool wine that lifts the spirit?"

"That sounds good, thanks. I'll have half a glass with pleasure."

Sidoti went into the kitchen, picked up a bottle and two glasses, and put them all down on the table. He uncorked the bottle, filled a glass halfway, handed it to the inspector, then served himself. They toasted.

"To our health!"

The wine went down smooth as silk.

"I phoned Ernesto," said Sidoti.

"Sabatello?"

"Yes. I've known him since he was a little kid, so we're on very familiar terms."

"And what did he say to you?"

"He said to do everything you asked."

"Did he explain why I need to talk to you?"

"No, sir, he didn't."

"And you didn't ask?"

"No, sir."

Montalbano felt curious. "And why not?"

The old man looked at him with his childlike eyes. "Because life has taught me that the fewer questions you ask, the better off you are. And I'm ready to answer without asking."

All Montalbano had to do was to begin.

"Do you remember the morning when Emanuele killed himself?"

"How could I forget?"

"Can you tell me about it?"

"Sure. So, that morning, since the housekeeper didn't come to work, the lady of the house had to go into town to buy groceries and gave Ernesto a lift to school. At around eight-thirty, Don Ciccino[1] called me and asked me to give him a hand in the garden."

"Was Emanuele with him?"

"No, because Don Ciccino said his brother'd had a bad night, and so he'd told him to stay in bed and rest."

"But didn't Don Ciccino have a regular job?"

"Don Ciccino ran his own practice. He had his office on Via Vittorio Emanuele. Since he didn't need to work, because of his family fortune, he could just stay at home if he didn't feel like going to the office."

"OK, go on."

"Wait, just to finish what I was saying, I wanted to tell you that towards the end there, Don Ciccino wasn't

---

[1] That is, Francesco (translator's note).

doing so good with his health and all, and so he went to see some doctors in Rome and Milan. He was very worried, and so working at the office was the last thing on his mind."

"Did his illness change him?"

"What can I say, Inspector? . . . His head was full of worries, really serious worries . . . he didn't laugh any more, and sometimes he seemed to talk nonsense . . . You'd say something to him and he wouldn't even listen."

"Let's go back to that morning."

"When we had finished with the garden, a little after ten o'clock, Don Ciccino wanted us to go and look at the gauges that we'd installed in an area of the boundary wall where a big crack had appeared opposite the garage."

"So, you mean behind the villa?"

"Exactly. He told me to go on ahead, and he was going to check up on Emanuele and see how he was doing. I started walking toward the gate . . ."

"Wasn't there another exit in the rear?"

"No, sir. To go in and out you had to go through that single gate. After I was past it, I turned and started walking back toward the villa, hugging the outside of the wall to see if there was any other damage. Then I came to the spot where the crack was."

"How long did it take you to walk down the path, go through the gate, and get to the place where the crack was?"

Sidoti did some quick calculations in his head.

"Ten minutes, at the most. It was a big park. Then, seeing that Don Ciccino wasn't coming, I sat down on the ground. And I suddenly heard the bang and sprung to my feet."

"Did you realize at once that it was a shot from a revolver?"

"Yes, sir."

"What did you do?"

"I just stood there for a second, feeling confused. Then I heard Don Ciccino's voice calling me desperately. So I started running toward the villa."

"And what did you see?"

"It's burned into my head, Inspector. I got to around halfway down the long side of the villa when I saw Don Ciccino with his right knee on the ground and his brother's head resting on his left leg. He was embracing him with one arm, face to face, and with the other hand he was trying to clean the blood off him with a handkerchief."

"A handkerchief?"

"Yes, sir. I don't really remember, but it must've been one of those big kerchiefs like the ones women use to wrap their heads," said Sidoti, falling silent. Then he resumed: "Don Ciccino then looked up for a second. It was like he was the one who'd been shot, that's how much blood he had on him. And then he said to me: 'He killed himself. Call the carabinieri.'"

"Did you see where the revolver was?"

"Yes, sir. It was on the ground, next to Don Ciccino's leg, the one kneeling. But it wasn't a revolver. It was an automatic."

"Did it belong to Don Ciccino?"

"Yes. He kept it in a drawer in his bedside table, but without the magazine inserted, because he was worried the kid might find it and start playing with it."

"Was the cartridge case ever found?"

"No, it wasn't. Don Ciccino looked everywhere for it, and so did I, and so did the carabinieri, too, but nothing doing . . ."

"What did Don Ciccino tell the carabinieri?"

"He said that he'd gone upstairs and found his brother lying down but awake. And so he asked him if he wanted to get dressed and come with him, but Emanuele said he didn't feel up to it. So Don Ciccino went back downstairs and was already outside, almost at the gate, when he heard the gunshot, which came from behind the house. The carabinieri marshal then gave his opinion of what he thought had happened, and Don Ciccino said he agreed."

"And what was that?"

"He said that, right after Don Ciccino went out of the house, Emanuele, barefoot and in his pyjamas, must have run into Don Ciccino's room, grabbed the pistol, and gone down the stairs, but, instead of going out of the front door, where his brother, who was still on the main path, would have seen him, he went down to the bathroom on the ground floor, climbed out of the window, and, once outside, shot himself, right there."

Montalbano hesitated.

"Wait a second," he said. "But didn't he shoot himself near the tool shed?"

"When I got there, they were both right under the bathroom window, the living man and the dead man."

Montalbano felt like someone who, approaching the beach, exhausted after a long swim, finds himself towed back out to the open sea by a strong riptide.

Then why did Francesco repeatedly film that patch of wall if it had nothing to do with Emanuele's suicide?

". . . every so often he would wail," said Sidoti.

"Eh?" said the inspector, who'd been distracted.

"I was saying that Don Ciccino wouldn't give himself no rest. Every so often he would wail to himself: 'I should never have left him alone that morning!'"

"So Francesco used to take his brother along with him even to work?"

"Yes, sir. He wasn't any bother, really," Sidoti paused, then resumed: "But sometimes — even if it wasn't very often — he would leave him alone all day, and in those cases it was up to me to look in on Emanuele and give him a hand."

"Was that when Don Ciccino used to go out of town for work?"

"No, if he had to go out of town he would take Emanuele with him."

"So in what circumstances would he leave him behind?"

"You must already know that Don Ciccino had a great passion."

"A woman?"

Sidoti started laughing.

"Woman? That's a good one! Hunting! That was his passion! Every so often he had to go out hunting with his friends. He couldn't help it."

"But Don Ciccino could easily have taken his brother along, no?"

"It wasn't that Don Ciccino didn't want him."

"So it was Emanuele who didn't want to go?"

"That's right."

"And why not?"

"Because he was afraid of guns."

"Can you explain a little better?"

"What's to explain, Inspector? He was scared to death of 'em. The minute he saw a rifle he would start shaking all over. I remember when he pissed his pants once because Ernestino'd pointed his toy rifle at him, the kind with the cork bullet."

"What kind of man was Francesco, can you tell me?"

"I wish there was more like him around! He was a real gentleman, and very generous. For example, in my case, in his will he left me a parcel of land out Montereale way, which allowed me to live my life without any worries. He was just a little over-fussy."

"How so?"

"He was very precise and attentive to detail, and would write down everything he spent and everything he did, really."

"Do you know what ever happened to his papers?"

"Well, when his wife decided to move to Palermo, I filled up five crates with papers and took them up to the attic of the house that Don Ciccino had in Vigàta. But I don't know if Ernesto kept them or got rid of them."

Then he looked at the inspector and said:

"If you don't have any more questions, I should probably start making lunch."

"I'm finished," said Montalbano, standing up. "Cooking anything interesting?"

"I bought myself a big pig's liver I'm going to cut up and roast on skewers."

"With each piece of liver wrapped in pig-gut?"

"Of course."

"Oh, it's been so long since I've eaten that!" the inspector blurted out.

Sidoti didn't think twice.

"Well, if you'd do me the honour of joining me . . ."

"I wouldn't want to intrude . . ."

"It's no intrusion at all! It'll be a pleasure! In fact, why don't you come into the kitchen and lend me a hand?"

Five minutes later, Montalbano was in shirtsleeves, protected by an apron, extricating and stretching out, with the palms of his hands, the delicate, netlike pig intestine, while Sidoti was cutting the liver up into little cubes.

And when the first aroma of liver scented with bay leaves and onions began to fill the kitchen, Montalbano realized that this meal, so simple and genuine, was going to be something to remember.

Almost immediately after driving a few miles in the direction of Palermo Airport, he became convinced that it was going to be hell. The traffic was dense, chaotic, and on edge. It was as if dozens and dozens of insane or drug-addicted or drunken people had decided all at once to get in their cars and drive to Palermo.

At one point, three cars tried, all at the same time, to pass one another, leading to one ending up in the opposite lane and crashing into an oncoming truck.

Everything ground to a halt for half an hour.

Fifteen minutes after the traffic started moving again, a dog appeared out of nowhere and cut in front of the inspector's car. To avoid running him over, Montalbano swerved left, inevitably scraping the vehicle rolling along next to him.

Introductions followed.

"Cretin!"

"Moron!"

Another twenty minutes lost exchanging insurance information.

Just a few miles outside the airport, the car started to skid. He realized he'd had a blowout.

He felt like crying. Never in a million years would he be able to change the tyre.

Dejected, he got out of the car and leaned against the bonnet.

A car drove past and immediately came to a halt.

"Inspector! What are you doing here?"

It was Pasqualino, Adelina's son. He changed Montalbano's tyre in the twinkling of an eye.

Onwards and upwards! the inspector thought to himself. He raced into the car park, got out of the car, and started running towards the entrance, but halfway there he realized he'd left his suitcase and mobile phone in the car. If he turned back, he was sure to miss the flight. He kept on running. After all, he had plenty of underwear and clean shirts at Livia's place.

As soon as he went in, he was nabbed by Inspector Parisi of the Airport Police.

"Come with me."

And he got into a police car that drove him all the way to the foot of the air stairs outside the plane. He climbed the stairs, found his seat, and collapsed into it, out of breath.

CHAPTER
EIGHT

By the time he arrived outside Livia's door, it was almost nine o'clock. He had a set of keys to the apartment but preferred ringing the doorbell. Selene started barking immediately in reply.

Then, from behind the door came the voice of a suspicious Livia, who wasn't expecting any visitors at that hour.

"Who's there?"

"Police!" he said, trying to change the sound of his voice. But Livia didn't fall for it.

"Salvo!" she cried, fumbling about to open the door.

As soon as it came open, the first to try to throw her arms around him was the joyously barking Selene, but Livia quickly pushed her away and squeezed Montalbano tight. They stood that way for a moment without saying anything. Then she took his hand and led him into the apartment.

"Don't you have a suitcase?"

"I forgot it in the car at Palermo Airport, along with my mobile phone. I would have missed the flight if I'd gone back to get them."

"You've got a full wardrobe here," said Livia. "And if they need you back in Vigàta, they can always reach you on my land line."

"I don't think they'll be needing me."

"How long do you plan to stay?"

"For four days, at the very least. But if nothing's going on down there, I could stretch that out to a week."

"That's wonderful!" Livia shouted, hugging him anew.

Then: "Have you had any dinner?"

"I didn't have time."

"If you'd be happy with a fried egg, some cheese, and some salami . . ."

"That'd be fine with me."

Then, just in case Livia suddenly felt inspired to cook something up the following day:

"I'll make up for it tomorrow at the restaurant."

They went into the kitchen. The inspector sat down at the table, and Livia set a place for him and served him the egg. She watched him eat without saying a word. She didn't open her mouth until Montalbano also had dispatched the salami and cheese.

"Listen, Salvo, of all those stories you told me over the phone . . . and there were really a lot . . ."

"But they weren't made up. They were —"

"They were whatever they were. But, of all those stories, I'm only interested in one."

"Which one?"

"The one about what happened between Mimì and Beba. Is it true that Beba wanted to talk to a lawyer?"

Montalbano ran one hand over his conscience.

Precisely where his conscience was located was another matter. He didn't know, but it must have been somewhere between his stomach and the bottom of his ribcage. He decided to tell her the truth. But a slightly adjusted truth.

Because, no matter how you looked at it, an adjusted truth was always more convincing than the hard, naked truth.

"She probably said that without really meaning it. But she became so exasperated with Mimì that she scratched his face. He really screwed up this time."

"Tell me about it."

Montalbano told her everything in great detail, including the show he'd put on at the restaurant and the revenge he'd taken by robbing Mimì of a night of sleep.

"Shall we go out on the balcony?" he asked when he'd finished. "It's such a nice evening . . ."

On the bedroom's balcony, from which you could see the sea, there was room enough for two chairs and a stool, which served as a small table. Livia set a bottle of whisky, a glass, and an ashtray down on it; Montalbano added a pack of cigarettes and a lighter. Selene, who was a medium-sized dog, rolled onto Livia's feet.

The inspector got carried away, colourfully describing the carnival atmosphere created by the film shoots all over town, prompting an occasional guffaw from Livia.

"Well," she commented when he'd finished, "if nothing else, at least you didn't have any problems at the police station."

"Maybe not at the police station, but I did have what you might call a personal problem, and I still haven't worked out how to resolve it."

"Tell me about it."

"It's a long story, Livia. I'll tell it to you tomorrow. We've got all the time in the world."

"I want to hear it now."

Whenever Livia got something into her head, there was no getting it out of there.

"All right, then," Montalbano said in surrender, pouring himself half a glass of whisky.

"Wait just a second," said Livia. "I want to put on a sweater."

She got up, leaned over Salvo, gave him a kiss, went into the bedroom, came back, kissed Salvo again, and sat back down, all the while with Selene following behind her.

"OK, you can begin."

Montalbano started telling her about the home-movie reels shot by Engineer Sabatello's father and went on for over an hour. That was because after a while he realized that he wasn't telling the story to Livia any more, but to himself, in the sense that this was the first time he'd managed to have a full picture of the situation, thanks to what Sidoti had told him.

"You've made me sad," said Livia.

"You were the one insisting that I tell you."

"I know," she said.

And she sat there in silence, stroking Selene.

"Are you wondering why he shot all those reels?" Montalbano asked her.

"That's not what I'm interested in."

The inspector gave a start.

"But they're the most interesting part of the —"

"I still have in my possession a pebble from a river," said Livia. "It was a present from my first boyfriend. Are you interested?"

"What's that got to do with anything?"

"It's the same sort of thing. Filming that wall was an exercise of remembrance."

"Remembering what?"

"That is what you, sooner or later, will have to find out. But, actually, I meant Emanuele."

"And his unhappy life?"

"That, too. But mostly his death."

"Tell me what you're thinking."

"I don't really know. It's just a rather confused impression. A feeling that none of it makes any sense."

"Could you be more precise?"

"Well, for example, I wonder how it is that Francesco never noticed that his brother had reached such a state of desperation. He should have been able to feel it inside, in his own body . . ."

Montalbano had asked himself this same question, but been unable to answer it.

"A desperation so great, so absolute that he would take a gun into his hand even though he was scared to death of guns . . . Can you imagine what kind of deep, dark fears he had to bear as he was raising the gun to his head?"

She heaved a long sigh. "It's late," she said.

"Did I tire you out with all my talking?"

"No. You made me happy."

At around three o'clock in the morning, Montalbano woke up. Livia was sleeping soundly. It was she who'd found the hole in the weave of the story he'd told her: namely, the weapon Emanuele chose to kill himself with.

There were countless ways to end one's own life without having to resort to a knife or a firearm.

In this particular case, Emanuele could have climbed to the top of the turret and thrown himself off.

Or else hanged himself from a tree.

Or jumped into the well in the middle of the garden. Or killed himself with rat poison.

Whereas . . .

He went and grabbed a weapon the mere sight of which made him piss his pants in terror.

Wait a second. It was an automatic, not a revolver, as Sidoti had taken care to point out.

A pistol that Francesco Sabatello kept around without the magazine inserted.

Which meant that Emanuele had not only inserted the magazine but had also loaded the bullet, pulling the slide back and then letting it forward again.

But those were movements one learned. They were not things you did instinctively.

118

Therefore Emanuele must have seen someone else make them.

But was seeing someone make them once or twice enough to allow a handicapped man like Emanuele to repeat them without making any mistakes?

And if, on the other hand, someone had taught them to him, how had they managed to convince him to pick up a gun?

And to hold it in his hand and not let go?

Wouldn't he have fainted in fright?

The inspector fell back to sleep, convinced of one thing. That he would never manage to discover the reason for the films if he didn't first understand with certainty how Emanuele had committed suicide.

He was woken by the sound of the front door closing. Through the half-shuttered balcony window, the light of a beautiful morning filtered in.

"Livia, is that you?"

"Yes, I took Selene out."

He felt confused. What time was it, anyway? He looked at his watch. Almost nine. He jumped out of bed, ran into the kitchen, and gave Livia a kiss.

"Why didn't you wake me up? I would have gone with you . . ."

"You were sleeping so soundly . . . I didn't have the heart to wake you. I put a change of underwear and a clean shirt for you in the bathroom."

"Have you had breakfast already?"

"Yes. And I've already brewed you a good four cups' worth of coffee. Think that'll be enough?"

"I'll make it be enough."

Before going into the bathroom he drank a first demitasse as a test. It was good. Coffee, at least, was one thing Livia knew how to make.

"So, what's the plan for this morning?" he asked, appearing before Livia all clean and shiny.

"That depends."

"On what?"

"On whether you want to stay at home or go out."

"I'd rather go out."

"Then let's do this. We'll all get in the car, you, me, and Selene. Since I have a few errands to run, I'll drop you and Selene off at the park. That way you can get a little better acquainted. But be sure to keep her on the lead the whole time. I'll come by and pick you up about an hour later, or maybe a little more."

"And then what?"

"And then we'll see whether we want to go straight to the restaurant or come briefly back home."

The inspector rather liked this last part of the plan.

With Selene on the lead, he headed towards a group of four benches arranged in a circle. Only one was free, and he sat down on it.

Selene was restless, tugging and whimpering and generally making it clear that she wanted to be set free to have a nice run. But if he let her off the lead, would she return when he called her? Or would he be forced to go looking for her?

As he sat there unable to make up his mind, he noticed that an old man, with a long beard halfway down his chest, had stopped in front of him and was looking at him intensely. What the hell did he want?

"I'm sorry, can I help you with something?"

"Yes. My bench."

"Excuse me, which bench?"

"The one you're sitting on."

Montalbano was at a loss.

"But it's a public bench! How can it be yours?"

"By usucaption. For the past twenty-five years, I've been sitting there from eleven a.m. to one p.m., and from four p.m. to six p.m."

Montalbano tried to compromise.

"There's more than enough room for you here. Just sit down beside me."

"I never share my bench with anyone."

The inspector didn't feel like getting into a squabble with an insane old man. Luckily an elderly couple sitting on the bench next to them got up and left. Montalbano dashed over and sat down on it.

And was immediately overwhelmed by a wave of melancholy.

How much time did he have left before retirement? Almost none at all — no, actually, if he'd wanted to, he could have already retired.

Was this the kind of future that awaited him? Taking Selene on walks in the park and scuffling with other geezers over a place on a sunlit bench?

And then, evenings, nodding off in front of the TV set, waking up numbskulled, calling for Livia, who's lying there in an even deeper stupor in the armchair beside him, and finally, each helping the other, staggering off to bed?

Too advanced in years to make new friends, or to accept Livia's friends, he was sure to have a desolate, lonely old age. He didn't feel like sitting there any longer. A strong desire to start walking came over him. So he got up, took three steps, and froze. Where was Selene?

She'd run away, lead and all. He broke out in a cold sweat. He looked around. No sign at all of her.

"Are you looking for your dog?" asked the usucaption codger with a malicious grin.

"Yes."

"It went over that way," the old man said, vaguely pointing in a north-north-east direction.

Montalbano, who knew the human soul well, headed off in a south-westerly direction, calling desperately.

"Selene! Selene!"

At last he saw her. She was playing with a little boy barely three years old, before the loving eyes of his mother, an attractive, well-dressed woman of about forty.

"I've come to retrieve my dog," said Montalbano.

"Please go ahead."

Easier said than done. As soon as he drew near, Selene would scamper away. After five minutes of vain attempts, the good-looking lady joined the hunt, but with no results, either.

"You haven't trained him very well, apparently," the woman reproached him.

Montalbano was about to reply when he heard a voice. "Salvo . . . Selene?"

Selene shot off like a rocket towards the spot where Livia's voice had come from.

Montalbano half bowed to the unknown woman in as dignified a manner as he could muster.

"Did Selene behave?" Livia asked when they were in the car.

"Behave? Are you kidding?" the inspector cried, venting his frustration. "First, taking advantage of a moment of distraction on my part —"

"I do hope you're not going to blame Selene for your being distracted," Livia said with irritation, interrupting him.

"I wouldn't dare. I just meant to say that she ran away, and when I went looking for her and called her name, she didn't come."

"And why should she come?"

"Because I was calling her!"

"And who are you to her? An acquaintance, someone who every so often comes to see me . . ."

Stop right there, Montalbano! Trouble ahead. The conversation was on the verge of taking a very dangerous turn. Better change the subject at once.

"So where are you going to take me now?"

"I have no choice but to go home first. I have to put some stuff in the freezer and prepare Selene's food."

"And what about me?"

"You can either come with me or go for a walk and we can meet outside my place in half an hour."

As he was strolling about town, he noticed a display of pure white roses called Queen of the Snows in a florist's window. Unable to restrain himself, he went inside.

"I'd like a dozen of those white roses," he said.

He also noticed some dark red roses with long stems inside the shop.

"And a dozen of these red ones as well."

"In a single bouquet?"

"Yes."

He walked back to Livia's place somewhat awkwardly, his view rather limited by the enormous bouquet he was carrying.

The moment Livia came out and saw Montalbano with the roses, she buried her face in her hands and started crying. The tears were genuine, and unstoppable, her shoulders heaving as she sobbed.

Montalbano went up to her, managing to hold the huge bouquet in one hand, so he could stroke her hair.

"C'mon, Livia, don't be like that."

But then she reopened the front door and went back inside, followed by Montalbano. She kept crying until they were inside the apartment, where she ran and locked herself in the bathroom.

Montalbano felt that his only option was to let her have all the time she needed to get it out of her system, and so he put the roses down on the table and went and smoked a cigarette on the bedroom's little balcony. Then he finally heard Livia calling him.

She was still in the bathroom, but she'd already put herself back together. Salvo had barely entered when she ran up to him and hugged him very tight, keeping her head pressed against his chest.

They stayed that way for a spell, in silence. Then she whispered:

"Thank you."

Raising her head, she kissed him on the chin.

"For what?" Montalbano asked confusedly.

"For being here with me."

Not knowing what to say, he squeezed her tighter. Then, in a sudden, loving impulse, he decided to sacrifice himself.

"Would you rather we stayed home? It's all the same to me, maybe even preferable . . . You can make me something to eat — say, a plate of spaghetti, and then —"

"Absolutely not," Livia said firmly. "We're going to eat out, as we decided."

They released their embrace.

"But first you must help me put these roses in some vases."

The inspector was beginning to feel rather hungry. His supper of the night before hadn't exactly been rich.

"Let's just do it when we get —"

"No, they'll suffer, all bound up like that."

She untied the bouquet, cut the roses scattered across the table, then made a face.

"What's wrong? Don't you like them?"

"They're magnificent. But . . ."

"But what?"

"They look like a homage to fallen patriots."

"What?!"

"Just look: the green of the leaves, the red and white of the roses . . . It's the Italian flag."

Why could he never do anything right?

"But, luckily, you're alive and of sound mind. Come on, let's get this over with."

At last they were ready to leave. At that moment Montalbano realized that the home phone's receiver was off the hook and lying beside it. He pointed this out to Livia.

"I hadn't noticed," she said, going over and hanging it back up. "Who knows for how long it's been like that."

Saying goodbye to Selene, who was well aware she was about to be left at home alone, was an ordeal. Even Montalbano felt touched.

"Let's bring her with us."

"They won't let her in."

In the lift she asked him: "Shall we go on foot or would you rather drive?"

"Whatever you prefer."

In all honesty he would have shot through an underground pneumatic tube if it could get him to the restaurant any sooner.

"It's such a beautiful day!" said Livia. Which, translated, meant: Let's walk.

They headed off. After they'd taken three steps — no more, no less — Livia stopped and began rummaging through her purse.

"I can't find my phone. I must have left it at home."

"No problem. Who do you expect —"

"You never know. I'm going home to get it. Wait for me here, I'll be back in a flash."

Montalbano launched into a litany of curses in his head. Only women really knew the extra-fine art of wasting time. Maybe it was one of the things the snake taught Eve.

And with every minute that passed, his stomach made its displeasure felt even more.

He kept an eye on the front door, three paces away, but it remained closed.

Some flash! Livia was taking as long as a whole thunderstorm!

He lit a cigarette, and not until he'd finished it did the door open and Livia appear.

"I'm sorry, darling."

"You couldn't find it?"

"No, I found it right away. I had to change my shoes. The heel was falling off of one, and so . . ."

. . . *and so you took fifteen minutes to decide on what other pair to wear*, Montalbano completed her sentence in his mind. They entered the restaurant. The television was on, broadcasting the news. After casting a glance at it, the inspector turned to stone.

On the screen was the face of Mimì Augello, in a tight close-up.

CHAPTER
NINE

Seeing Montalbano's eyes popping out of his head, Livia followed the direction of his gaze and was equally flabbergasted.

"And that's about it," said Mimì.

"Thank you, Inspector Augello," said a voice off camera.

"Glad to oblige," replied Mimì.

Then he disappeared. In his place a talking head appeared and said:

"And that's the latest news. We now leave you to the following scheduled programme, which . . ."

Dozens of thoughts were arising in Montalbano's brain at the speed of lightning, intertwining with one another until they formed a skein.

Livia was the first to react. Only two tables were occupied, one by a solitary customer, and the other by two men of about fifty. Livia, whom the inspector followed like a robot, walked over to the single man.

"I'm sorry, but did you by any chance hear the last story on the news programme?"

The solitary man, apparently a typical Ligurian grumbler, replied brusquely:

"Neither the last nor the first. I mind my own business."

She had better luck with the people at the second table.

"I heard a bit of it," said one of them. "We were talking about it . . . apparently there was a school shooting, in some town in Sicily . . ."

"Were there any dead or injured?"

"I couldn't say."

"It's all the fault of the Americans!" burst out the other one, who hadn't yet spoken.

"What've the Americans got to do with it?" his friend asked.

"They're always exporting all their most disgusting things to us, from Halloween to school shootings!"

Montalbano, who'd basically recovered from his initial shock, took Livia by the arm. "Let's get out of here," Then: "If you hadn't wasted all that time, we could have heard the news."

Livia said nothing. Next door to the restaurant was a block of flats with the main door open, but no doorman. The inspector went inside.

"Give me your mobile phone."

Livia handed it to him. But she didn't miss her chance for revenge.

"If I'd left it at home, as you wanted . . ."

"It's engaged," said the inspector.

"Are you feeling all right? You're as pale as a corpse."

"How am I supposed to feel? I'm very worried."

He tried calling the station again. Still busy. He tried Fazio: unreachable. Augello likewise. He couldn't remember any other phone numbers. With each minute that passed, the inspector felt more and more prey to an impotent rage and terror at the thought of what might have happened.

"Could you hand me the phone for a second?" asked Livia.

"Right now?"

"Yes."

Montalbano gave it to her reluctantly, and Livia stepped aside. To the inspector her phone call seemed endless, but he didn't have the courage to snatch the phone out of her hand. As soon as it was back in his possession, however, he dialled the station's number again. This time the unmistakable voice of Catarella answered.

"Montalbano here."

"*O matre santissima!* O swee' blessed Jesus!"

"Cat . . ."

"O holiest o' voigins! O saints in 'eaven!"

"Be quiet, Cat! That's an order!"

But he wasn't even listening.

"Iss so good to hear yer verce at last, Chief! I been tryin' a reach yiz all mornin'! Yer mobble phone jess rings an' rings, an Miss Livia's phone's like off the hook, an' 'en alluva sudden iss back onna hook, bu' nobuddy ansers . . ."

"Shut up!" the inspector yelled.

The flow of Catarella's words suddenly stopped, as if the power had been cut off.

"You must only speak to answer my questions. Are there any dead or injured?"

"Nossir, Chief, none. By the Lord's goo' grace, wha' happened is —"

"Sshhh! Get me Fazio or Inspector Augello."

"'Ey ain't onna premisses, Chief."

"Where are they?"

"Who?"

"What do you mean, who? Augello and Fazio."

"Ya gotta 'scuse me, Chief, bu' since I'm a little upsitt . . . I tought ya wannit a know where the premisses was . . . Fazio was called in by the Dicos, an' Isspecter Augello's in canfrince wit' Hizzoner the C'mishner."

"Can you tell me, in just a few words, exactly what happened?"

"I c'n try, Chief. So, 'iss mornin' jest a li'l afore ten, two individdles belongin' to the maskiline persuasion ennered the Luici Pirinnello School . . . Ya know which one I'm talkin' about?"

"Yes. Go on."

"An' 'en 'ey boist inna the classroom Tree B, inwheres 'ey astracted 'eir guns an' tol' ivryone a put their hands up, an' 'at 'at was an order. An' since the studints got all ascared an' summuvm started cryin', summuvm callin' fer help, the gunmen shot tree or four times inna air, an' 'at only addit to the confusion. An' at this point, Isspecter Augello —"

"Wait a second, let me get this straight. So Augello was already there?"

"Yessir, Chief, 'e went a talk to the teacher 'cuz 'is boy was in class Tree B."

"OK, got it. Go on."

"An' at 'at point, Augello tried a calm the kids down, but one o' the individdles belongin' to the maskiline sex punched 'im inna face and trettened a kill 'im."

"And then what?"

"An' 'en one o' the two said to the kids, 'Careful ya don't do nuttin' stupid, or we'll come back an' wipe yiz all out.' An' 'en 'ey left. But Isspecter Augello chased after 'em an' as soon as 'ey was inna courtyard, 'e took out 'is gun and said: 'Halt! Police!' an' 'en 'ere was a schange o' gunfires, bu' the two manitched t'ascape."

"Well done, Cat, thanks."

"But what're ya gonna do yisself, Chief? Ain't ya comin' back? We need yiz roun' here, Chief, jess like we need air!"

"I'll call you back in a little bit."

He summarized for Livia what Catarella had just told him.

"What do you plan to do?" Livia asked, naturally.

Before answering, Montalbano took her into his arms. "You have no idea how much I regret this," he said. "But I think it's my duty to —"

"No need to say any more," said Livia.

"Why?"

"Because I already knew how you would react. That was why I asked you for the phone. In ninety minutes there's a flight for Palermo."

Montalbano wasn't even able to thank her. He was all choked up and couldn't manage to speak.

"Shall I order a couple of panini for you?" asked Livia.

"I don't really feel like eating any more."

"Then let's get the car. I'll drive you to the airport."

Nobody'd touched his car. The phone was exactly where he'd left it; the suitcase was in the boot. He heaved a sigh of relief. True, he'd left it in the police car park, but the way things were going these days . . .

On the drive home he was stopped three times — by the police, by the customs officers, and by the carabinieri, respectively. The checkpoints meant they hadn't yet arrested the two men who'd attacked the school.

Heading for the station's car park, he noticed a crowd of photographers, cameramen, and journalists outside the front door, being kept at bay by Mazzarella and Borruso, two of their uniformed officers. Without getting out of his car, he phoned Catarella and asked him to unlock the back door to the building. That way he might just manage to make it into his office without being seen. But he ran out of time. One newsman spotted him and started yelling.

"Montalbano's here!"

In the twinkling of an eye he found himself surrounded by people shouting and flashes popping. Luckily Mazzarella and Borruso were quick to intervene, pushing and kicking in every direction, clearing a path for the inspector to arrive safe and sound inside the building.

Where he was greeted by a sort of wail that sounded like a cross between a howling dog and a braying ass and turned out to be Catarella welcoming him back.

"'E's baaaack! Omygaaaad 'e's baaaack!"

"Come with me."

Catarella leapt out from his cubbyhole and followed behind him, emitting a sort of whining sound.

Once the inspector was sitting in his chair, in his office, among his customary objects, he felt his fit of agitation passing.

He knew he was now lucid and calm. "Are Augello and Fazio here?"

"'Ey haven't retoined to the premisses yet, Chief. Fazio was summonsed by Hizzoner the C'mishner poissonally in poisson, an' Isspecter Augello, after 'e was done wit' 'Izzoner the C'mishner, 'adda go an' see Prassecutor Riccadonna. Bu' I tol' both of 'em — both of 'em bein' Fazio an' Isspecter Augello — 'at you was on yer way 'ere."

Montalbano twisted up his mouth. Pietropaolo Riccadonna had never seemed like a terribly brilliant mind to him.

"Is there any news?"

"Yessir, Chief. One of our patrools foun' the car the two school attackers ascaped in 'at Isspecter Augello got the number plate for."

"Where'd they find it?"

"In Montelusa, roun' the train station. Toins out it was stolen yisterday mornin' in Montelusa."

"Can you tell me anything else?"

"Wha' can I say, Chief? Iss only jess now I manitched a get away fro' the tiliphone! Alia noosepapers always callin' continuatiously! Even from the French part of France! And the Joiman Joimany! I

134

ain't even had the time — if you'll ascuse my 'Talian — to relieve my blatter!"

"You can go now, and then get back to the switchboard."

Catarella saluted and dashed out of the room.

The inspector rang Livia, told her he'd had a good flight, and hung up. At that moment Fazio appeared.

Montalbano had never seen him look so tired.

"Can I hug you?" Fazio asked.

The inspector stood up and opened his arms. Then they both sat down.

"Feel like telling me what happened?"

"I do."

"Careful, though: I only want to know the part that involves you. That is, how you found out about the school incident and what you did."

"OK. This morning, when I came in, Catarella told me Inspector Augello had left word that he would come in to the office around ten-thirty. Then, a little before ten o'clock, Catarella put a call through to me. At that moment Officers Spinoccia and Catalano were with me. The man on the phone sounded scared out of his wits. 'There's been a shooting at the Pirandello School,' he said. 'Come right away.' So we all grabbed our guns and ran out. Ten minutes later, we were at the school but had no idea what was going on."

"Why not?"

"Because, Chief, dozens and dozens of children were pouring out of the building crying, screaming, calling for help, running away with their teachers. While, in the meantime, all the people who'd heard about the shooting — mothers, fathers, brothers, sisters, relatives — were rushing in from the street. To cut a long story short, the only way we were able to get inside the school was through a first-floor window. Once we were in the hallway, we saw Inspector Augello come out of one of the classrooms, which took us by surprise. His pistol was stuck in his belt, and he was talking on his phone. He had such a look on his face that for a second I thought that something must have happened to his son, Salvuzzo. Then, a couple of seconds later, luckily, I saw his kid come out of the same classroom.

"I asked Augello what he was doing there, and he explained everything to me and said he'd immediately alerted Montelusa Central and the carabinieri. Then he asked me to do whatever was needed to try to calm things down inside the school and especially outside the school, adding that nobody'd been killed or injured, and that everyone was safe, kids as well as teachers. He told me all this with Salvuzzo hanging on his arm the whole time. I'll let Augello tell you what happened inside the classroom."

"What did the Digos want from you?"

"The Digos? No, Chief, it was the counterterrorism unit that questioned me. But I couldn't tell them anything, 'cause it's not like I actually saw the two perpetrators."

"And did Counterterrorism have any ideas about the whole thing?"

"None at all. They don't know what to think."

"And what did the commissioner want?"

"The commissioner wanted to know exactly the same things you've just asked me about, since he's under siege not only by the media but also by the politicians."

"And what do you think about the whole thing?" Montalbano asked him.

"Chief, to me the whole thing's neither here nor there, but if I have to put it somewhere, I'll put it here, because in my opinion the Mafia's got to have something to do with this."

"Give me one reason."

"Well, first you're going to have to authorize me to talk about something in which I didn't directly take part."

"OK. You have my authorization."

"I've learned — and Inspector Augello can confirm this — that the two men who entered the school headed straight for classroom III B without asking directions from the caretaker, who in fact was right there inside the front door. So therefore they knew where they were going."

"And so?"

"And so, the first thing to do would be to find out the first and last names, and family relations, of all the kids in III B."

"And are you leaving the teacher conducting class at that moment out of this?"

"No, Chief. And this is not something to waste any time over. I'll get on it right away. See you tomorrow."

He got up and went out. At that same moment the telephone rang.

"Chief, 'at'd be Isspecter Augello onna line."

"Put him through."

"Welcome back, Salvo. I really mean it."

"Tell me everything, Mimì."

"I wanted to ask you something. Since I've finished what I was doing here, could you wait for me there? I could be there in twenty minutes, max."

"All right."

Montalbano realized that Mimì Augello was going well out of his way, especially after the kind of day he'd just had. It must be something really serious.

Augello fell into the chair opposite Montalbano's desk with the weight of a boulder.

"I'm completely drained."

Then he raised his left arm and sniffed his armpit. "And I stink, too. I haven't had a moment's rest since this morning."

"If you want, we can talk tomorrow . . ."

"No. Just give me five minutes to wash and freshen up a little."

"Go ahead."

As soon as Mimì went out, something occurred to Montalbano. He rang Catarella.

"Come into my office, would you, Cat?"

Catarella materialized in a flash.

"Yer orders, sah!"

"Are there still newsmen about?"

"Yessir, Chief 'Ere's still about ten lookin' like famitched dogs waitin' fer a bone."

"Then it's better if I don't let them see me. Here, take my car keys, open the boot, and bring the suitcase that's in there to Inspector Augello and tell him he can put on whatever clothes of mine he needs."

Ten minutes later Mimì was sitting opposite the inspector's desk again. He'd put on one of Montalbano's clean shirts and seemed clearly to have revived.

"So, why did you want me to wait for you?" the inspector began.

"First of all, to give you a report. And secondly because I need to tell you something about Riccadonna that I didn't like at all. But I'd rather tell you after I've told you what happened this morning."

"If you feel up to it . . ."

"I feel up to it, don't you worry about that."

He paused a moment, took a deep breath, and began. "You should know that in my son's class there are three nasty boys, three little bullies who —"

"I know that part already, so you can skip it," Montalbano interrupted him.

Augello was taken aback.

"You know it? Who told you?"

"Beba told me."

Augello looked at him askance but didn't press the matter. "This morning at nine o'clock I went to the school to talk to the head teacher, to bring to her attention that there have been some instances of bullying in class III B. You have no idea how she reacted! She denied everything, said that her school was a model school, 'in conformity with all the latest legislation' — those were her exact words — and she took me on a tour of the toilets. After a while I got fed up and asked for her permission to go and talk to one of the teachers. Which she granted, specifying that at that moment class III B was having its maths lesson with Mr Puleo."

"Did you already know this Puleo?"

"No, but Salvuzzo had said good things about him. Class III B is on the ground floor, at the far end of the corridor at the other end of which is the main entrance. You follow?"

"I follow."

"Since the head teacher's office is on the first floor, I headed downstairs towards the classroom. Out of the corner of my eye I noticed two people coming into the school. I knocked on the door, Puleo said to come in, and so I entered the classroom and closed the door.

"I hadn't told Salvuzzo I was coming, so he was pleasantly surprised to see me and called out, 'Hello, Papa.' I introduced myself to Puleo, told him the head teacher had given me permission to come there, and said I needed to talk to him. The teacher said that the class was almost over, and if I would just be so kind as to wait for him outside, in the hallway . . . So I said, fine, and turned around to go out, and at that exact moment, the door opened and two people —"

"Stop for a second. Were their faces covered?"

"Yes. They were both wearing the same mask."

"Some kind of carnival mask?"

"No. Puleo did a sketch of it. Counterterrorism's got it."

"How were they dressed?"

"Almost exactly alike. Greenish sweatshirts, baggy trousers, plimsolls."

140

"And physically what were they like?"

"One was skinny, about five foot eleven, with black curly hair. The other was blond and about three inches shorter."

"Were they speaking Italian or dialect?"

"Italian."

"Any particular accent?"

"Not that I could tell. Maybe Puleo . . ."

"How old do you think they were?"

"I'd say both were under thirty."

"Go on."

"They came in brandishing their pistols, closed the door behind them, and then the taller one said in a very soft but cold and determined voice: 'Everybody get their hands up and nobody breathe!' And then something happened."

"What?"

"Two or three students started laughing. They thought it was a game. And so I, since I was already on my way out and just a step away from them, I said: 'Cut it out, guys!' By way of reply the blond one punched me right in the face and ordered me to go and stand next to Puleo with my hands up."

"And what did you do?"

"Well, since I was armed, my natural instinct was to use it. But I controlled myself."

"How did you manage to do that?"

"I thought of all the kids, who at this point were scared out of their wits. If I followed my natural instinct, it could've triggered a shoot-out, in a classroom with thirty kids! Can you imagine that? It could have turned into a massacre! Puleo was great. He never once lost his nerve, and he kept repeating to his pupils not to get upset, and not to move."

"Mimi, let me tell you something, and I mean it with all my heart. Puleo may have been great, but you were even greater. You remained perfectly lucid, you made the right decision. Well done!"

"I have to confess that it cost me a lot. Not so much for my own sake, but for my son's."

"Because he saw you being humiliated?"

"Yes. After the guy punched me, I looked over at Salvuzzo. He'd covered his eyes so he couldn't see, and he was crying . . . Let me think . . . At this point the tall thin guy took a step forward, but staying still close to the door, and said: 'Now listen up,' and he gave a little speech."

"Do you remember what he said?"

"How could I forget? While he was talking I made a special effort to concentrate so I could commit his words to memory. He said: 'We represent order and justice. We will not tolerate disorder, injustice, and abuse of power. Those who do not respect our principles we consider our enemies. If in the future these principles are not respected, we will return, and the fate of our enemies will be the following.' And at that point they both fired a shot in the air. Then, as all hell broke loose in the class, they opened the door and ran down the corridor and finally out of the school. I shouted to Puleo to look after the kids, and then dashed out in pursuit."

142

CHAPTER
TEN

"Hold on a second. Were they only armed with pistols?"

"Pistols is all I saw."

"What kind?"

"Ordinary Berettas."

"Which you couldn't really say are the favourite weapons of terrorists."

"And in fact the counterterrorism guys are completely befuddled. So, as I was saying, I started chasing after them. I could have tried to stop them while they were still at the end of the hallway, but I didn't. It was too dangerous."

"For whom?"

"Those two shots they fired had stirred up a lot of commotion. There were about ten people in the hallway, counting students and teachers. If the two gunmen had opened fire, they would certainly have killed somebody."

"You did exactly the right thing."

"But as soon as I came out into the schoolyard and realized it was empty, I yelled: 'Stop! Police!' The two guys, who in the meantime had almost reached the gate, then turned around and shot at me, so I fell to the ground and returned fire. They started crawling

143

backwards, shooting all the while, and finally went out through the gate and got into a car that was waiting for them with its doors open. I stood up and was able to get the number plate. Which I immediately communicated to Montelusa Central and the carabinieri. And that's about it."

"Did they still have their masks on when they were shooting at you?"

"They never once took them off."

"So nobody ever saw their faces?"

"One did. The caretaker at the school entrance. Because the taller guy, when he came in, told him they were scouting the place in preparation for shooting a scene from the TV movie there, and that they had the administration's permission. They probably were hiding their masks under their sweatshirts."

"They didn't ask him where classroom III B was?"

"No."

"Did the caretaker say anything else?"

"Yes. He said that the blond man had a scar on his forehead over his left eye."

"Who was it that called our station?"

"Puleo, as soon as he heard the shots being fired in the schoolyard."

"Tell me a little about Riccadonna . . ."

"He's a complete idiot. And I feel personally insulted by what he said to me after I told him the whole story."

"And what was that?"

"He said he was going to ask the commissioner to keep me out of this investigation."

The inspector did a double take. "Why?"

"He said, and I quote: 'For your shamefully submissive attitude in the face of the two aggressors.'"

"Let me get this straight. He's blaming you for not reacting to being punched?"

"That's correct."

Two big tears rolled down Augello's cheeks. Which he wiped away in rage with one hand and then said in a quavering voice:

"And God knows what it cost me to hold myself back . . . With my son there covering his eyes in shame . . ."

Montalbano felt a stifling rage rising up inside him but controlled himself.

"Mimì, you have my word that Riccadonna will be forced to apologize to you. And for now you should stop thinking about it. Take my advice. Just go home now and rest. We'll talk again tomorrow."

Mimì rose wearily to his feet.

"Don't forget that there's a press conference at the commissioner's office at noon tomorrow. I'll be seeing you. Have a good night."

After Mimì went out, the hunger the inspector had been ignoring for the past two days attacked him like a mad dog. He glanced at his watch: almost ten. He realized that a few remaining members of the film crew might still be at Enzo's; on the other hand, he really didn't feel like fasting all night. It was worth a try.

"Montalbano here, Enzo. Are there still people there?"

"No, Inspector."

"Is there still time for me to come by and get something to eat?"

"The restaurant's closed, Inspector, but if you want to come and sit down at our table, we made a wonderful fish soup with the leftovers from the day."

"I'll be there in an instant," said Montalbano.

The first thing he did upon entering his office the following morning was to call the commissioner.

"Good morning, sir. I wanted to let you know that I came back from my leave yesterday evening to make myself totally available to the force. I also wanted to ask you if I could come and talk to you before the press conference at noon."

"I appreciate your conscientiousness, Montalbano. You can consider yourself exempted from attending, since —"

"Thank you, but I absolutely have to talk to you."

"But is it something concerning what happened yesterday?"

"Yes, Mr Commissioner."

"Then come to my office at eleven."

"Thank you."

Moments later, Fazio walked in.

"Were you able to get some rest?"

"Enough. But I didn't get home until past midnight."

"Why? Where were you?"

"Out gathering information on Mr Puleo, the teacher."

"And what can you tell me?"

"Giuseppe Puleo . . ." He stopped and looked at Montalbano. "Can I have a look at my notes?"

"Sure, just so long as you don't launch into a full account of Puleo's family tree."

"OK."

With a satisfied air, Fazio pulled a folded sheet of paper out of his jacket pocket, unfolded it, and started reading.

"Giuseppe Puleo, forty-eight years old, born in Montelusa. Has taught mathematics for the past five years at the Pirandello School. Married with three sons, and all good kids. He's widely admired as a serious, balanced, reserved person, and as far as we are concerned, he has no police record, no 41 bis, and no friends of 41 bis in his family."

He folded the page up again and put it back in his pocket.

"Mimì told me," said Montalbano, "that Puleo was exemplary in his behaviour during the disruption in his classroom and never once lost his nerve. I would like to talk to this schoolteacher, and to the caretaker who saw the culprits' faces. I would also like to have a look at the school early this afternoon."

"The school is closed by court injunction. But if you want, I can ask both of them to come by around twelve thirty."

"OK. Go and call them right away." As Fazio was leaving, Augello came in.

In his hand he was holding a transparent plastic bag containing the shirt that Montalbano had lent him the previous evening. All nice and clean and ironed and good as new. He set it down on the desk.

"There was no need to make work for Beba. You could have just given it back to me the way it was."

"Actually the poor thing had to work double-time, because when she hung it out to dry after the first

147

washing, a pigeon made a point of shitting on it, and so she had to wash it again by hand and then dry it with a hair dryer. Anyway, here it is."

Montalbano took it and put it in a drawer of his desk. "I've been exempted," he said, "from attending the press conference."

"Well, I haven't, unfortunately," said Augello.

"But the commissioner will be expecting me at eleven, and I want to talk to him about this Riccadonna business."

"Thanks. I had trouble falling asleep last night," Augello continued. "I kept thinking about the little speech the taller man made."

"And did you draw any conclusions?"

"Yes. The more I thought about it, the more I realized that what he said seemed to concern everything and nothing at the same time. He might have been referring to class III B, or I A, or even to the town hall, the local fish business, or the problem of the homeless. And just to stay on the subject of school, what kind of injustice and abuse of power could he be talking about?"

The only injustices that came into the inspector's mind were small things: an undeserved low mark, a bad recommendation, excessive favouritism, but nothing that might cause such pandemonium.

"On the other hand," Mimi resumed, "those two guys' only purpose was to scare everybody to death. They certainly didn't want to kill the teacher or any of the students. It was basically all smoke and mirrors."

Montalbano looked at him, and sat there for a moment without opening his mouth. Then he began:

"No, Mimì, you're not taking into account the fact that the school incident breaks down into two parts. Let's try to clearly define what we're talking about. You're right about the first part, but the second part involved not so much smoke and mirrors but a couple of real-life gunshots, which changes the picture entirely. When they fired their guns in the schoolyard, were they shooting in the air or aiming at you?"

"They were aiming at me. I was lucky they didn't hit me."

"You see?" Montalbano continued. "The second part adds to the gravity of the first. Let me give you another example. Something you yourself said. You didn't react to being punched because you were mathematically certain that they would have responded by firing their guns. To conclude, what I mean is that what they did was a genuine act of violence. You were able to avert the worst, and you did it to protect the kids in the classroom; but you weren't able to do the same in the schoolyard. So my question is: what happened in that classroom to trigger such a reaction?"

"You're absolutely right. Except that your division of the event into two parts implies that the first part was planned and the second part unforeseen. And the unforeseen element is me. Because if I hadn't been there, the extreme violence you mention would not have broken out."

"Now you're right where I want you. What you've just said completely rules out the hypothesis that those two guys might be terrorists. Because that is almost certainly what they'll be talking about at the press conference today."

"What makes you think that?"

"Because terrorists act completely differently from the way those two young men did. Terrorists shoot and kill first, then lay claim to their butchery with their slogans. Those two came into a classroom, made their little speech, then fired two symbolic shots into the air, to underscore what they'd just said. According to their plans, the whole matter was to have ended there."

"And so?"

"And so nothing, at least for now. There's only one thing I feel I can say for certain at the moment, which is that their incursion into the school has a number of inconsistencies about it, if we're supposed to be considering it an act of terrorism."

"So what do you think it was, then?"

"I tend to think it was some kind of violent attempt at intimidation."

"Which would make a huge difference," commented Augello.

Commissioner Bonetti-Alderighi's face had the shattered look of someone who'd lost a lot of sleep. And in a strange, unprecedented turn, he was almost cordial with Montalbano. He held out his hand, sat him down, and said:

"I really appreciate your decision to cut your holiday short to return to service."

What was happening to the man? He must be scared to death to be behaving so lamblike.

"Though I am often forced to criticize you for your methods, I have to admit that your presence reassures me. You, naturally, will now take over the investigation, while remaining of course in close contact with the counterterrorism unit."

"Thank you, Mr Commissioner."

"Why did you want to see me?"

"My second-in-command, Domenico Augello, told me that Prosecutor Riccadonna intends to . . ."

Bonetti-Alderighi raised his hand. The inspector trailed off. "I already know everything. Are you in agreement with Riccadonna?" asked the commissioner.

"Not in the least! Inspector Augello acted in an exemplary fashion! I do not understand how . . ."

The commissioner raised his hand again.

"There have been some developments you're unaware of. Yesterday evening, Riccadonna phoned me to ask that Inspector Augello be dismissed from the case for the reasons you know. I tried to explain to him that he was wrong about that, but he was stubborn. So I called the chief prosecutor and laid out the whole situation for him. Which is that I was intending, at the press conference, to nominate Inspector Augello for a citation of honour, and that therefore my words were going to be in direct conflict with what Riccadonna was going to say. The journalists would have gone to town with it. A short while later the chief prosecutor called back to tell me that Riccadonna, after some arm-twisting, had withdrawn his request."

"Are we so sure that Riccadonna won't blurt out some unpleasant assertions during the press conference?"

"If he does, I'll be ready to rebut them."

"I appreciate that."

Bonetti-Alderighi then leaned all the way forward in his chair, and said in a soft voice:

"But, in all honesty, Montalbano, have you come up with any possible explanation for what happened?"

Montalbano looked him in the eye, dead serious. "In all honesty, sir, no."

"Well, keep me informed of any positive developments, even the most minuscule. I mean it. I'm being bombarded from Rome with pressures, demands . . . If there was one little thing I could give them, however small . . ."

He was clearly scared. Naturally, he felt his career was in jeopardy.

It was almost noon when the inspector got to the station. He barely had time to go into Augello's office and turn on the television to the Free Channel. There, on the screen, behind a long table, sat Augello, Marchica — who was the chief of the counterterrorism unit — Bonetti-Alderighi, Riccadonna, and Liberati of the Flying Squad. The commissioner, who was the first to speak, said that this was going to be a communique for the press, not a conference. Therefore, given the sensitive nature of the ongoing investigations, no questions would be permitted. There was a buzz of discontented muttering among the mob of journalists present. Hearing those words, the inspector became convinced that there had been another spat between the commissioner and Riccadonna and that the press conference, or whatever it was, could very well take a bad turn, or almost. And, indeed, Riccadonna, whose turn came next, was off like a rocket.

He announced that the prosecutor's office, as was their duty, were following every lead, but they were favouring one in particular: the terrorism angle, and they could only regret that the police, at the moment of the assault on the school, had not acted as decisively as might have been hoped. And he sat back down. As pale as a corpse, Augello was about to stand up, but Fazio, who was standing behind him, put a hand on his shoulder, forcing him to remain seated. Then Marchica stood up and explained that the mask the two assailants were wearing was the trademark of Anonymous, an international organization operating via the internet that coordinated individual as well as group actions against things they deemed unjust. According to Marchica, however, the two men wearing Anonymous masks had behaved in a manner inconsistent with the group's general pattern.

Liberati explained how they'd found the car the two gunmen had stolen, and then the commissioner resumed speaking. He told how Inspector Domenico Augello, of Vigàta Police, happened purely by chance to be engaged in a discussion with a teacher at the school when the two armed men suddenly burst into the classroom. The only thought in Inspector Augello's head was to be sure, even at the cost of personal

153

humiliation, to avoid any chance of an exchange of fire in that classroom with thirty children in it. He did, on the other hand, open fire on the two men once they were in a relatively safe area with no danger to bystanders. And for his bravery, lucidity, and the deep sense of responsibility he had shown in protecting the students, he was recommending Inspector Augello for a well-deserved citation of honour and recognition by the Ministry of Justice.

He then thanked the journalists gathered, adjourned the meeting, and went out, followed by everyone else.

Everyone had blown his own trumpet, and each trumpet had a different sound. As the commissioner had foreseen, the newsmen now had a great deal to feast on.

Montalbano went to get his car and then drove to the Pirandello School.

He parked outside the front gate, walked through the schoolyard in which the exchange of gunfire had taken place, and then returned the greeting of the police officer standing at the entrance.

"Have the caretaker and Mr Puleo arrived yet?" he asked him.

"They went out to get some coffee. They'll be right back."

The inspector went in, climbed three broad stairs, and found himself at one end of a long, wide corridor that had a large window at the far end. On his right were a table and chair, which must have normally been the caretaker's post for keeping an eye on people coming in and going out. The staircase leading upstairs began about halfway down the hallway, on the left-hand side. He began walking down the hall, reading the nameplates outside each door. He had to walk the entire length of the corridor, since III B was the last classroom on the right, just beside the large window.

He turned the doorknob and went in.

The room was in a state of indescribable chaos. Benches on their sides or overturned, legs in the air, the blackboard on the floor next to the teacher's desk, which was resting on one side. All resulting from the panic that had broken out after the two men had fired their guns. The inspector looked up and saw the damage done by the two shots. He couldn't help but think of how good Mimì had been to protect all the kids, including his own son, at all costs.

He went back out, turned his back, and saw a pair of men approaching who looked rather like Don Quixote and Sancho Panza. One was tall, lanky, and very thin, the other short and round as a barrel. He went up to them and introduced himself.

The barrel said his name was Vitantonio Camastra, and called himself the "school manager" — in plain language, the caretaker. Mr Puleo simply shook the inspector's hand, saying his surname under his breath.

"Where can we talk?" Montalbano asked.

"We can talk in the staffroom," replied the caretaker, setting out down the hall.

He opened a door halfway down and stepped aside to let the other two in.

It was a large room with a long table in the middle, surrounded by a great many chairs.

"Who do you want to start with?" asked the teacher.

"I'll start with Mr Camastra, but if you feel like staying . . ."

"I'm happy to stay."

They sat down.

"I'm told," the inspector began, "that you contributed descriptions to the artist's reconstruction of the two gunmen. Did they stop to talk to you for long?"

"No, not at all," replied Camastra.

"So then how were you able —"

"The head teacher says I have a photographic memory. And it's true."

"Can you repeat to me with any precision what they said when they came in?"

"Actually, I spoke first. When I saw them come in, I asked what they wanted. The taller guy replied that they were part of the film crew and were supposed to scout the place, and they had the head teacher's permission. And then he started digging in his pocket for something. At that point I asked him, 'Do you know where to go?' and the tall guy said, 'Yes,' and so I said, 'OK, you can go on in.' I kept on watching them as they headed down to the end of the hallway, then a man appeared and said he'd come to pick up his son."

"You're very observant. So I'd like you to make a little effort to search your memory. When you asked them if they knew where to go, did the taller guy immediately say yes?"

The little barrel gave him a strange look, openmouthed, a bit like Lou Ravi in a nativity scene. "How'd you guess?"

"What did they do?" asked Puleo.

Then, a bit shyly, the caretaker said:

"Sorry, sorry. They looked at each other, and the blond guy gave a little laugh. A stupid little laugh. To the point that I thought: 'What's so funny, anyway?'"

"And did you hear the gunshots?"

"Of course, but I was upstairs, since I'd accompanied the boy's father to the classroom where he could find his son."

"When the two gunmen entered room III B, they were wearing masks. Were you able to see where they'd been hiding them?"

"They were probably inside the cases they wore around their necks. You know, the kind used for carrying small cameras and that sort of thing."

"In your opinion, was the man who spoke Italian or a foreigner?"

"If you ask me, he was Italian. But Italian Italian."

"You mean he wasn't Sicilian?"

"Right, not Sicilian, nor Calabrian, nor Apulian, nor Neapolitan. And not even Roman."

"Are there any other details you can give me, using your photographic memory?"

"What can I say! The blond guy looked lost. His eyes looked like he was in a daze. Like he was hypnotized. The other guy, the one who talked, when I saw him walking from behind, looked like he was on a ship on rough seas."

"Explain what you mean."

"He walked weird, leaning from side to side, first to the right, then to the left, then forward, then back."

"Do you think they were drugged?"

"I have no idea. But I know one thing: they sure weren't normal. But I didn't get suspicious because I thought . . . well, you know what those movie and TV people are like . . . they're weird!"

"After you heard the shots, what did you do?"

"I went downstairs in a hurry, but when I got there the two guys were already outside. And inside there was panic, everybody running every which way, screaming and crying. I didn't know which ones to help first. Then there was a teacher, Mrs Arnone, who seemed like she'd gone out of her mind. She started yelling: 'Fire! Fire!' I don't why she got this idea that there was a fire. 'Everybody run to the fire escapes! Use the extinguishers! Break the glass with the hammers!' It took me a little while to convince her there wasn't a fire. And then I did the only thing I felt it was my duty to do. When I saw the two guys at the end of the corridor about to go out, I ran first into III A, then into III B, and then, just to be sure, I went into all the other classrooms in that hallway, and when I was sure there weren't any more kids or teachers or injured or dead, and only then, I sat down on the floor."

"All right, thanks. That will suffice for now."

CHAPTER
ELEVEN

"Does that mean you don't need me no more?" asked Camastra.

"Yes, that's right," said Montalbano. "For the moment I have no more questions for you."

Camastra stood up.

"Then I'm going to go. School reopens tomorrow, and so if you need me, you can find me here."

He said goodbye to Puleo and the inspector and went out.

Left alone in the room, the two men looked each other in the eye for a moment, and that brief glance expressed a shared sense of dissatisfaction. Camastra's account did nothing to advance the investigation by as much as one step.

"I don't think," said the schoolteacher, as if he'd read the inspector's mind, "that I can really add anything to what you already know, either."

"Well, let's try anyway. Were you able to tell whether or not the two gunmen spoke with northern inflections? And if so, from where?"

The schoolteacher thought about this for a moment, then said:

"To be perfectly honest with you, I had exactly the opposite impression from the caretaker."

"Meaning?"

"To me they seemed like two southerners doing everything possible to try not to seem like southerners. There was a certain lack of spontaneity in the way they pronounced their words."

Montalbano pressed him further.

"You, I'm told, are an astute observer, to the point that you were able to draw the masks they used to cover their faces. My question now is: could you tell whether they were drugged or otherwise in some sort of altered state?"

"They certainly weren't normal, but I couldn't really say whether it was because of drugs or the tenseness of the situation. I do remember clearly, however, that the man who didn't talk seemed subservient to the other one. He depended on him not only verbally but also in his actions, to know 'what moves to make'."

"Well, that's sort of normal. Apparently the taller guy was the boss."

"Yes," said Puleo, "but to me it looked like something more than just a hierarchical thing. It was as if the two men were linked by something else, something I can't define. And it wasn't just camaraderie. The look in the blond guy's eyes was . . . wait, let me think . . . it was a look of devoted submission. That's it."

Montalbano's thoughts went back for a moment to the photo of the Sabatello brothers. Maybe the two gunmen were also related.

160

"Thank you for your observations," he said, "but as of this moment, I want us to proceed as if we were just chatting freely. Neither of us should feel the need to ask questions or provide answers. Is that OK with you?"

"It's OK with me."

"I know just about everything that happened from the moment the two entered the classroom. My second-in-command, Mimì Augello, told me all about it. Therefore —"

"I'm taking advantage of your instructions, so please forgive me for interrupting," said Puleo. "But in all the time that's passed since that moment, among the thousands of other questions I've been pointlessly asking myself, there's one, perhaps, that you might be able to answer."

"What is it?"

"Do you know why your second-in-command, Salvo Augello's father, came to talk to me?"

"Yes," said the inspector. "I think I do. He wanted to alert you to the fact that there'd been some unpleasant cases of bullying in class III B."

Puleo looked at him with surprise. "Really?"

"Yes, really."

"But how did Augello find out? Was Salvo perhaps directly involved?"

"No, he's not the one being bullied," said Montalbano. "Apparently there are three boys in the class who are picking on one of their classmates. One day Salvo tried to defend him and ended up paying for it, coming home with a black eye and his clothes all torn. So you didn't hear anything about any of this?"

161

Puleo was genuinely astonished. "Nothing whatsoever."

Montalbano remembered what Augello had said about the teacher — about the man he'd shown himself to be when the assailants burst in. Certainly no young toughs were going to start acting like idiots or bullies in front of him.

"Maybe," said the inspector, "it's because these things occur outside class."

"Probably," Puleo added. "But I assure you that none of my colleagues has mentioned anything of that nature."

He sat there for a moment, absorbed in thought. Montalbano resumed.

"Back to us. Going by what the caretaker said — and you heard him yourself — the two assailants already knew the location of classroom III B in the building. And they headed straight for it. Do you agree with me about that?"

"Yes."

"So, in every classroom, you have the teacher on the one hand, the students on the other. In your opinion, when the gunmen issued their threats, before shooting their guns, to whom were the threats directed?"

As soon as he'd formulated his question, the door opened and Fazio came in, greeted them both, and went and sat in a chair a bit further away.

"When I saw them come in," said Puleo, after returning Fazio's glance of greeting, "armed and masked, my first thought was that their target must be me."

"Why did you think that?"

Puleo made a slight grin.

"Certainly not because I thought I was guilty of anything."

"Why, then?"

"Inspector, at that moment, my mind was unable to conceive that so violent and terrifying a threat could possibly be directed at my kids. But I had to revise my opinion. And I had proof of it almost immediately."

"How?" asked Montalbano.

"I'll explain. Let's say you come into this room, the staffroom, during a meeting. You look directly at the person you intend to threaten, no? It's perfectly natural. Well, neither of those two guys ever looked at me. Not once did either of them ever turn their eyes to me. Actually they acted the same way our head teacher does when she wants to reprimand the class. She comes in, closes the door, remains close to it, looks over at me — she, at least, does — then addresses the class. She talks to them, not to me. Well, I had that exact feeling. I wasn't part of their plan."

"That makes sense to me," Montalbano admitted. "Unfortunately, however, it's not enough for me."

Puleo seemed surprised. "Why not?"

"Because personal convictions are never enough for me. I need to know, beyond your impressions, whether the two assailants really never looked at you, or whether their general focus on the class might not have been just a cover to hide their real purpose."

"I have no enemies," Puleo said without hesitation.

This time it was Montalbano who smiled.

"In an official interrogation, I would have asked you: my good professor, how could you think the two might have come for you if you have no enemies? You're contradicting yourself. But since we're just having a chat, I can tell you that I don't think there's a single man alive who can say he doesn't have any enemies. I'll grant that the word 'enemy' may be a bit excessive. But it's impossible for a man not to know a single person he might rub the wrong way, and who detests him for one reason or another, or maybe envies him, or somebody who, rightly or wrongly, thinks he did him a bad turn."

Puleo smiled.

"I did some very careful, detailed soul-searching to be able to make the statement I just did. But perhaps I should change the wording. I don't think I have ever elicited in any other party such resentment as would warrant taking armed action."

"But *you* are not on other people's minds, sir."

"You're right," Puleo said after a moment's pause, seeming a little less self-assured.

"To put it in your kind of language, there's no way you can be mathematically certain of what you're saying to me," Montalbano added for emphasis. "Nowadays, in a world as neurotic as ours, all it takes is the slightest thing to set a person off. How often have we read in the papers about situations, say, where someone steals someone else's parking spot, and the guy who feels cheated can't help but get out of the car and beat the other person to death?"

"Well," said Puleo, "at this point I give up. If that's the way it is, I would have to review every action I've ever taken in life and ask myself whether it might have yielded unforeseen and indeed unthinkable consequences. It is as if, in a quadratic equation . . ."

The mere mention of the word "equation" sufficed to make Montalbano break out into a sweat and see himself back in class with the teacher at the blackboard writing down letters and numbers about which he understood not a thing.

"Stop right there," he said out of the blue.

The room went silent, until the sound of Fazio's voice broke in.

"Er, Mr Puleo, about what you just said . . . I found out by chance that five or six years ago you published a book that stirred up some controversy . . ."

Mr Puleo first looked at him in wide-eyed bewilderment, then slapped himself on the forehead.

"You're right! But what are you thinking? I don't think that has any connection with . . ."

Montalbano, for his part, became immediately interested.

"No, no. That's up to us to decide. Do please tell us about it. I'm anxious to hear."

"A dear friend of mine opened a small publishing house in conjunction with his bookshop in Montelusa. And I wrote for him a sort of biography of a great Arab mathematician who'd served at the court of Frederick II in Palermo, and who gave a tremendous boost to mathematical scholarship by contributing a formula that I won't bother to explain to you. According to this mathematician, the inspiration for creating the formula, which is based on the plus sign, came to him in a

165

dream in the form of the Christian cross. And this was the basic reason that led him shortly thereafter to abjure his own faith and convert to Christianity. I don't know how, but my little book ended up in the hands of some Arab scholars, who basically dismissed the story of the conversion and the dream of the cross."

"The way things are these days," Fazio observed, "don't you think that might be a plausible motive?"

"No, I would rule that out."

"Why?"

"Because," Puleo said firmly, "the dismissal was couched in scholarly terms and contained no threatening tone or language. The letter simply cited evidence, and the disputation was quite civilized and never ventured outside of the realm of academic discourse."

Then he blurted out:

"That's all we need! For every scholarly, historical, or religious argument to end up in bombings and shoot-outs! Sicilian culture is also part Arab at its origins, after all! And where are we going to put Frederick II of Swabia? Who are we kidding?" Puleo carried on, nervously taking his glasses off and on several times. "Anyway, the two men didn't at all speak the way they should have. They spoke generically, whereas we know that terrorists always take the name of Allah in vain. But they didn't."

"I can't say you're wrong," said Montalbano, who had already come to the same conclusion on his own.

"On the other hand, what deeply disturbs me is how I managed not to notice that there was such a serious problem in my classroom. Could you tell me a little more about it?"

"I don't know any more than what I've told you," said the inspector. "Oh, wait. Yes, I also remember that Salvo says the friend of his who's the target of the bullying is a computer wizard."

"Luigino Sciarabba!" the teacher said at once. Then, as if to himself: "I would never have imagined it."

"Why not?"

"Because, well, he never let anything show during class time. I've never seen him upset, angry, or particularly nervous . . . How odd, how very odd . . . But who are these bullies, anyway? How long has this been going on? Who knows about it? . . . I thank you for informing me. From now on I'm going to keep my eyes open . . . Please tell Salvo's father that I'm entirely at his disposal, and would really like to know more about the whole situation . . . I don't feel like asking the kids about it."

Montalbano was rather struck by the sincerity of Puleo's concern.

"I will of course do everything I can to learn more about this and I'll pass any new information on to my second-in-command. I'll keep you posted."

He then returned to what interested him most.

"Tell me something: are there computers in the school?"

"Of course there are computers! As in all Italian schools. What's a shame is that, as in all Italian schools, they're hardly ever used. There's not enough money to pay technicians, and our computers have just been

167

sitting there for years, gathering dust. Luckily the electronic blackboard hasn't yet arrived here in the south . . ."

With a hand gesture, Montalbano put an end to the schoolteacher's grousing about school-related matters. Otherwise it might go on for ever. He returned to the main subject.

"So how did word get out about this Sciarabba kid's talents?"

"I can see, Inspector, that you think there's still a need for computers, screens, hardware, plugs . . . But the kids now all have smartphones, tablets, and every manner of gadget perpetually connected to the internet, and Luigino, being quite the expert in all that, is always being consulted by everyone for help and advice. That's how word got out about him. The kids talk about him among themselves, and they talk about him in class . . ."

Montalbano couldn't think of anything else to ask him. "Well, Professor, I thank you for your help. We'll be seeing each other again soon, since starting tomorrow I want to talk to the kids. Actually, Fazio, get the head teacher to assign a room to you that we can use for our talks."

Fazio looked doubtful.

"What's wrong?" asked the inspector.

"I'm sorry, Chief, but shouldn't the parents also be present for these talks?"

"My intention is not to have genuine interrogations, and neither to record the transcripts of our discussions. I just want each of them to describe to me what they saw when those two burst into the classroom, what they felt, what they noticed in particular. I am sure they will each have a different perspective . . ."

He stopped and looked questioningly at Puleo.

"I think you'll be able to do your job without any problem, and without any parents or psychologists having to be there," said the schoolteacher.

They both smiled. Montalbano held out his hand. Puleo shook it and said:

"I really would like to be present at these meetings, if you think that would be possible."

"I'd love nothing more, but I fear your presence might in some way inhibit the kids from speaking freely. In their eyes you're still Mr Puleo, the maths teacher. Know what I mean?"

"I know what you mean."

"But I promise to keep you informed as to how my talks are going, and I'm sure I'll be needing your advice."

After Puleo went out, Fazio asked:

"How are you going to talk to these kids? One at a time? Two at a time? All at the same time?"

"Do you know how many are in that class?"

Fazio stuck one hand in his jacket pocket, pulled out a sheet of paper folded in four, unfolded it, looked at it, and said:

"Twenty-six."

"What've you got there?"

"I asked for a list of all the students in class III B."

Montalbano looked at him in admiration.

"And I'm sure you also asked whether there were any absences that day."

"They were all present."

The inspector smiled.

"Does any name jump out at you?"

"Not really. But if you don't need me at the moment, I think I'll drop in at the records office after lunch. So I can check on family relations, cousins, grandparents, nephews, nieces, and so on."

The inspector was about to say "good idea", but at the sound of the word "lunch" he felt a hunger pang so powerful that all he could do was pat Fazio on the shoulder and run out of the room.

He was about to get in his car and race off to Enzo's when he noticed a dozen or so tables on the pavement opposite the school, most of them occupied by kids who looked about fifteen years old and who were joking around, laughing, talking, and eating pizza.

Montalbano looked up and read the sign: *Pizza and Sfincione*. It was clear this pizzeria was a meeting place for these teenagers, even though the school was closed.

Lately he'd been speaking of nothing but teenagers, but he'd never actually heard these teenagers talking.

He locked the car and went into the establishment.

He ordered two piping-hot slices of *sfincione* with meat, which were promptly served on a plate, and holding a glass of beer in his other hand, he went and sat down at one of the tables outside.

While eating he kept his ears pricked up to listen to what the kids at the table next to his were saying. But he didn't understand a word of it.

Maybe if he'd lived a little longer with François . . . But he immediately slammed that door shut.

Good God, how long had it been since he'd had anything to do with adolescents?

How did they talk nowadays? How did they think?

What were their interests?

And here he'd been thinking it would be so easy to question them!

This represented a new problem.

The *sfincione*, on the other hand, was good. He stood up and got himself another hefty serving.

When he went to sit back down, the hum of voices died down a little, and Montalbano was able to hear a few phrases of what the two boys sitting close to him were saying.

"Why, don't you think that's the raddest thing?"

"No, I think it's more hot than rad."

"Speaking of hot, I got a WhatsApp from Maria."

"Oh, goody! So you joined, too."

Now, Montalbano more or less knew what they meant by "hot", but "rad" was entirely new to his ears. And a *wotsap* was something he couldn't even conceive.

The new problem was growing before his very eyes. Perhaps he should ask Salvuzzo to act as his interpreter.

All of a sudden, like a flock of birds, in response to some sort of signal, all the kids got up and ran out, yelling and laughing, headed down to the end of the street, turned the corner, and disappeared.

Left to himself, Montalbano finished eating and got in his car to drive to the harbour, to take his customary stroll.

As he was about to set out onto the jetty, however, he was stopped by a barrier of wire fences. At this point a sort of rustic King Kong bore down hard on him.

"You got it? You got it?"

"What am I supposed to got?"

"A pass. You got it?"

Montalbano suddenly remembered the TV movie, turned around without answering, and walked away.

He'd just driven past the Caffè Castiglione when he suddenly slammed on the brakes. He'd noticed another group of teenagers hanging around outside the cafe, some of them sitting, some standing. Without getting out of the car, he started watching them. He sat there for a while that way, then started the car back up and returned to the station.

He parked the car, but instead of going into his office, he went back out into the street and retraced his path on foot, slowly, one step at a time, back to the Caffè Castiglione.

Stopping a short distance away, he lit a cigarette and started watching again.

These kids, unlike the ones at the pizzeria, who were the same age, were scattered about, some closer to the cafe, some farther away, but each in his or her own world, isolated. And they seemed so hypnotized by what they were doing that they never even raised their heads to look at one another.

But what were they doing?

Montalbano noticed that they all had more or less the same posture. Chin resting on the chest, elbows tucked tightly into the waist, both hands squeezing something they were caressing with their thumbs, the only part of their bodies that was moving.

He went closer.

He stepped onto the pavement. He was in their midst.

The silence was unreal. He felt as if he was in an aquarium. Then he forced himself to look at their faces and managed to see their eyes. All of them had pinpoint pupils and looked lost.

Nobody dared raise his or her head, as would have been natural, feeling oneself being eyed by another person.

On the contrary, it seemed as if his extraneous presence among them made them flee even further into their personal bubbles of isolation.

If the kids at the pizzeria were speaking a language Montalbano couldn't understand, he felt even more excluded from these youths who never opened their mouths.

He was discouraged.

How would he ever manage to grasp the slightest thing about the way they thought and acted?

As he walked away, he had one question in his head. How was it possible, in the age of global communication, when all cultural, linguistic, geographical, and economic borders had been erased from the face of the earth, that this vast new realm had only created a multitude of loners, infinite numbers of lonely people in communication with one another, yes, but still in a state of utter solitude?

CHAPTER
TWELVE

At the office he found Augello waiting for him. One look was enough to tell him that every pore in Mimì's body was exuding pure and total satisfaction.

He was clearly keen to talk, so Montalbano gave him the green light.

"Tell me what happened after the press conference."

Augello, who wanted nothing more, smiled and took a deep breath, like an actor before stepping onto the stage.

"What happened was that Riccadonna didn't keep his word. Contrary to what had been agreed, during the press conference he made a point of finding fault with my behaviour. And the commissioner was so upset about it that he not only replied publicly, but, after the conference was over, he locked himself in a room with the chief prosecutor, and when they came back out, both frowning, the journalists, who'd got a whiff of something odd and therefore hadn't budged from the premises, were told that Riccadonna had been replaced by his colleague, Prosecutor Terranova."

"Congratulations on your sweet revenge! And for the commissioner's words of praise," said Montalbano.

Then, continuing: "Terranova seems to me like an honest person who understands things."

"And who doesn't attack people for no reason," added Augello.

Afterwards, the inspector informed him as to his meetings that morning with the caretaker and the schoolteacher.

"So, in essence, no new developments," was Mimì's final comment. "Let's hope the kids give some answers . . ."

"Well, that's just the problem," said Montalbano.

"Why do you say that? What problem is that?"

"I've come to the conclusion it's going to be very hard to talk to them. You know how when you start thinking intensely about something, you end up seeing it everywhere? Well, ever since the classroom incident, I see teenagers everywhere. I ran into some earlier, both before lunch and after, on my way here. I watched them, studied them, and listened to them, and the conclusion I came to was that they represent a world that is entirely foreign to me. I can't even understand them when they speak."

"You're telling me!" Mimì blurted out. "The same thing happens to me with Salvuzzo. Beba is constantly reproaching me for not talking enough to my son. I try, I swear to you, I try, but he always answers as if he has no idea what I'm talking about. I've started to wonder whether he's stupid or just does it on purpose. And so, I end up losing patience and raising my voice, and he just clams up and that's the end of that. Such is the daily situation at my house."

After knocking, Fazio came in.

"Did you speak to the head teacher?"

"Yeah, Chief But there's a big problem."

"Namely?"

"The head teacher says she has to play by the rules, and that therefore, to talk to the students from class III B, the parents and one psychologist must be present."

"What a pain in the arse!" said Montalbano.

"As far as the parents are concerned, the head teacher is willing to look the other way," Fazio went on, "but she won't budge on the psychologist."

"And so?"

"And so we have to wait two or three days, for the head teacher to submit the request to the school board, or whatever it's called, and for her to get an answer and a board-appointed psychologist for the task. Which, in plain language, means, knowing how these things go, that it's going to waste at least a week."

Montalbano reacted furiously.

"Are they insane? With all this chaos of journalists, police commissioners, and ministers demanding updates and evidence, we can't even afford a few days without any news. We'll be branded incompetent at the very least!"

"In the meantime," Mimì cut in, "there is something we could do."

"And what's that?"

"We can start by talking to Salvuzzo. You can come to dinner at our place this evening and stay and talk to my son for as long as you like."

"Wrong," said Montalbano.

"Why?"

"Because you've just finished telling me about your difficulty in relating to Salvuzzo. You can't possibly think he's going to open up to me with you and Beba present."

"There's a way to get around that," said Mimì. "As soon as we've finished eating, Beba and I will go out to the movies. That way you'll even be doing us a favour, since we've been needing a little time together alone."

Considering the fact that Beba was a good cook, the inspector accepted without hesitation.

"You've got yourself a deal," he said.

"Eight-thirty OK with you?" Augello asked, standing up.

"Fine," said Montalbano.

"Guess what? A complete waste of time," said Fazio, after Augello had left.

"Explain."

"I checked the names of all the kids in class III B at the records office. I have to revise my opinion. Not one of them had any blood relations to Mafia families. What's so strange is that normally everyone around here's got someone in Ucciardone prison, except for the kids in this class."

The moment he stepped out of the office he was faced with a dilemma: should he buy a dozen roses for Beba, or a dozen super-fresh cannoli?

He settled the question by heading straight for the Caffè Castiglione. He'd just ordered the pastries when Engineer Sabatello, who'd been sitting at a table with two friends, joined him at the bar, leaning on a crutch. They exchanged a warm greeting.

"I imagine you've got other things on your mind these days, and so I beg your pardon, but I just can't control my curiosity. Did you learn anything new from Sidoti?"

Montalbano, who'd practically forgotten all about the mystery of the wall, needed a few seconds before answering. Then he said:

"He gave me a few details about what he saw at the scene of the suicide."

As he was saying it, the word "details" triggered a sort of short circuit in his brain. Details.

That was it. Sidoti had told him something that might be an important detail, or not, though at the time he had paid it no mind. Now, however, that detail seemed so alive and present in his memory, and in need of explanation, that the words rolled off his tongue before his brain had actually formulated the question.

"Was your father bald?"

Sabatello was momentarily taken aback, then said: "Yes, he was, bald as a billiard ball. But why do you ask?"

He had him there. Montalbano didn't know why he'd asked, and preferred to turn back to what Sidoti had said to him without answering Sabatello's question.

"*. . . and with the other hand he was trying to clean the blood off him with a handkerchief.*"

"*A handkerchief?*"

178

"Yes, sir. I don't really remember, but it must've been one of those big kerchiefs like the ones women use to wrap their heads . . ."

"How did your father normally cover his head, when he went out to work in the garden?"

Sabatello seemed even more taken aback.

"Well . . . wait . . . he had a big straw hat. Yes, that's it! Wow, that really brings back the memories!"

"Didn't he ever cover his head with one of those big, colourful handkerchiefs that peasant women use —"

"No," Sabatello interrupted him. "If he ever wore something like that, it was Mamma who put it on him."

The barman of the cafe gave the inspector a packet with the cannoli.

Sabatello held his hand out to Montalbano.

"You know something, in the attic there are five wooden chests containing Papa's papers. They were taken from the villa. I decided to open them and have a look inside. Can I let you know if I find anything interesting?"

"Whenever and however you like," said the inspector, shaking the engineer's hand.

Nobody talked much during dinner. More than once during the meal, Beba — who'd cooked a delicious timbale of pasta rings and aubergine — tried to spark a discussion of what had happened at the school, but her words were always met with silence from the two men, who were anxious to finish eating, and with almost total indifference from Salvuzzo, as though he didn't even know what they were talking about.

179

Finally, Beba, indignant that she hadn't even heard so much as a word of thanks, cleared the table, put on a little makeup, and dragged Mimì out of the house.

Salvuzzo and Montalbano didn't even look at each other.

Not until they heard the front door closing did they start speaking, and it was the boy who spoke first.

"Did Papa tell you what happened at the school?"

"Yes."

"And now you want to know more from me?"

It certainly wasn't the best of starts, but Montalbano didn't lose heart and decided that the best approach was to go on the offensive.

"Your dad told me you actually started crying. Why? Were you scared?"

Salvuzzo gave a start, and then looked Montalbano in the eye.

"I wasn't scared. I was offended."

"Why?"

"Because I saw my father being punched around and not having the courage to fight back."

This was exactly the answer Montalbano had been expecting when he asked his question.

"Are you so sure your father didn't have the courage?"

"No. I realized almost immediately why he didn't react."

"Tell me, too."

"Because he wanted to protect us kids."

At this point the inspector knew he had opened a breach in Salvuzzo's defences.

Satisfied, he stood up and, as if in his own home, went over to the glass liquor case, poured himself three fingers' worth of whisky, and was about to sit back down when Salvuzzo said:

"Could you come into my room for a minute, Uncle?"

"I'd be glad to."

Salvuzzo's bedroom was in a state of nearly inconceivable chaos, but this very fact seemed to give it a reason for being.

The desk was like the showcase of an electronics shop, with a television, computer, iPod, iPad, three mobile phones, a battery charger for all tastes, books upon books upon books, and notebooks large and small. Beside it was a chair so piled up with clothes that it looked like a home version of Pistoletto's *Venus of the Rags*. Completely at ease, Salvuzzo invited Montalbano to sit down on the bed — but not before having pushed aside the hundreds of CDs, DVDs, socks, and small backpacks littered across it. The inspector settled in under a Beatles poster.

Reassured by the fraternal presence of *Yellow Submarine*, he took his first sip of whisky.

"Can you give me five minutes, Uncle?"

"Of course."

Salvuzzo sat down at his desk, turned on the screen of his PC, and with a speed that left Montalbano wide-eyed, he opened a few icons as windows, closed them, wrote a message, answered another message, asked a question, meanwhile reading the messages on his mobile phone and composing replies to them, as noises, sounds, and words came in as he fiddled with all the many different devices he had on his desktop.

He did a hundred things all at the same time, his fingers dancing with a lightness reminiscent of a ballerina's feet.

What a difference from when he, Montalbano, was his age! In his own childhood bedroom he'd had a desk with only a lamp on it, always in the same place. He would study one book at a time, or at most with the help of a dictionary.

And his interest never strayed outside the cone of light cast by the lamp.

How had these kids' brains developed over time? They were capable of maintaining a simultaneous interest in a thousand different stimuli: music, images, words, sounds, symbols, noises . . . And they seemed able to absorb it all with an ease that was probably only superficial, but involved a vast, all-encompassing surface, the surface of the whole world.

He, for his part, had been taught to dive deep, whereas they had learned to navigate on the open seas.

He was casting no judgement, but merely taking stock of the fact, since deep down he thought that maybe in a hundred years the kids would be better equipped than they were in his day.

Then, after a while, Salvuzzo stopped poking around with his fingers, turned to Montalbano, and said: "I'm all yours."

"The first thing I would like to know," said the inspector, "is whether you've talked about the incident with your classmates."

Salvuzzo shook his head.

"No, Uncle, since school's been closed —"

"But what need is there for you to see one another in order to talk when you've got all these phones and computers?" Montalbano asked, cutting him off. "You're glued to them day and night!"

"No, Uncle," said Salvuzzo. "We haven't been in touch because, after what happened, three or four of my friends came down with a fever from the fright. And some of the other kids have been forbidden by their parents to say a single word about it, and are being kept locked up at home like they were in jail. Other parents took their kids' phones and computers away and drove them out to the country. The only one I've managed to talk to is Tindaro."

"And who's Tindaro?"

"He's my best friend. We see each other every day, do our homework together, and also share a desk at school."

"And when talking to Tindaro, have you two come up with any explanation for what happened?"

"Well, we've certainly thought and talked a lot about it. But in the end we always come up empty. We just don't get it."

The boy suddenly smiled.

"What are you thinking?" the inspector asked.

"Actually, Tindaro had a theory. But it's so far-fetched that he was the first to tear it apart, and we ended up laughing about it for the rest of the day."

"Let me have a laugh, too."

"Since the TV crews need to shoot a scene inside a school classroom with students in it, last week they did some screen tests with kids from class III A and III B. They ended up choosing us, and they even made us try on some fifties-style clothes. You guys were really sharp when you were young, Uncle!"

Montalbano protested.

"Well, for your information, I wasn't so sharp. I wasn't even born! Now go on."

"Anyway, Tindaro got this idea that the two men that came into the class might've been on some kind of vendetta by class III A. But that really doesn't make any sense."

"You're right, I agree with you," said the inspector. "Even though nowadays some people are capable of doing just about anything to get on TV."

He changed the subject and got straight to the point.

"Can you tell me what your first thought was when you saw those two guys come in?"

Salvuzzo only needed a second.

"I wasn't thinking anything, Uncle. I was just kind of shocked. I just sat there with my mouth hanging open. And then I was scared."

"You realized it was something serious?"

"Yes."

"Why?"

"Because I immediately realized those were real guns they had. I know guns."

"And what did you do?"

"Well, when I heard Tindaro beside me whisper, 'Oh, my God, these guys are going to kill us,' I squeezed his hand under the desk to give him courage."

"And then what?"

"And then I witnessed my dad getting punched, and I started crying . . ."

"And then?"

"And then I just sat there, like this, with my hands covering my face."

"Until it was over?"

"No. I was watching them through my fingers."

"Did you notice anything in particular?"

"I did notice one thing, but I don't know if it wasn't just my impression, and so —"

"And so you'll tell me just the same."

"Well, I had the impression that the shorter guy was scared."

"And what gave you that impression?"

"I could see he was sweating. There were little drops of sweat all along his hairline."

Montalbano was fairly impressed at Salvuzzo's powers of observation. Nobody else — not Puleo, not Mimì — had noticed that very important detail. He continued along the same lines.

"Whereas the taller guy seemed more decisive and self-assured?"

"I can't really say. Maybe he just had better self-control. Which scared me even more."

"Why?"

"They seemed . . . I mean, I would have felt safer . . . I don't know how to put it . . . They seemed like they were improvising, like they were doing something they weren't used to doing, and therefore they were afraid of making a false move . . ."

"I see . . ." Montalbano said pensively.

There was a brief pause, and then the inspector changed the subject again.

"I'm told there were some cases of bullying against a classmate of yours. Is that true?"

"Yes."

"Are the bullies in your class?"

"Yeah. They've got it in for Luigino. Luigino Sciarabba."

Despite the fact that Salvuzzo's unease was plain to see, Montalbano continued.

"Tell me something. Is it true you intervened in his defence?"

"Who told you that?" the boy asked, surprised.

"Your mother."

"Well, it's like this, Uncle. One morning in the schoolyard they started taunting him a lot more than usual. So he reacted, and they attacked him, and it turned into a kind of free-for-all. Since it was three against one, it seemed like the right thing for me to go and help him out, and then Tindaro joined in."

"Why, is Tindaro his friend, too?"

"No, he's my friend, and seeing me joining the fight he followed me. But we got the worst of it. I came out with a black eye and Tindaro took a kick in the knee that had him limping for three days."

"And can you tell me the names of these three bullies?" Montalbano asked point-blank.

If Salvuzzo had seemed ill at ease moments before, it was now clear that he didn't want to talk any more about the whole thing. He just stared at the inspector without answering.

"Are you going to tell me or not?"

"No. I ain't no snitch."

"I'm not asking you to be a snitch," Montalbano retorted. "I simply want the names of three bastards who like to push other people around for no reason and have no right to do so. And since you don't feel like answering, I want to explain something to you. Reporting those three violent bastards is not dishonourable, my friend; on the contrary: it's an act of courage. The same kind of courage you showed when you defended your friend, and the same as your father showed when he took that punch without breathing a word. But let's forget about that. In your opinion, what do those three boys have against Sciarabba?"

"Well . . . in my opinion, it's because they're . . . retarded."

"What do you mean?"

"Well, the whole class knows what to do with computers, smartphones, iPads. Except for them. They're a little . . . well, slow. They just can't manage. So it's possible they feel envious. They're envious of Luigino because he's better than all of us at that stuff And we always turn to him for advice. Know what I mean? I think they act that way out of envy. That's all."

"You may be right, but I don't think that's a strong enough motive. Does Tindaro think the same as you?"

"Tindaro also thinks those three have it in for him because one of them has got a crush on a girl from our class who doesn't know he even exists because she's always chasing after Luigino."

"And does Luigino feel the same way about her?"

"Luigino doesn't even notice. He's always got his head in the clouds. It's not like he has a lot of friends . . . Luigino is a loner, even though he's never alone. I don't know how to explain, but if you ask him something, or want a favour from him, he'll bend over backwards for you. But then he goes straight back to his little island, closing himself off in his own world."

"Listen, there's something I'm curious about. Given the fact that this business has been going on for a while, how come Luigino never went and talked to the head teacher about it, or to someone like Mr Puleo, who seems like a real man to me?"

"Come on, Uncle, a teacher? The poor teachers can barely even manage to maintain order in the classroom so they can teach! Some days I feel more like I'm at the market than at school. It's a madhouse!"

Montalbano was convinced that Salvuzzo had nothing more to tell him. And at the same time, to his great surprise, he realized that he and the boy had spoken freely and normally, and that the problem of communicating with his class, which he had anticipated, was not a real problem. This reassured him. These kids used their own lingo among themselves, but with others they used a universal language comprehensible to all.

Feeling relieved, he said out of the blue: "I'd like to speak to Tindaro, if I can."

"No problem, as far as that goes," said Salvuzzo. Then, without addressing anyone, but speaking out loud, he added: "Tindaro! You OK with talking to the inspector?"

"Yes," said another voice inside the room. Montalbano looked around, completely flummoxed. Where was that voice coming from?

Then he understood.

Tindaro's "yes" had come from inside the computer.

CHAPTER
THIRTEEN

At the sound of that "yes", Salvuzzo, who was at his desk, pushed himself away from the desktop with his hand so that the inspector could see the screen. Only then was Montalbano, half standing up, able to glimpse the chubby, pimply face of a teenage boy smiling at him.

"Hello," said Tindaro.

"Hello," replied the inspector, still confused.

"Maybe it's better if you sit here, Uncle," said Salvuzzo, undoing the Pistoletto work to make room for Montalbano and then settling in beside him.

The inspector felt extremely awkward. The novelty of the situation had left him momentarily speechless. He felt quite uncomfortable talking to a person he could only see part of, just the head and the tops of his shoulders, being professionally accustomed to watching the way the person in front of him moved his toes. But he was being invited to dance, and he danced with utter assurance, perhaps out of a desire not to look bad in front of the two youths.

"Did you hear all of our conversation?"

"Yes. All of it."

"Good. So now let me ask you what you were thinking when you saw the two men enter the classroom."

"To tell you the truth, Inspector, what scared me wasn't the guns but the masks. You know, those masks with that frozen smile that never changes. I felt like I was in some kind of American horror movie. Only the voice of the guy who was talking made me realize we weren't in a movie."

"Did you also have the impression the two men were scared?"

"No, 'cause I was too scared myself. Anyway, just to reassure myself, I looked over at Mr Puleo and saw him looking very serious and worried, which made me think that they had come to kill the whole class. Like the crazies you read about in the news . . . and so I looked around."

"And what did you see?"

"Inspector, we've been together in that class for three years. I thought I knew everybody's faces, but, I swear, when I looked at them then, I didn't recognize a single one of them. That's how upset they were. Their faces were transformed. Some of them were crying, some covering their mouths with their hands to keep from screaming, some with their hands in their hair, some with their hands in the air. Lorusso was hugging Fiori, and I remember Portolano was teetering in his chair."

Increasingly impressed with these kids' powers of observation, Montalbano interrupted him.

191

"Let me ask you another question: do you remember if there was anyone in particular who seemed more afraid than the others?"

"No, Inspector, I don't think so. We were all equally terrified. Or, if anything, there was maybe someone who seemed less afraid."

"Who?"

"Luigino, the same kid you two were just talking about."

"And why did you think he was less scared than the others?"

"He was the only one whose face I could still recognize, Inspector."

"What was it like? Expressionless? Indifferent?"

"No, sir. Neither Expressionless nor indifferent. I don't really know how to put it. He wasn't scared; he was attentive. Yes, that's it. Extremely attentive."

"Listen, Tindaro, by the way, why do you think those three bullies have it in for Luigino? Salvuzzo says they feel stupid compared to him. You think it's some kind of rivalry over a girl. But now that I've got you both here with me, I want you to brainstorm a little. Could there be another motive?"

The two looked at each other through the screen and remained silent. Then Tindaro said:

"It's an old story, Inspector. It started last year when Peppe Portolano got this idea in his head that Luigino had to change his marks in the electronic register. But Luigi flatly refused."

"Aaahhh," exclaimed Salvuzzo.

"What's wrong?"

192

"You said one of the bullies' names!" Montalbano answered, smiling.

At this point they all started laughing.

"All right, then, I'll say the others, too: two Portolanos and one Michele Giacalone."

"Why are there two Portolanos?" asked Montalbano.

"Because there's Peppe, who's the ringleader, and then there's Saro Portolano, who was held back."

"Tell me, Tindaro, since you're not a policeman's son —"

"I may not be a policeman's son," Tindaro interrupted, "but since the first year I've been the best friend of a policeman's son, and we've been playing at being policemen for years."

"How do you do that?" asked Montalbano, feeling curious and amused.

"Well, for example, there's the scene of the crime. When we go into a place we've never been to before, we pretend that somebody's been murdered there. So we look around for fifteen seconds, then close our eyes, and whoever can remember the most details wins. Sometimes I play the detective and Salvuzzo's my assistant, and sometimes we switch roles. Or, just to give you another example, sometimes when getting off the city bus we have to remember the colour of the jacket the lady sitting behind the driver was wearing. Stuff like that."

The inspector smiled and asked: "And would you like to keep doing that when you grow up?"

"No," Salvuzzo said decisively.

"I think it's better to keep it just a game," said Tindaro.

Montalbano felt simultaneously disappointed and relieved. The two lads would have made excellent policemen, but the way things were these days, they were better off choosing another path in life. And so he went back to the subject that most interested him.

"But tell me something: do either of you know whether this Luigino has talked to his mother or father about what's been happening at school?"

It was Tindaro who answered:

"Actually, Inspector, I know Luigino's family pretty well. They live just across the landing from my grandmother. His father works for the European Union and is more often in Brussels than at home. And his mother's afraid of her own shadow. For example, she often asks my grandmother to go shopping for her, because on certain days she's terrified at the mere thought of sticking her nose out of the door . . ."

On the computer screen Tindaro could be seen looking down at something.

"Wait just a second," he said. "Luigino may not know it yet, but the situation has changed."

"Why? What happened?" Salvo and Salvuzzo asked in chorus.

"Gilda, the prettiest girl in the class, just messaged me about something that happened right after the two men burst in, but which hardly anybody noticed."

"What?" said the two Salvos, again in tandem.

"Apparently in all the chaos that followed, Peppe fell to the floor and his brother thought he'd been shot and

194

started shouting desperately. It was none other than Luigino, who'd come running to help, who realized that he'd merely passed out in fright and had to drag him outside, with the help of Saro and Giacalone. Which basically means the whole business is over. Peppe and the other two morons that follow him around can now go fuck themselves. Also because Filippo Lupo filmed the whole scene with his mobile phone. Wait, wait. He's uploading it to me. I'll play it for you in a second."

At that point Salvuzzo sprang to his feet and went and leaned against the desktop, practically sticking his head inside the computer. When the first images began to elicit uncontrollable laughter and ferocious commentaries from the two youths, Montalbano realized his presence was no longer needed.

So he got up, left the room, went into the kitchen, poured himself two more fingers of whisky, and waited for Beba and Mimì to come home.

He poured himself another two fingers of whisky once he got home and sipped them out on the veranda. The discussion with Salvuzzo and Tindaro had made a strong impression on him. The two youths not only had described to him perfectly what had happened in the classroom, but they'd also displayed extraordinary powers of observation. Despite all this, however, they'd been unable to come up with any reason for the attack on their class. Therefore, what was the point of meeting the other students, if Salvuzzo and Tindaro, despite all their practice, couldn't think of any explanation? But if that was how it was, who could he now turn to in

195

search of some lead, however minor, that might help in determining a possible motive?

However hard he tried, no light came on in his brain. Maybe, with his increasing age, the old, incandescent bulb had been replaced by a new, low-energy one that took hours to reach full brightness.

This was an idea that until recently could be rather dangerous, as it could open the door to useless lamentations over imminent old age. Now, however, that had changed, because having spent the whole evening talking to two intelligent lads had injected into his veins, as in some kind of vampiric transfusion, a minimal but sufficient amount of fresh, invigorating blood. And at that moment the phone rang.

Livia's first question naturally concerned what had happened at the school. Montalbano told her everything, in fine detail, and when he'd finished he came to the conclusion that he hadn't been able to come to any conclusion.

"And yet there must be one," said Livia, "because an act as extraordinary as that has to be motivated by something."

"Congratulations on your discovery," Montalbano retorted. "The problem is finding out what."

But that certainly wasn't Livia's problem, and, as proof of this, she immediately started talking about Selene's latest feats.

They talked a little while longer, then wished each other good night.

After he got into bed Montalbano spent a long time tossing and turning.

He had two cases on his hands, and he couldn't work out a motive for either one: why Francesco Sabatello had filmed that wall, or why those two men had terrorized that classroom. There was something strange, however. Despite the fact that the first case had featured a suicide and the second a shoot-out, the two events nevertheless had one point in common: no fresh new deaths had resulted from them, and he therefore had had no need to call in the pathologist, Dr Pasquano.

Wrapping himself up in this thought, he was finally able to fall asleep.

He woke with the firm intention of taking things easy, and in fact remained in bed for another half-hour, not bothering to open the shutters and staring at the ceiling, where some reflected light was moving slowly and rhythmically, like the surf. Then he got up, went into the kitchen, and, yawning, waited for the coffee to bubble up. After drinking a cup full to the brim, he went and opened the French windows to the veranda. The colours of the day stunned him with their intensity, and the sea seemed to whisper to him: *Come on, dive in, I'm waiting for you.*

"I'll be right there," he replied, heading into the house to change into his swimming trunks.

At that moment the telephone rang.

"Mornin', Chief, beck yer partin fer the distoibance."

"Did somebody get killed?"

"Nah, Chief."

"Then it's not a disturbance. What is it?"

"I wannit a tell yiz 'at hizzoner the prassecuter Atterraora called jess now sayin' as how 'e'll be waitin' f 'yiz in 'is poissonal affice in Montelusa in a hour. An' so I decided a senn Gallo to yer 'ouse straightaways. Wazzat a mistake?"

"No, no mistake," Montalbano said bitterly, starting to take off his trunks.

Upon arriving, Gallo had to wait fifteen minutes before the inspector was ready to leave, and therefore felt dutybound to drive at 180 kph on the road to Montelusa.

As Montalbano entered Terranova's office, he found Counterterrorism Chief Marchica and Liberati of the Flying Squad also there.

They exchanged greetings, and after shaking everybody's hand, Montalbano sat in the only free chair remaining, opposite Terranova's desk, atop which towered a computer with a very large screen.

"Please excuse me for calling this unscheduled meeting," Terranova began, "but there are some new developments that I think will prove useful to the investigation. Inspector Marchica has sent me the document, which you'll see in just a moment. Here is the transcript."

He handed a sheet of paper to Liberati and Montalbano, and then clicked something on the computer.

On the screen appeared first a rotating globe, except that this globe was caged behind a grid of bars. Then the globe turned into a circle of light surrounded by a laurel wreath, with, in the middle, the silhouette of a

198

clerk with the requisite white shirt and black tie but, in the place of his head, a question mark. The whole thing accompanied by some rather lugubrious music. Then, finally, a frame with the famous Anonymous Guy Fawkes mask appeared, worn by a hooded man. A mechanical voice began to speak.

Citizens of the World, We are Anonymous.

There has been some recent confusion in the media over something that happened in a Sicilian school.

We must point out that one does not speak for all. Many do not speak for everyone.

We are one. We are legion. We do not forgive. We do not forget.

Anonymous is not interested in personalized appeals.

Anonymous pays no attention to private requests.

Anonymous cannot be labelled, accused, or used.

Anonymous is a space in the cosmic consciousness.

To attribute responsibility to Anonymous would be to attribute responsibility to the citizens of the world.

No cosmic consciousness entered that Sicilian school.

The image suddenly vanished. Terranova turned the screen off, looked at the three men before him, and asked:

"Any comments?"

Liberati was the first to speak.

"Are we sure this document is authentic?" he asked, turning to Marchica.

"We're ninety-nine per cent certain. There still remains a minimum of uncertainty, even though Rome assures us it's an official video. At any rate, both the logo and the style belong to what you could call the Italian section of the organization."

"In other words," Liberati continued, "they're saying they had nothing to do with this."

"So it would seem," said Marchica.

At this point Prosecutor Terranova intervened.

"Still, we have to be careful with these people. It's perfectly possible they are indeed saying this action didn't involve them, but it could also be that they had some misgivings after the fact that led them to disavow what some of their comrades from the same section had done. I'm not sure I'm being clear."

"Perfectly clear," said Liberati.

"Whatever the case, however, the fact remains that they have now officially distanced themselves."

"Yes," said Terranova.

Montalbano hadn't yet opened his mouth. And he kept it shut.

"At any rate," said Marchica, trying to make a point, "I should remind you that from the very start I had serious doubts that Anonymous was behind this act."

"Why's that?" asked Liberati.

"There's a big difference in the language used, my friend. You just now heard their communique, didn't you? Did you pay any attention to their choice of words? Good. I've listened to dozens of these messages, and they all seem to use — how should I say? — a single, common vocabulary, whether we're talking about the English section, the French section, or the German section of Anonymous. Whereas the two men who entered the school used an essentially different kind of language, and they emphasized their threat by firing two shots into the air. In short, the *modus operandi* and *modus dicendi* of the two men, from the start, did not seem to me to match the methods and words of Anonymous. And there you have it. And this latest communique seems to confirm my doubts rather definitively."

Since Montalbano continued to remain silent, Terranova addressed him directly.

"And what do *you* think, Inspector? I'm anxious to hear your opinion."

Montalbano paused a moment to think before answering.

"I think that this communique, whether or not it's genuine, doesn't change the essence of the problem much."

"What do you mean?" Terranova insisted.

"I mean that I'm not interested in assigning the two men a label. If the most likely label could provide us with a lead for arriving at some hint of an explanation for what happened, then its contribution to the investigation would be far from negligible. But it's irrelevant whether the two belong to one organization or another, if such an association doesn't provide us with a lead for making some progress on the case. Therefore, in my opinion, nothing has changed from before this communique was issued."

"Leaving aside these observations of yours, which I agree with," said Terranova, "I would like you to comment more concretely on the purpose of this meeting. In other words: is this communique enough, in your opinion, to justify us entirely abandoning the Anonymous lead?"

"At this point, if Marchica thinks it's appropriate, I would be for letting that lead slide," replied Montalbano.

"So we're all in agreement?" asked the prosecutor.

"I've still got some lingering doubts," said Liberati.

"About what?" asked the inspector.

"I ask myself why they decided to wear masks that were so recognizable. Why the two men laid claim to a brand, even while knowing that the real owners of the brand would inevitably deny they had anything to do with it."

"Well," Marchica ventured, "probably because they wanted to throw us off the trail by leading us in a specific direction."

"Yes," retorted Liberati, "but I still don't understand. We would have followed the false lead for two or three days, but it was still going to come out that they weren't part of Anonymous. Therefore . . ."

Since everyone remained silent, being fully aware that none of them were in a position to dismiss Liberati's doubts, Terranova decided it was a good moment to adjourn the meeting.

They all said goodbye and left in a state of mild confusion.

"I'll notifize Isspecter Augello 'at ya just arrived onna premisses," Catarella said as Montalbano walked in.

"Does he want to talk to me?"

"Yessir."

"No need to trouble yourself. I'll notarize him myself."

Halfway down the corridor, he stopped, knocked on the door to Mimì's office, turned the handle, opened it, and, leaning into the room, asked: "Got something to tell me?"

"Yes. Give me two minutes, and I'll come to you."

Montalbano had time enough to sit down and glance worriedly at the precarious balance of the huge pile of documents to be signed on his desk before Augello came in with some sheets of paper in his hand. He sat down opposite the desk and said:

"What can you tell me about the meeting with the prosecutor?"

"We came to the conclusion that Anonymous had nothing to do with the episode. I'll spare you the details. And what about you? What have you got to tell me?"

"Well, since it seems that all your attention has been on the two that entered the school, I've been devoting myself to the third figure in the . . . let's call it the commando unit."

Montalbano looked him straight in the eye, a bit taken aback. Then he smacked himself in the forehead.

"Damn, you're right! You mean the third accomplice, the one that came and picked them up in a car?"

"Exactly. The car, as you know, turns out to have been stolen in Montelusa, and it was found again in Montelusa, in the square outside the railway station. Based on my research, I can say that the first time this car appeared in Vigàta was on the morning of the assault on the school, a little before nine-thirty. That's what I was told by the waiter in the pizzeria outside the school. Apparently they were driving around, casing the area.

"The second time it was seen was when the car stopped a block away from the school, but on the opposite side of the street. According to a credible eyewitness, two people got out of the car and started walking towards the school. Five minutes later, the driver got out of the car and went into the tobacconist's he'd parked in front of. The man — who was a youth of about twenty-five, of short, stocky build — went in and asked for a pack of cigarettes. Apparently he spoke with a Bolognese accent. Upon his request, the person who was in the shop, who is my witness, replied that it wasn't a real tobacconist's, but had just been done up as one for the TV movie.

"The kid got really confused and asked where the closest real tobacconist's was. My witness told him, and the kid replied that it was too far away and, racing out of the store, he went and sat in the car with the engine still running.

"A few minutes went by, and then my witness thought he heard some gunshots, but he didn't budge at first, because he thought it might be something to do with the TV movie. But when he saw the car suddenly shoot off like a rocket, cutting in front of all the other cars going in the same direction, he started to have some doubts, and decided it was best to stay inside his shop."

"Well done, Mimì," Montalbano said quite sincerely.

"But," Mimì continued, "also thanks to my witness, we now have an identikit for all three men who formed the commando."

He set the three sheets of paper in his hand down for Montalbano to see. They contained artists' reconstructions of the three men's likenesses.

"Forensics were able to reconstruct two likenesses from the testimony of Camastra, the caretaker. The third is the one I've been telling you about. These likenesses have now been sent out to police stations all over Italy."

Montalbano thought of the thousands of photographs and artist's reconstructions that made their way through all the police stations of the republic without ever achieving the slightest results, but he didn't want to disappoint Mimì.

"Excellent work, Mimì," he said.

"Now," Mimì continued, "since the checkpoints were set up less than half an hour after the shoot-out and got no results, I would like, if you'll allow me, to try to reconstruct the path those three may have taken. I'll look into the train and bus schedules, the flights . . ."

"Yes," said Montalbano, "go right ahead, you have my full blessing."

CHAPTER
FOURTEEN

After Mimì went out, he glanced at his watch. There was still an hour to go before he could leave the station, and so, sighing despondently, he reached out and took a number of papers from the pile to be signed. And he continued in this fashion until he thought he'd done enough, at which point he got up and was on his way out to his car, but then stopped outside the cubbyhole in which Catarella had his switchboard.

Red in the face, Catarella was muttering to himself and insulting the computer.

"Damn damn damn this horny-toed son of a bee!"

"Who you cursing at, Cat?" asked Montalbano.

Catarella looked up, saw the inspector, and, if it was possible, got even redder in the face, going from red-pepper to tomato-paste red.

"Wha', Chief? D'jou hear me?"

"Of course."

"Ya gotta 'scuse me, Chief, bu' I loss my patience."

"Why, what happened?"

"Wha' happened izzat at a soitan point, I's jess typin' som'n an' 'en the machine et it! It was gone! An when I ast 'help' it jess takes me back to the same point!"

"Cat, I'm afraid this is all beyond my ken."

"Be on yer wha', Chief?"

"I wish you the best of luck," Montalbano then said, patting Catarella on the shoulder. And he went out.

He'd taken three steps towards his car when his path was blocked by another car.

"We came to get you!"

It was Ingrid. In the passenger's seat was the blond bear, the director of the TV movie, who greeted him with a nod and a smile.

"Where are we going?"

"Since it's the last week of shooting, all the Vigàta personnel who took part in the production have organized a great big luncheon on their boats."

"I'm not sure I understand," said Montalbano. "Are we going out on the water to eat from the lunch boxes of the production team?"

"Don't be silly. The whole thing was organized by the fishermen of Vigàta and their families. And so —"

"And so I'd be delighted to join you," Montalbano cut her off, suddenly feeling his heart warm.

The blond bear got out of the car and into the back seat, respecting the hierarchical order.

Montalbano expressed his appreciation with a nod and sat down in front.

They pulled up at the quay and got out of the car.

Montalbano felt wonderstruck and touched by what he saw. They'd even outdone the preparations for the feast of Our Lady of the Sea!

The centre of the harbour was teeming with trawlers, motorboats, yachts, rowing boats, and every manner of craft, all adorned with banners and bunting of the Italian and Swedish flags, and from the congregation came festive shouts and cries, greetings, and, above all — as the inspector's nostrils were quick to note — the wondrous scent of fried fish.

A small shallop awaited them. They climbed aboard, and five minutes later they reached the central boat, a large deep-sea trawler. Montalbano and the blond bear were greeted with applause.

"Come and sit down over here," the ship's captain said to them.

A whole row of hot grills had been set up, one beside the other, on the stern of the ship, and were being constantly re-fed with mullet, prawns, baby octopus, anchovies, and sardines. The fishermen would then fill metal trays up with fish, salt the fish, and pass them on from hand to hand until they reached the other boats surrounding the main one.

Beside the grills, in two great pots placed over a pair of gas burners, boiled the pasta water, while a large soup tureen full of sea-urchin sauce was ready to receive the spaghetti.

And, just to make sure nothing was missing, in an enormous frying pan a number of oversized mullet, mackerel, and sole were quietly sizzling.

The feast was so satisfying for Montalbano that by the end he found himself embracing the blond bear, having reconciled himself to the constant pain in the arse the TV movie had been for him.

Then, after saying goodbye to everyone, he was about to step down into the boat when Ingrid said: "Can I come back with you?"

"But I'm not going into town. I'm just going to ask him to take me out there," he said, pointing to his customary flat rock directly under the lighthouse.

"It doesn't matter," said Ingrid. "I want to come anyway. I can walk back."

They got into the boat, and the sailor started rowing towards the rock. Halfway there, however, they spotted an empty bottle floating in the water beside the boat.

"Grab it! Grab it!" Ingrid shouted to Montalbano.

"Why?"

"Maybe there's a message inside," she said, laughing. Ingrid was particularly sensitive to Sicilian wine.

Just to play along, Montalbano reached down, grabbed the bottle, and turned it upside down. It was empty. Ingrid snatched it from his hands and, laughing, shook it violently and then threw it back into the water.

The sailor pulled up at the flat rock.

"If you put one foot on this rock in front of us, you'll find it easier to climb from rock to rock until you reach the jetty."

"You get out first," Montalbano said to Ingrid.

As soon as she set her foot on the rock, she shrieked, lost her balance, and would have fallen into the sea if Montalbano hadn't caught her in time.

"Maybe it's better if you go back in the boat," said the inspector.

"Yeah, maybe it's better," said Ingrid.

She gave him a kiss, climbed back into the boat, and headed off.

He watched the boats slowly pull away from the big trawler, which then started its engine and began to make its way out of the harbour. Perhaps to throw all the rubbish they'd produced into the sea.

Poor sea!

Of course, compared to all the stuff discharged daily into that body of water — plastic waste, toxic runoff, sewage — that little bit of rubbish wasn't going to hurt the sea too much. And of course it had already suffered much more from the thousands and thousands of corpses of desperate souls who'd met their end on the water, hoping to reach Italian shores to escape from the wars at home or to try to earn a little daily bread.

A dark cloud of melancholy began to descend on the inspector, but he forced himself to dispel it, since, after that tremendous pig-out, any tears he might shed would surely have been crocodile tears.

Carried by the current, the empty bottle was now knocking rhythmically against the rock, pulled by the undertow. Montalbano sat there watching it.

Little by little, the bottle came under the sway of another current, drifted away from the rock, and started to navigate towards the mouth of the harbour and the open sea beyond.

The open sea.

The open sea, and everything in it: ships, boats, rubbish, corpses, surfing to their dubious destinations. The open sea.

Why did one use the same terms — surfing, navigating — for the internet as for the sea?

Certainly the World Wide Web served to connect millions of people to one another through their computers; but, just like the sea, the internet, if you don't know it well, can take you down the wrong path, crash you against some unknown, possibly booby-trapped shoals. So the expressions were, in fact, appropriate. The sea and the net are places for everybody and nobody. Skilful navigators know how to sail safely to the right port. Those without skill might stray from their course and end up in the wrong port. But what kind of compass existed to guide you in your navigations across the internet? Well, the only compass was probably the very reason for which one put one's questions to the computer: a desire for information, to look for new people, make new contacts, find answers. Maybe even to call for help.

Right, the way Catarella asked for help from his computer.

Help! SOS. Mayday, Mayday . . .

How does one ask the internet for help?

The inspector stopped for a moment to think. He stuck a hand in his jacket pocket and pulled out a sheet of paper folded in four. He opened it and read:

Citizens of the World, We are Anonymous.
There has been some recent confusion in the media over something that happened in a Sicilian school.

We must point out that one does not speak for all. Many do not speak for everyone.

We are one. We are legion. We do not forgive. We do not forget.

Anonymous is not interested in personalized appeals.

Anonymous pays no attention to private requests.

Anonymous cannot be labelled, accused, or used.

Anonymous is a space in the cosmic consciousness.

To attribute responsibility to Anonymous would be to attribute responsibility to the citizens of the world.

No cosmic consciousness entered that Sicilian school.

Anonymous is not interested in personalized appeals. Anonymous pays no attention to private requests. Anonymous cannot be labelled, accused, or used.

All of which meant — and no one had paid any mind to this during the morning meeting — that Anonymous had refused to intervene in a personal matter, a private request. They didn't want to be accused, labelled, or used. So there had indeed been a request for something. For help, perhaps? And if such a request was made, who could have made it?

A flash went off in his brain.

And a name appeared, which he immediately dismissed. Impossible. It was a crazy conjecture, totally

212

off the wall. He, anyway, was a good navigator. Careful, though: on the open seas, across the great ocean one can run into pirates, or ships sailing under assumed names and flying flags of countries that don't even exist. So how can one tell the real from the fake?

No, no, no. Too complex. Too complicated. He should get the idea out of his head.

He got up slowly from the rock and made his way back to the station.

"Did the computer give you the help you wanted?" he asked Catarella when entering.

"Yessir, Chief, it did. The 'pewter was jest askin' fer protection. It was scared a virus was gonna 'tack it. An' so I 'adda hupdate the hanti-virus."

Montalbano didn't understand a word of this, and so changed the subject.

"But where has Fazio gone to, anyway? I haven't seen him in ages."

"'E got back jess now," said Catarella.

"Send him to me."

Two minutes later Fazio was sitting in front of the inspector's desk.

"So, did you meet Inspector Augello's son?"

"Yes. And I was also able to talk to a schoolmate of his. Smart lads, both of them. One of these days they might just steal your job!"

"Why? What did they say?"

"First of all, that the attackers seemed frightened by what they were doing. Which is something that nobody else had noticed. And second — and this is something that caught me completely by surprise — that during the chaos of the incursion, there was only one person who sat still at his desk, almost calm, but paying close attention to what was going on. And that person was Luigino Sciarabba."

"What? The computer wizard?"

"That's right. None other."

"Maybe he's just a cold fish," said Fazio.

"Maybe. So, what have you got to tell me?"

"Well, Chief, just as I'd done with the names on the class register, I went and dug up all the names of the teachers of class III B."

"And so?"

"And so I know everything there is to know about them and their families."

"And the result?"

"Chief, the whole class looks like something cooked up in a Swedish statistical laboratory. They're all fine, upstanding individuals, involved in social causes, with families all in order, no vices, no weaknesses, no police records, and all with respectable jobs. And that's not all! There's nobody, no one at all, not even second cousins, with any blots on their records. It's enough to drive a man crazy! I've been forming a question in my head that I'm embarrassed even to mention to you."

"If you're so embarrassed you can cover your face with your hands when you tell me."

"Well, since we haven't been able to come up with the slightest motive for the crime, isn't it possible that the attackers went to the wrong address?"

"The wrong address, no. If anything, the wrong classroom. Because they told the caretaker they knew where to go."

"OK, Chief, but it's not like that changes things very much. So, not the wrong address, but the wrong classroom."

"If your hypothesis is true, Fazio, do you realize how much work we'll have on our hands? How many students are there at the Pirandello, anyway? And how many teachers? No, thanks. I am absolutely certain that those two knew where to go and that we have the motive right under our noses but can't see it."

"Well, then, Chief, you tell me what moves I should make, because I just don't know what to think any more!"

Montalbano thought about this for a moment.

"Nothing. Don't do anything. It's better to wait for the wind to pick up before we set the sails."

"What do you mean?"

"I mean we're going to sit tight."

"Whatever you say," said Fazio, getting up and leaving.

Montalbano sat there for a long time, staring at the door that Fazio had just closed.

And a question popped into his head: if the wind never picked up, wasn't it better to give the boat a little push? He thought a long time about how he might set that boat in motion.

Slowly, the image of the bottle sluggishly making its way out of the harbour, to the open sea, became projected on the white of the door as on a movie screen. Was it possible, as he had done in the boat with Ingrid, to intercept a bottle sailing on a different kind of sea? And, if so, how would you track the bottle back to the person who'd thrown it in? There might be a way.

Of course there was no guarantee that the bottle sailing across the internet was empty, like the one he'd watched floating out to sea.

These were questions he would never be able to answer. However . . .

He quickly picked up the phone and dialled. "Cat, get in here right away."

He hadn't finished speaking when the door flew open and crashed against the wall with the force of a cannon blast.

"Sorry 'bout tat, Chief, my 'and slipped."

"Come in and close the door behind you."

Catarella did as he was asked, and then stood stiff as a pole in front of the inspector's desk.

"Have a seat," said Montalbano.

"I can't, Chief."

"That's an order."

Catarella, deeply offended, settled onto the very edge of the chair.

"What I'm about to ask you must remain between us," the inspector began, looking him severely in the eye.

Catarella's eyes filled with tears from the emotion.

And he raised his right hand and closed it, while leaving his fore and middle fingers still extended, which

216

he brought to his lips, kissed them on the back, then turned them around kissed them on the front as well.

"Till death do us part." It was a solemn oath.

Finally he wiped away his tears with his left hand, then sat there staring at the inspector.

"Tell you what. I'm going to stay here and sign papers, and after everyone goes home, I want you to come back here, to my office, and bring your computer with you."

Catarella nodded assent. Then he stood up, but was so overwhelmed with emotion that it took him a long time to reach the door. His legs were stiff, his arms open and extended à la Frankenstein, and it was hard for him to move his feet.

He didn't know how long he'd been signing papers when the phone rang.

"Ahh, Chief, 'at'd be the 'nchineer Sabatobello onna line wantin' a talk t'yiz poissonally in poisson."

"Good evening, sir, what can I do for you?"

"I'm sorry to bother you, Inspector. I am truly mortified, in fact. I realize you have problems far more serious than mine, but I nevertheless had to tell you. I opened up the chests containing Papa's old papers, and found something that seemed very important to me. If you can give me five minutes, I'd like to talk to you about it."

Montalbano didn't hesitate.

"Mr Sabatello, I'm sorry, but as you stated correctly, I'm extremely busy these days. Tell you what: as soon as

I manage to find a little free time, I'll get in touch with you."

"Is that a promise?"

"That's a promise. It's in my own interest, too."

"Oh, by the way," said Sabatello. "Have you heard what happened to poor old Sidoti?"

"No, what happened to him?"

"He was hit by a car and is in very grave condition. The doctors are giving up hope of saving him. I went to see him at San Giovanni Hospital a few hours ago, and will be going back tomorrow."

Montalbano was very sorry to hear this, and of course had not forgotten the wonderful meal he'd had with Sidoti.

"Please keep me informed as to his condition."

"All right. Till next time."

"Till next time."

The knock at the door was so soft that Montalbano wasn't sure there'd been one. All the same, he said:

"Come in."

The door opened extremely slowly, and then half of Catarella's face appeared behind it, looking around with an air more conspiratorial than a Carbonaro in the days of Mazzini.

"Come in, come in."

Catarella took two steps forward and closed the door behind him. He had his computer in his hand. Then he said softly:

"Everybody's gone. We's alone, Chief."

"And who's manning the switchboard?"

218

"I left Costamagna at it an' tol' 'im not to put any phone calls troo to the phone. Did I do good?"

"You did good. And now, do me a favour and find a chair and sit down next to me."

Catarella, who was just then taking a step, froze at the sound of the words "next to me", his left foot in midair, thunderstruck. A statue.

"Cat! What's wrong?"

"*Matre santa!* Sit down nex' to youse! What a honour! *Matre santissima*, what a honour!"

"C'mon, Cat, let's stop wasting time."

With great effort, and all sweaty and red in the face, Catarella came forward, took a chair, and dragged it behind the desk, though at a considerable distance from the inspector's.

"Come closer," Montalbano ordered him.

"*Maria santissimissima!*" Catarella wailed, moving his chair a little bit closer to the inspector's.

Then he picked up the computer and held it suspended over the desk.

"May I, Chief? May I?"

"Yes, you may."

Catarella set the computer down.

"Now listen to me, Cat. Cat! Can you hear me???"

Catarella's eyes were staring into the void, lost.

"Catarella!!!" the inspector yelled, grabbing his assistant's chin with his left hand and turning it towards him so he could look him in the eye. "Cat! Now listen carefully!"

"Yessir, Chief, I'm all ears."

"I need to get in touch with somebody through the computer. OK? You got that?"

"Yessir, Chief, got it."

But it was clear that he was having great difficulty snapping out of his trance.

"All right, then, ask me all the questions you need to ask to conduct this operation."

"Yessir, Chief," said Catarella, lifting the lid of the computer. "Ah, lissen. Does this poisson got a blog?"

"I don't know."

"Is 'e a tweeter?"

"No, he only eats threes. What kind of a question is that?!"

"Nah, nah, Chief, I mean summon 'at tweets on Twitter."

"What are you talking about! Must one be a twit to tweet?"

"Nah, nah, 'a'ss not it, neither, Chief, it jess means ya can't write more than a hunnert-forty carataracts at a time."

"Ah, I see. No, I don't think a hundred and forty characters would be enough for this person."

"Well, if 'e ain't a tweeter, then I'm sure 'e's on Fessebook. Whattya tink, Chief? Is 'e onnit er nat?"

"I would guess he probably is on Facebook, Cat."

"Ah, well, 'a'ss awriddy sum'n, Chief. So wha'ss 'iss poisson's name?"

"Luigi Sciarabba," said Montalbano.

CHAPTER
FIFTEEN

"Awright, then, we'll ax the 'pewter to 'elp us," said Catarella, starting to poke around on the keyboard.

Montalbano leaned forward to see whether he'd written the name correctly.

A minute later, Catarella said:

"Well, well, Chief! I found five o' these Sciarabbis!"

Confused, Montalbano asked:

"So how are we going to find the one I'm looking for?"

"Iss easy, Chief. Where's 'iss Sciarabba got 'is risidence?"

"Here in Vigàta."

"'Ere's two of 'em 'ere in Vigàta, an' bote of 'em's called Luici. But one's a legalized adult an' the utter's a minoritarian. Which one's we innerested in?"

"The minoritarian," said Montalbano.

Catarella poked around again and then cried out: "Oh, man! 'A'ss bad, bad luck!"

"What is?"

"Google's tellin' me 'iss kid's Fessebook account was scancilled tree days ago."

"Are you sure about those three days?"

"Yeah, says so right 'ere."

221

Montalbano realized the account was cancelled on the same day the school was attacked.

"So there's nothing else we can do?" he asked.

Catarella threw his hands up disconsolately.

"Chief, wittout a account I dunno what to do."

Montalbano suddenly had an idea. He reached out, picked up the phone, and then stopped.

Should he or shouldn't he? He had no other choice.

He dialled Augello's home phone, and Beba answered. "Hello, Salvo. Mimì's not back yet . . ."

"That's OK, Beba, sorry to bother you, but I wanted to talk to Salvuzzo."

A second later he heard the boy's voice. "Hello, Uncle. I'm all yours."

"Listen carefully, Salvù. I'm going to ask you something that nobody — not even your father and mother — must know about."

"OK, Uncle."

"Man to man. How do I get in touch with the computer whiz kid?"

"Do you want me to give you Luigino's phone number?"

"No, no. No phones. Don't you have his email address?"

"Sure I do."

He gave it to him.

"Thanks, Salvu. Good night."

"Good night, Uncle."

"OK, Cat, we've done it. I have Sciarabba's email address," and he dictated it to him.

222

A smile lit up Catarella's face like sunlight, as he resumed poking around on the keyboard again.

Montalbano stopped him.

"Wait a second. Will the kid know who sent him the email?"

"O' course, Chief. See? *From:* . . ."

"Then it's not going to work," Montalbano said decisively.

But Catarella, who was already off and running, went on:

"But, Chief, if ya don wanna be rec'nized, 'ere's sum'n we can do: open a 'nomynous account 'at can't be idinnified an' 'll remain top secret. 'At way, we c'n write to this minoritant from tha' account."

For whatever reason, the mere mention of the words "top secret" made Montalbano think of James Bond, who in his super-equipped London office was always given, along with the requisite beautiful blonde, the latest technological gadgets to help him do his job, whereas he, Montalbano, was there in a stinky room with Catarella, using a computer from the previous century.

"But is this something we can do right away?"

"Assolutely straightaways, Chief. Alls we gotta do is make up a fake name for our two-poisson account."

"OK, you make something up," said Montalbano, who was starting to lose patience.

"I got an idea, but I'm ambarrassed to say it."

"C'mon, Cat, let's not waste any time."

"What if you an' me got married?"

"What the hell are you talking about, Cat!"

223

"Beckin' yer partin, Chief, bu' I jess meant we could marry our lass names. We cou' call our account Montarella or Catalbano, or som'n like 'at."

The idea made Montalbano want to drop the whole thing. But he restrained himself and said, through clenched teeth:

"Call it Montarella."

Two tears sprang from Catarella's adoring eyes. "Tanks, Chief, tanks so much. An', whiles we're at it, fer the passwoid we c'n do a crass 'tween our boit dates."

"Do whatever you want, but just hurry up."

Catarella started writing, repeating aloud what he was writing:

"From . . . ; To . . . ; Subject . . . ," and then he looked over at the inspector.

"For 'Subject'," said Montalbano, "write 'from a friend'."

"OK. Now star' dictatin'."

"Dear Luigi, you've been found out. If you don't do what I say at once, I will report you to the police for the chaos you caused at the school. Do not reply to this message. More soon."

"Done," said Catarella.

Montalbano reread the message. "OK, you can send it."

"Done," Catarella repeated proudly a moment later.

"Thanks," said Montalbano. "That's all for now."

Catarella asked permission to use their "marritch account" in exceptional circumstances, and only exceptional circumstances, which the inspector granted, but only on the condition that Catarella leave his office. The problem was that Catarella was now as limp as an empty bag, and Montalbano had to accompany him to the door, holding him up.

So he'd cast his bottle into the sea. This time it would not get lost among the waves, but go where it had to go.

He was unlocking his car, getting ready to go home to Marinella, when Catarella appeared in the doorway and called out to him.

"Chief! Chief!"

"What is it?"

"'Ere's Missis Sciosciostrom onna line an' she wants a talk t'yiz poissonally in poisson."

Montalbano went back inside, stopped in front of Catarella's cubbyhole, and took the receiver Catarella was holding out to him.

"Hello, Ingrid, what's up?"

"Listen, Salvo, did you by any chance go home this afternoon?"

"No, why do you ask?"

"Because if you had, you would have noticed that there's work being done for the film there."

"For tonight?"

"Yes. We have to shoot a scene that's going to last all night, right in front of your house."

A punch in the face would surely have had less of an effect, and he would have absorbed it much better. The whole thing seemed to him an out-and-out desecration, which he wanted no part of whatsoever.

"What are you saying?" he asked, incredulous.

"As I said, we'll be shooting all night long, right in front of your house. So, the director and I were thinking that maybe, during a break, we could come in and see you."

A lie of defence rolled off his tongue at once.

"But I ... tonight I won't be at home, unfortunately."

"You won't?"

"No, we've been given word that there's a fugitive at large in the area, and we're going to have to set up some stakeouts. I'm sorry."

"Me, too," said Ingrid. "Oh, listen, since you won't be there, could we use your veranda for making up the extras?"

"OK, OK," said Montalbano.

"Have fun on your stakeout."

"Work well," the inspector replied, then hung up.

And now what? Should he go and stay in a hotel? No way. His only option was to go home but make sure nobody saw him.

"Listen, Cat. Is Gallo around?"

"Yessir."

"Ring him and tell him I need him to drive me home to Marinella."

"Straightaways, Chief."

Gallo arrived almost at once. Montalbano got in the car, and they drove off. Near the road that led to his house, Montalbano said:

"Turn off the headlights and go down the drive with the engine off."

226

Gallo looked at him in shock. "Why?"

"Because it never snows in Cuba."

Gallo rolled with the punch and did as he was told.

"And I want you to come and get me tomorrow morning at eight," Montalbano said before getting out of the car.

"OK," said Gallo.

The inspector opened the front door of the house very carefully, without turning on any lights.

He made his way through the darkness into the dining room and looked outside onto the veranda. Through the slats in the shutter, by the glow of the spotlights illuminating the set like daylight, he could see that they'd set up a sort of very long railway track parallel to the water's edge.

There weren't any actors around yet, but he could see members of the crew running about at high speed between two trucks, unloading movie cameras, costumes, scenery, and props, and generally creating a great deal of confusion.

The inspector calculated that there were two rather dangerous places in the house, the ones facing the beach: the French windows to the veranda and the bedroom window. Whereas in the kitchen and bathroom he could turn on the light without any worry, because the windows did not give onto the seaside. And so he went into the kitchen, turned on the light, and opened the fridge. Not a thing inside. Disappointed but still hopeful, he ran over to the oven and opened it, and at once bells started ringing in his head in celebration. Mullet with Adelina's special sauce!

The mere sight of it dispelled his bad mood.

And as the fish was warming in the oven, he laid the table in the kitchen and went and looked again to see what was going on outside. Now there was no less than a yacht there, having been brought on a sort of HGV, and the crew was building a slipway to guide it into the water.

He took the casserole, sat down at the table, and decided that he would better appreciate the flavour of the fish by eating them just like that, without a proper plate.

With the first forkful he brought to his lips, he had the impression the fish had a strange taste. He took another bite. Worse than the first. The fish was decidedly bitterish. How could Adelina have possibly gone so wrong? He took a third bite and, closing his eyes, scientifically analysed the flavour between his palate and tongue.

No! It wasn't the fish or the sauce. They were fine; indeed marvellous.

It was his mouth that tasted bitter.

And he knew why his mouth wasn't functioning properly. He'd wanted to keep the reason for his unease, and thus for that nasty taste, hidden from himself, but it nevertheless rose up from the depths of his consciousness to the surface. And if he was ever going to be able to eat his mullet in peace, it was best to let the idea come out in full. And to give it some thought. It was possible that, by dint of reflection, his mouth would get rid of the bitter taste.

228

Stop kidding yourself, Montalbà. The reason is that right after sending the message to Luigino, you felt ashamed of yourself and what you had done.

You've laid traps and played tricks on dozens and dozens of people over the years, but they were always crooks, people with skins thick as armour or who didn't want to tell the truth.

Never, never with a little kid. Never with a thirteen-year-old boy.

That was beneath you. That was beneath you. So why did you do it?

Well, Montalbà, you did it because you had no other paths open to you that might lead you to a solution.

And yet . . . And yet . . .

He was ashamed of his act and deeply worried about it. Because the reactions of a killer, a crook, a man accustomed to dealing with the law, were one thing. But the way a young kid might react — a kid still naïve, still whole and lacking armour against adversaries — was something else entirely.

And so?

And so, in short, he decided that the only thing he could do at the moment was to eat his mullet just the same, despite the unpleasant taste . . .

When he'd finished, he went into the bathroom, turned on the light, showered, and dried himself off. As he was getting into bed, he heard the phone ring.

He blindly walked into the dining room and picked up the receiver. It was Livia.

"Hello, Livia," he said in a muffled voice.

"Why are you talking like that?"

"Because I'm a ghost."

"Cut the clowning."

"I'm not joking, Livia."

And he told her about the shoot and everything that was going on around him. Livia laughed heartily.

"Well, then, I won't keep you. I hope they let you sleep."

"Me, too. Good night."

And he went and lay down in bed, thinking primarily of how the kid would react upon receiving his message and what kind of countermoves he might make. But he realized that it was going to be hard to think, because suddenly it was as if a dozen people had entered the dining room, laughing and shouting rudely. He imagined it was the extras getting dressed and made up on the veranda. Shit. All that racket was going to prevent him not only from thinking, but from sleeping as well. So he got up, went into the bathroom, opened the medicine chest, took two balls of cotton, and stuffed them in his ears. All the noise on the veranda now became muffled. And tolerable.

So, if Luigino had perchance resolved to — A sudden, violent, blinding white light inundated the room, blazing through the shutter slats. Apparently they'd pointed the spotlights directly at his house. What next? How was he going to sleep with that light shining in? The worst of it was that even when he closed his eyes, the light filtered in through his eyelids. He was positive that even with his eyes sealed shut he would never manage to fall asleep. Cursing the saints, he got up out of bed again and went and opened the wardrobe. He started looking for something, and after throwing underpants, shirts, and socks all over the floor, he finally found a pair of Livia's silk scarves, took one, and covered his eyes with it, knotting it behind his head. Then he got back into bed.

A waste of time. The light came through just the same. He got up again, this time stringing together a litany of curses, opened the wardrobe again, took out the other scarf, and doubled his blindfold with it. The light was now just a faint glow that wouldn't be any bother.

At that point he started thinking of something he wasn't able at first to bring into focus, and it didn't have anything to do with Luigino. So what was it? Then he remembered the dream he'd had a few nights before. Actually, truth be told, the dream about Livia's dream. Because he'd dreamt that Livia was telling him about a dream she'd had about a blindfolded man who was running away from another man who wanted to kill him. No, no, wait. The man in Livia's dream wasn't blindfolded but running with a large woman's kerchief on his head. But what did this have to do with anything? Nothing at all.

He thrashed about in bed for a long time. Then, he didn't know when or how, he was snatched away by sleep's talons and cast deep down into a dense, black, leaden liquid.

When he woke up, he sensed that it was already morning. But then why didn't he hear the splashing of the surf? Total silence. Why was no light filtering in through the window? Pitch blackness. What was happening? Had he gone deaf and blind during the night? All at once? Maybe he'd had some kind of stroke. He broke out in a cold sweat, terrified. Then he remembered the great fuss he'd gone to the previous evening, untied the two scarves around his eyes, thinking what an idiot he was, and removed the cotton from his ears. Relieved, he took a deep breath and glanced over at the clock. It was almost seven and the alarm was about to ring. He didn't get out of bed in time before it started ringing.

"Already taken care of," he said, borrowing Fazio's expression.

Before he went into the kitchen to make coffee, there was something extremely urgent he had to do. He grabbed the phone.

"Chief. What's going on?" asked Fazio, a bit alarmed.

"I need the phone number of Mr Puleo, the schoolteacher."

"OK, give me a minute and I'll get it for you."

As soon as he got the number, he rang Puleo.

"Hello, who is this?"

"Montalbano here."

"Good morning, Inspector. What can I do for you?"

"Sorry to bother you first thing in the morning, but —"

"No bother at all. I was just getting ready to go to school."

"Well, in fact, that's exactly what I wanted to talk to you about. Are you teaching class III B today?"

"Yes, my first class of the day."

"Excellent. I'd like to ask a favour of you . . ."

"Go right ahead."

But Montalbano didn't have the words ready to describe the anxiety he felt inside, and therefore his voice came out hesitant.

"Well, what I'd like is for you to keep an eye on a student of yours, Luigi Sciarabba."

Silence. Apparently surprised, Mr Puleo let a few moments pass before speaking.

"About that bullying business you told me about?"

"Yes," said Montalbano, taking advantage of the pretext being offered him.

"What exactly would you want me to do?"

"Nothing, actually. I simply would like you to report to me on Luigi. If he seemed normal today, more nervous, more distracted, that kind of thing. It's just a silly idea I had."

"All right, then," said Puleo. "I'll give you a ring as soon as the class gets out."

"Thank you," said Montalbano, hanging up.

He went and opened the French windows to the veranda. A few workers had finished dismantling the mini-railway, while others were loading the parts onto a truck. But even after the truck eventually left, the traces of the night before would remain visible. Indeed the whole beach looked as if it had been raped, dug out, bombed. Luckily a bit of wind was rising.

And little by little, the sea, too, would erase the damage that man had done.

He went into the kitchen with the firm intention of drinking at least two big mugs of espresso.

Since it took Gallo only ten minutes to drive him from Marinella to the police station in Vigàta, the inspector got to work just a few minutes past eight o'clock.

"Fazio in?" he asked Catarella.

"Nah, Chief, 'e ain't onna premisses."

"How about Augello?"

"'E ain't onna premisses, neither."

"OK, whoever is the first to come in, tell him to come to my office."

Catarella gave him a bewildered look. "An' wha' do I tell the seckin' one?"

"Tell him the same thing."

He went into his office then, all at once, the door flew open and crashed loudly against the wall.

"Sorry, Chief. My 'and slipped again! I fergat to tell yi' som'n."

"So tell me."

"I fergat to tell yiz 'at jess a few seccuns ago Mr Muleo the schoolteacher ast if 'yiz onna phone."

"Puleo?" Montalbano asked, not comprehending. Hadn't they left it that he was going to call after the first class?

"And what did he say?"

"'E said 'e wannit a talk t'yiz rilly oigently an' poissonally in poisson an' 'e leff me 'is mobble phone number in case ya wannit a call 'im back yisself."

"All right, then, call him and then put it through to me."

Catarella vanished. And Montalbano was overcome with anguish. What could this early phone call mean? Why didn't he wait to call?

The telephone rang. He snatched the receiver. "Mr Puleo?"

"Yes, it's me, Inspector. There's something I have to tell you. You may not know that ever since there was the attack on the school, we've been . . . well, we've been in a state of alert. The head teacher has asked us teachers and the students' families to inform her of any absences so we can monitor the situation."

"And so?"

"And so this morning there were two children absent from class III B," said Puleo.

"Who?"

"Giuseppe Portolano, whose father phoned in an excuse; the other one is our same Luigi Sciarabba, who, however . . ."

"However?"

"Well . . . it's a little strange," said Puleo. "He called in person to give his reasons. He said he had a slight temperature and was going to stay at home and rest."

"Thank you, Mr Puleo," said Montalbano, his mouth dry.

He called in person to give his reasons. A thirteen-year-old kid calls the school's head teacher to say he can't come to class? No, it made no sense. Anyway, he could very well have been lying. It was anybody's guess where he was calling from.

Montalbano feared that the push he'd given the boat had been a bit too strong.

CHAPTER
SIXTEEN

He couldn't remain hanging in the air like that much longer, in the midst of uncertainty. He had to find a solution at once. OK, but what? He sat there for five minutes racking his brain, and then he remembered that Salvuzzo's friend, Tindaro, had told him something about his grandmother, something to do with Luigi's mother . . . Right, that was it: Tindaro's grandmother lived right across the landing from the Sciarabbas. Not wasting one second, the inspector seized the telephone and rang Beba.

"Hello, Salvo. Mimì is —"

"I don't care where Mimì is —"

"But Salvuzzo's not here, either. He went to school —"

"Beba, let me speak for a second. I need you. Now listen closely: I remember that Tindaro said his grandmother is a friend of Luigino Sciarabba's mother."

"Luigino, the computer wizard? Yes, that's true, but why do you ask? Has something happened to him?"

"No, nothing's happened to him, but I need to know if Luigino is ill and if that's why he didn't go to school today."

"Salvo," said Beba, interrupting him, "the head teacher asked us all to call in if any of our kids were going to be absent, so if you call the school —"

"No, this is something private. I need to know whether Luigino is at home or not."

"But what can I do about it? You want me to give you the Sciarabbas' home phone number?"

"Good God, no. I wouldn't want to upset Luigino's mother. That's why I was asking you about Tindaro's grandmother. Do you know her?"

"Sure, absolutely. Her name is Anna, Anna Amato, she's a wonderful woman. Just think, once, before the summer, she took half the class on a field trip to Tindari at her own expense. If you want I can give you her number and address."

Montalbano, meanwhile, was lost in his thoughts. Anna Amato?!

Want to bet this was the same beautiful Anna Amato he'd met shortly after first moving to Vigàta? And whom he'd almost lost his head over? The one who'd worked as a waitress at the San Calogero restaurant?

Anna Amato, a grandmother?

And why not? He remembered she had a fifteen-year-old daughter at the time, and then he did a quick mental calculation. Yes! Anna Amato could very easily be a grandmother now. Just as he, too, could have been a grandfather.

"Hello?!" said Beba. "Hello?!"

"Oh, sorry. I was thinking of something else. OK, go ahead."

He wrote down the number and address on the same sheet of paper with the kid's email, but he already knew he would never have the courage to go and see Anna Amato the grandmother.

"Listen, Beba. You're the mother of a good future police officer and the wife of a police inspector, and so a bit of coppishness must have rubbed off on you, too. Do you feel up to asking this Anna whether Luigi is at home or not? Without arousing her suspicions, of course."

"There's no need to be a cop, Salvo. It's enough just to be a woman," Beba said, laughing. "I'll call you back as soon as I know something."

He was unable to sit there, doing nothing. So he got up, went over to the window, and smoked a cigarette. Then he lit a second one with the butt of the first. To chase the dark thoughts from his head he started reciting the poet Trilussa's "La vispa Teresa" and got to the point where Teresa repents and goes into church to pray to the Lord, when the Lord made the phone on his desk ring. He ran over to it. It was Beba.

"You know, Salvo, it was easier than I thought. Anna, among other things, even told me that she ran into Luigino in the stairwell on his way to school. Is that enough for you?"

"Yes," Montalbano said bitterly, and he thanked her.

It wasn't just enough, it was too much. In fact, it was confirmation that Luigino had worked out a detailed plan: he'd told his mother he was going to school and phoned the head teacher to tell her he was staying at home, so it was in fact anyone's guess where he might be now and what he was doing. And it was also possible that in carrying out his plan he would fuck up big-time. And the responsibility would be all his — that is, it would fall entirely on the brilliant but ever so slightly doddering Inspector Montalbano, because of those damn words he'd sent through cyberspace.

"May I?" asked Mimì, appearing in the doorway with Fazio behind him.

"Come on in, close the door, and sit down," Montalbano said gloomily.

But when he had the two of them sitting in front of his desk, words suddenly failed him. He didn't know where to start.

"What's wrong, Inspector?" asked Fazio, who knew him well.

"I got some troubling news just now, and I'm worried the situation might be dire."

"Meaning?"

"Meaning that, this morning, Luigino Sciarabba —"

"Salvuzzo's friend?" Augello interrupted him.

"Yes, that's right. He didn't go to school today."

The others looked at him wide-eyed.

"So?" asked Mimì.

"So, the situation seems troubling to me."

"Why?" asked Augello, raising his voice.

"Because the kid called the head teacher himself to excuse his absence. He said he had a slight temperature. But he's not at home."

This time Fazio and Augello looked at each other wide-eyed. Then they turned towards the inspector.

"I'm sorry, but are you feeling all right?" asked Mimi.

"I feel fine. Why do you ask?"

"Because you seem to be making no sense," Mimi said by way of reply. "What the hell do you care if Luigino told his head teacher a lie? Want to know how often I used to play hooky and then fake my dad's signature when I brought in my excuse? What are you so worried about?"

"I'm just worried, that's all."

"Oh, no, you don't," Mimi went on. "I smell something fishy here. You'd better give us a better explanation, otherwise I really don't care whether Luigino skipped school, and Fazio probably doesn't, either."

Montalbano said nothing.

"Chief," said Fazio, looking him in the eye. "Do you think there might be a connection between the kid's lie and the attack on the school?"

Reluctantly, Montalbano nodded.

"And what would that be?" Augello pressed him.

"I think that this kid, one way or another, is up to his neck in the whole business of the attack."

"I don't understand anything any more," said Fazio. "So what happened to this Luigino?"

"He's the boy from Salvuzzo's class who's been bullied by three classmates. He's never told anyone about the problem. Apparently he's an easy-going boy with an outstanding talent for computers. I can't really give you any logical explanation for it, but I had an idea. Yesterday I started thinking that maybe there was some connection between the two men who attacked the school and this Luigino, who communicates with the whole world through his computer. I can't really tell you more than that. I just got that idea, that's all."

"Well, that's not all for me," said Augello. "What connection are you talking about anyway? I was there, and the two attackers didn't address anyone in the class in particular. So your suspicions must be based on something else that you don't want to tell us."

Mimì's reasoning made perfect sense. Montalbano had his back to the wall.

"When I talked to Salvuzzo and his friend Tindaro, they started talking about this Luigino, his family, and the fact that he's really very solitary. My curiosity was aroused when they told me that, during the attack, Luigino was the only one in the class who didn't seem scared. He merely seemed very attentive, showing none of the fear, surprise, or confusion all his other classmates were feeling."

"Damn!" said Augello. "My son told you all that? I don't think he's spoken that many words to me in the last three years!"

"And I'm telling you that it was in fact the boys' words that raised the question in my mind: what if Luigi was expecting that attack on the class? That was my starting point. And so, wanting to pursue this idea and see if it was justified . . ."

"What did you do?"

"Well, to make the kid come out in the open, yesterday evening, after you all left, I called Catarella and got him to help me send an email to Luigi. An anonymous email."

"What?" said Mimì, shocked, sticking his hands in his hair.

"You heard right. Catarella and I wrote an anonymous email," replied the inspector, in a tone at once resigned and dismissive.

"And what did you say to him in the email?"

"I blackmailed him. I don't remember exactly what I said . . . Something like: 'You've been discovered, we know it was you who organized the attack on the school, and if you don't do what we say we'll report you to the police.' I think that was it, more or less. And, yes, I know, it was the wrong thing to do, stupid as fuck. OK? I'll say it first, before you do. And now I'm scared to death that the kid got freaked out by my message, ran away from home, and is going to do something stupid. And there you have it."

"My heartfelt congratulations," said Mimì, "on your approach to this investigation, which you're conducting with the valorous help of Catarella and my son. What do you plan to do next time? Resort to seances? Ask for help from a medium?"

Montalbano ignored the insults. His head was too full of dark thoughts.

"What can we do, Chief?" asked Fazio. "Shall we issue a general alert?"

"No, no, no. Only as a last resort. The best thing to do, for now, is for the three of us to try to find him, but be as quiet as possible about it."

"I agree," said Fazio.

"Then here's what we'll do. We'll each of us get in his car and start driving around town to try to —"

"What I'm going do," said Fazio, interrupting him, "is, as soon as I get the address, I'm going to travel, on foot, the route the kid usually takes from home to school, and maybe ask the people who normally see him walk by if they have any information . . ."

"That's a good idea. I've got the address right here. Copy it."

He handed him the piece of paper with the numbers that Beba had given him.

"And then what?"

"You, Mimì, should instead drive slowly around the side streets, to see —"

"Wait a second," said Mimì. "I know Luigino Sciarabba; Fazio doesn't. Just wait here a second. I'll be right back."

He went out of the room and returned a moment later with a photograph of the class, which he handed to Fazio.

"Luigino's the fourth on the left in the second row," he said.

Fazio studied it.

"Let me see, too," said Montalbano.

Luigino was a tall kid, with a head of bushy blond hair and round glasses like Harry Potter's.

"Everyone's addresses and phone numbers are on the back of the photo," said Augello.

Fazio wrote down Luigino's number, which the inspector then copied down on the paper he had with all the other numbers.

"OK," said Montalbano, bringing his hand down on the desktop by way of conclusion. "Now let's not waste any time. We'll meet back up here in two hours, keeping in touch with one another all the while via our mobile phones."

"And what are you going to do?" asked Augello.

"I," said Montalbano, "am going to poke around in the upper part of town, in Piano Lanterna."

And such was his purpose until he got in his car, put the key in the ignition, and thought of something. He took the road to Montelusa. When he got there, he parked in the Central Police building's main car park and headed towards the new wing, where he knew the Postal Police had their offices. The new section had a separate entrance of its own, which delighted the inspector, since he was unlikely to run into anyone unpleasant. And, in fact, he didn't see a living soul. It was as if the building was uninhabited. He didn't hear any voices, telephones ringing, or footsteps in the hallways. He might be looking at one of those buildings the need for which lay entirely with the construction firm that had built it.

After crossing a ghostly corridor, he finally found a sign at the foot of a staircase saying that the offices of the Postal Police were located on the second floor. Climbing two flights of stairs, he came to a landing with a desk and a uniformed policeman sitting at it.

"May I help you?"

"I'm Inspector Montalbano."

The man stood up and said: "I beg your pardon. I didn't recognize you. What can I do for you?"

"I would like to speak to someone from the Postal Police."

"All right, Inspector. Just go down the hallway on the left, and it'll be the third door on the right. There'll be an officer there to help you."

"Thank you very much," said Montalbano, and he went and knocked at the appointed door.

"Come in," said a woman's voice.

Montalbano turned the doorknob and went in.

The first thing he saw was a great mass of red hair set aflame by the light pouring in from the window behind the female figure sitting at the desk.

Then he saw the woman's facial features and turned to stone, because she looked exactly like Anna Amato.

So, was it true, after all, that when you mention someone after a great many years, that person will suddenly appear in the flesh? Except for the fact that while the young woman in front of him was indeed Anna Amato, she was Anna as a girl thirty years ago.

The same Anna Amato whose memory he had so well preserved that he'd felt troubled at the idea of having to see her again after thirty years, inevitably changed by the passage of time.

Meanwhile the girl had stood up and was coming towards him with her hand extended.

"You're Inspector Montalbano, aren't you? I'm so pleased to meet you. Please come and sit down."

Still feeling a bit numb, Montalbano sat down in front of the desk. The girl took her place in the other chair next to the inspector, who still hadn't recovered.

"I've come to ask for some information."

"What would you like to know?"

"A lady friend of mine called me, a woman who tends to get easily worried, and she's very upset that her son didn't show up at school today, even though he'd said that was where he was going."

The redhead smiled.

"We've all played hooky at one time or another, haven't we?"

"Yes, of course, but, you see, the fact is that this boy, who's thirteen, has never done so before. And since he's from the class where the two masked gunmen broke in . . . in short, those kids all went through a troubling experience. So I just wanted to say that I'm a little anxious myself."

"I understand," said the young woman. "So how can I help you?"

"That's just it. I wanted to know . . . whether, by any chance, it might be possible to locate him through his mobile phone or computer."

The red-haired Venus smiled a thousand-watt smile. "Inspector, unfortunately we're not in an American TV movie. If you can give me a little information on this boy, I can try to see what I can do, but I can't promise you anything. You want this to remain a private matter?"

"Absolutely."

"Then that limits my options somewhat. I'll try to do a little research on my own. Do you have any useful information you can give me?"

Montalbano took out the piece of paper on which he'd written all the data on Luigino and handed it to her.

The girl circled around to the back of the desk and copied the information down on the computer.

Then she said:

"I'm afraid there isn't much at all we can do. But, if you like, you can stay here with me and see what we can come up with."

It occurred to Montalbano that if he'd refused to see Anna Amato the grandmother, it would have been even more intolerable to sit there looking at Anna Amato the ravishing young woman.

So he stood up and said:

"I think I'd rather continue my search. Let's exchange mobile numbers. You can call me if you manage to find anything."

The girl took down his number, gave him hers, and then stood up. They shook hands.

Montalbano went out, closing the door behind him, and just stood there in the hall. He needed to recover from the shock. Walking ever so slowly, with the step of a battered dog, he said goodbye to the policeman at the desk and turned to head down the stairs. But then he froze and turned back.

"Excuse me," he said to the policeman, "but I've already forgotten the young woman's name . . ."

"Her name is Laura Infantino."

Montalbano thanked him, descended the stairs, went into the car park, got in his car, and headed off to Vigàta.

After he'd combed three or four streets in Piano Lanterna, his mobile phone rang. He answered without looking first at who it was.

"Hello," he said wearily.

"I'm sorry, Inspector. This is Mr Puleo. I got your number from the switchboard operator at the station. I'm afraid I have some bad news for you."

Out of the frying pan and into the fire, thought the inspector. "I'm all ears, sir. Is it about Luigino?"

"Indirectly," Puleo replied, adding: "I did something stupid."

"What did you do?"

"Well, your phone call got me a little worried, and so when class was over I called the Sciarabba home to find out where Luigino was. I know, I know, it was the wrong thing to do."

"Go on," the inspector said drily.

"The moment I told his mother that he hadn't come to school, she started wailing like a madwoman, as if I'd just said that Luigi was dead or something. She started yelling: 'Oh, my God, he's been kidnapped, probably murdered!' And so, not knowing what to do, I got in my car and dashed over to her place. But when I got there I saw that Luigino's mother was luckily being assisted by a neighbour, Mrs Amato, who was just great and managed to calm her down a little. She put her into bed, gave her a sedative, and called the doctor."

Montalbano's balls were in a tight spin. He'd done everything possible to leave Luigino's mother out of this affair, and now Mr Puleo had gone and . . .

"Yes, that was stupid, what you did," Montalbano said gruffly. "How is she now?"

"A little better. We're all waiting for the doctor to get here, and I decided it was my duty to stay with her until things calmed down a little."

Feeling more than defeated by this point, Montalbano cut him off.

"Very well, sir. Thank you very much for keeping me informed, but now I really have to go."

"Just a second," said Puleo. "I was wondering if maybe you yourself should also come here to Luigino's place, for just a few seconds, to try to calm his mother down a little more. Just to say a couple of words to her, to tell her that you're doing everything in your power to find the boy —"

"No, that would be a pointless waste of time. I have to continue my search," he said, even more harshly than before, cutting him off.

Meet Anna Amato the grandmother? What was this, a conspiracy? A plot to persecute him? He would never set foot in that apartment, not even dead.

"I beg you, just for a couple of minutes —"

"No. I said no. But I can assure you that as soon as we find Luigino — and I am certain that we will find him — the first thing I'll tell him to do is to call his mother to set her mind at rest. That's all I can do for you. Goodbye," and he hung up.

Since he already had his phone in his hand, he rang Fazio.

"Any news?"

"None whatsoever, Chief. But the newspaper seller, the one with the kiosk on the road to Luigino's school, told me that around eight-thirty this morning the kid stopped to buy his favourite computer magazine. He said he was the same as all the other times, nothing strange about him: backpack on his shoulders and computer in view. The kid said hello and then went on his way."

"Did he see what direction he went in?"

"No, he didn't. I asked him the same thing, but nothing."

The inspector then called Mimì.

And got the same dismaying reply. No news.

And so he started up the car and continued his search. He saw a computer shop, which he'd driven past hundreds of times before without ever experiencing the slightest desire to stop and look in the display window, which featured computers straight out of science-fiction movies and mobile phones capable of doing everything, even preparing your morning coffee. This time, however, following his instinct, he stopped, pulled up, got out of the car, and went inside.

"Good morning."

"Good morning, Inspector," said a well-dressed man of about fifty who was looking into a glowing computer screen.

"I need some information."

"If I can be of help . . ."

"Do you know a boy by the name of Luigi Sciarabba?"

"Luigino? Of course! He comes in here at least two, three times a week."

"What does he come for?"

"He likes to inform himself on the latest things. He's a real expert, you know."

"When was the last time you saw him?"

"Just this morning, he dropped in at around a quarter to nine."

"Did he ask for anything in particular?"

"Actually he came to bring me the solution to a technical problem a customer of mine has been having with his computer." The man smiled and continued: "Keep this between us, but sometimes I use Luigino as a consultant."

"And how did he seem this morning?"

The salesman gave him a confused look. "What do you mean by that, Inspector?"

"Didn't you ask him why he wasn't in school?"

"Of course. He said he'd be going in for the second class of the day. He seemed the same as always this morning. Why, has something happened?"

"No. I just needed to talk to him, but since he never went to school and isn't at home, either . . ."

"How strange," said the man. "Skipping school isn't really Luigi's style. Does this have anything to do with the shoot-out that occurred at the school the other day?"

"Yes," said Montalbano, leaving it at that. "Do you have any idea where he may have gone?"

"Inspector, all we ever talk about is computers. What I can tell you, though, is that he sometimes goes to the harbour in the afternoon."

CHAPTER
SEVENTEEN

The inspector's heart sank. "To the harbour?"

Maybe Luigino, through his computer, had got in contact with somebody in Tunisia or Morocco and embarked clandestinely on a ship. And was now navigating through real water, after the internet's open sea of virtuality.

And it was anyone's guess where they should poke their noses next.

"What does he do at the harbour?"

"I remember he once told me he had a lot of friends among the sailors on the trawlers."

"Thanks so much for your help," said Montalbano, and he rushed out of the shop, got in his car, and headed for the harbour.

What did it mean, that he was friends with the crewmen of the trawlers? It didn't make any sense. Maybe it was another lie. What did that kid really go and do at the harbour? With all the fantasies in his head, it could be anything.

Montalbano parked the car on the central quay in front of two freighters, got out, and started walking down the eastern one. Just like he normally did every day for his meditative-digestive stroll. Maybe the kid had wanted to be alone and was sitting out among the rocks. Halfway down, he saw the usual old man with his fishing rod, who'd become a friend.

"Hello, Toto."

"Hello, Inspector."

"They biting?"

"Not much."

"Listen, Toto, did you by any chance see a blond boy of about thirteen with a backpack and round glasses pass by this way?"

"Nah, Inspector. I've seen a lot of people go by, but no kids."

He thanked him, turned back, and walked along the side of the Lampedusa ferry. The gangway was still raised, meaning that it wasn't time for the passengers to start boarding.

He headed for the ticket office and went in.

Only one of three booths had a person working in it, a fiftyish woman with glasses.

"Hello, I'm Inspector Montalbano, police."

The woman looked at him without saying anything.

"Do you have a list of the passengers who've reserved places on this evening's ferry for Lampedusa?"

"Of course."

"All right, could you check and see whether a certain Luigi Sciarabba has reserved?"

The woman looked into the computer she had beside her. "No, there's no one named Sciarabba."

"Thank you," said the inspector.

"Mind you," the woman said, "that doesn't really mean much."

"Why do you say that?"

"Reservations are open until five o'clock this evening, and there are still plenty of vacancies. And someone arriving at the last minute can usually find a place after buying their ticket just before boarding. This isn't high season, after all."

"I see," said Montalbano, thanking her and going out.

The only thing left to do was to get back in his car and go to the end of central quay, where the fishing trawlers were tied up.

On the esplanade at the start of the quay he found only two fishermen sitting on the ground, repairing the damaged meshes of an extremely long net that they kept turning around and around.

He pulled up beside them, got out of the car, and said: "Hello. I'm Inspector Montalbano."

The two men didn't seem to have heard. Then the older of the two looked up and replied:

"If you're planning on arresting us, give us ten minutes to finish fixing the net."

"I'm not here to arrest anybody. I just want some information. Do either of you know a boy of thirteen named Luigino Sciarabba?"

"Sure!" replied the older man. "He often comes to see us in the afternoon. Says he likes to watch us work on the nets."

"Does he talk to you?"

"Of course he talks."

Apparently the fisherman needed a little push. "Listen," said Montalbano, who immediately realized the older man was playing his cards close to his chest in dealing with a policeman, "I have no desire whatsoever to do any harm to this boy. On the contrary. So you can tell me anything. What does he say to you when he comes here?"

"He tells us about his dad, says he can only see him once a year and is always waiting for him to come back. He's convinced that this time he'll return on a ship. And so, every time a big ship pulls into harbour, he races down here to see who comes off it."

"When did you last see him?"

"He came by just about an hour ago. And then he left."

"Did you see what direction he went in?"

"He went out towards the end of the quay, and I think he's still there 'cause I never saw him come back. D'you see him, Cicci?"

"Nah, I dint see him return, neither."

Without wasting another minute, Montalbano got back in his car and started driving slowly past the ten or so cold-storage warehouses that lined that part of the quay. No sign of Luigino. Pushing on, he ended up in the last section, about thirty or forty yards, where there were no more buildings and there was only the harbour wall, with its surrounding rocks. He drove at a crawl, and then all at once he spotted a human figure standing on the last rock, right under the small green light that marked the mouth of the harbour.

And so, he, too, still rolling very slowly, got as far as he could without driving his car into the water, and found himself just ten feet away from — he was sure of it now — Luigino Sciarabba. Another thing was also clear: that the kid was thinking things over before doing something really, really stupid. So the inspector had to tread very carefully.

Luigino was gazing out at the sea, and made no sign indicating that he'd heard the car pull up. Before opening his mouth, Montalbano took a deep breath, and only when he finally felt all the nerves in his body relaxing, leaving no residual trace of tension whatsoever, did he decide to lower the car window quietly, and in the calmest, most neutral tone of voice he could muster, he said:

"Hey there, Luigi."

The boy turned around slowly, then bent his knees a little to look into the car.

"Hello, Inspector," he said.

"You're right, I'm Inspector Salvo Montalbano, but I'm also the godfather of your friend Salvuzzo Augello. I've been looking for you all morning."

"Why were you looking for me?"

"Because I want to tell you a story. And you are the only person who can tell me whether this story is true or not," said Montalbano, opening the car door and stepping out.

"OK. But I would ask you to be so kind as to stay where you are and not come any closer."

With utter aplomb, Montalbano lit a cigarette.

He took his time smoking it, looking out at the sea all the while. This enabled him to see that the kid's backpack and computer were in a hollow in the rock, and that, although at first glance he'd seemed calm, Luigino's nerves, under his skin, were as taut as violin strings. How long could he resist that internal pressure? The inspector decided it was a good moment to make his move.

"It's really hot today," he said.

He took off his jacket, opened the car door, tossed it onto the back seat, closed the door again, and, as naturally as possible, took a few steps forward.

"Stop right there," Luigino ordered him.

Montalbano looked at him with surprise.

"But I can't very well shout the story I want to tell you. I have to come at least —"

"Then go there," said Luigino, indicating a rock a couple of yards away from him.

Hopping from rock to rock like a goat, Montalbano found himself on one that was impossible to sit down on. All he could do was remain standing in precarious balance. The boy was now before him, looking at him with curiosity.

"The story," Montalbano began, "is about a dog."

Luigino's surprise was immediately evident in his face.

"A dog," the inspector continued, "whose master would beat him every hour of the day for no reason at all. One day the dog couldn't stand it any longer and asked for help from a pack of wolves. He wanted them to frighten his master. But the wolves wouldn't listen to him. Then suddenly one day two wolves said they were ready to help him. But the dog didn't know they weren't real wolves. In fact, they were two stray dogs who wanted —"

"That's enough!" said the boy.

And he turned abruptly away, to face the sea. But he hadn't finished his motion before Montalbano had already left his feet and was flying through the air towards him. But the inspector must have calculated the distance incorrectly, because he landed with all his weight on the boy's back, prompting the surprised youth to cry out and fall forward. And so, just like that, they found themselves both in the sea, making a tremendous splash. Both bodies plunged deep underwater, then their heads re-emerged. By this point completely beside himself with rage, Montalbano grabbed Luigino by the shoulders, shook him so violently that the boy's head bobbed in and out of the water, and shouted:

"So you wanted to kill yourself, eh? You little shit! Eh, did you?"

Practically gasping for breath and spitting out some of the water in his mouth, the boy stammered:

"I wasn't going to jump into the water, I swear! It was you who pushed me and made me fall. I didn't want to kill myself, I swear it, I swear it!"

Montalbano felt so ashamed that he wished the sea would just swallow him up. Luigino was telling the truth.

"Let's get back on dry land," he said.

In two strokes, side by side, they reached the nearest rock, which luckily was low and flat. Giving each other a hand, they climbed onto it. And sat there for a spell, catching their breath. Then, all at once, Luigino started crying like a little boy and covered his face with his hands, repeating all the while:

"I can't take it any more, I can't take it any more."

The inspector realized the boy had lost his glasses. He got up and went over to the next rock to retrieve the computer and backpack, then returned.

"Let me help you," he said.

And taking him by his shoulder, he lifted him up. But since Luigino couldn't stand on his own two feet, he put his arms around the inspector. He'd gone back to being a thirteen-year-old boy, after an adventure that had been too grown-up for him.

By some miracle, nearly falling with every step, they managed to reach the car. Montalbano sat the boy in the front and threw the backpack and computer in the back. Then he started the engine and headed straight for Marinella.

He stopped a minute later, picked up his jacket from the back seat, extracted his mobile phone, and called Fazio, informing him that he'd found Luigino and that he should pass the news on to Augello.

"Are you on your way here to the station?" asked Fazio.

"No, I'm taking him home with me to Marinella. I don't know when I'll be coming to the office. I'll let you know."

A few minutes after he'd set off again, Luigino's head dropped into his lap. He'd fallen into a deep sleep.

Montalbano sat him up again, buckled his seat belt, and leaned the boy's head against the car window. It was a short but difficult journey, because every so often the boy's body would slide towards him and restrict his movements.

As soon as he pulled up in front of his house, the door opened and Adelina appeared, her little handbag dangling from her arm.

"I's a juss finishin' up, 'coz I comma late a this mornin', an' so . . ."

She trailed off and goggled her eyes at the sight of the inspector with his shirt all wet and his hair and moustache still dripping.

"*Matre santa*, wha' happen? Eh? Wha' happen a youse?" she asked.

"Nothing, Adeli," said Montalbano. "We were just sitting on a rock when a big wave . . ."

He grabbed his jacket, the computer, and the backpack, got out of the car, and said:

"Please give the boy a hand, if you would."

"I tekka goo' care o' him," said Adelina, fussing about to free the boy from the seat belt.

Montalbano went into his bedroom, threw everything in his hands onto the bed, and started getting undressed, worried because he was feeling chills running up his spine. All he needed now was to catch a cold.

He stripped naked and dried himself with the pillowcases, since he didn't feel like going into the bathroom. Then he got dressed again.

When he went into the kitchen about twenty minutes later, he saw Luigino sitting in a chair, still half-asleep, wearing a pair of his underpants and a T-shirt of the local tourist bureau, which Montalbano had always refused to put on because, among other things, it barely covered his belly button. Adelina had plugged in the iron and was drying his underwear with its heat. The boy's clothes were hanging outside in the sun.

"I wish I had my glasses," Luigino said plaintively.

"You lost them in the water," the inspector replied.

"I know, but I've got another pair in the backpack."

Montalbano went into his bedroom, returned with the computer and backpack, and handed the backpack to Luigino.

The boy opened it, took out a pair of glasses exactly like the other one, and put them on, seeming relieved.

"Come with me," said Montalbano. They went into the dining room.

"Now I want you to take this phone and call your mother to reassure her," he said.

"But what should I tell her?" asked Luigi.

"Tell her that on your way to school this morning you ran into me, and I picked you up and took you to the station, because I wanted to know a few more details about the attack on the school. And now you're at my place in Marinella and are going to have lunch with me, after which I'll drive you home. Then put me on."

He left him alone and went back into the kitchen. Adelina was busy at the stove.

"What are you doing?"

263

"Whattya mean what am I doin'? Don' ya wanna eata somma pasta?"

"Of course, but on one condition, that you sit and eat with us."

"Then please lay the table f' me," Adelina said, smiling. "An' whattya say I tekka six eggs an' a mekka *ova a piscitéddru?*"

"Excellent idea!" said Montalbano. "It's been ages since I last had *ova a piscitéddru!*"

He'd just finished laying the table when Luigi called to him:

"Inspector! Can you come to the phone?"

Then, as he was handing him the receiver, he said under his breath:

"I think I managed to calm her down."

"Hello, Mrs Sciarabba," the inspector said in an official tone.

"Salvo! It's so good to hear your voice!"

With his heart crashing down to his feet, Montalbano recognized who it was at the other end and tried desperately to remain equal to the situation.

"I beg your pardon, but who is this?"

"Oh, I'm sorry, Salvo. It's Anna. Anna Amato. Do you remember? The Trattoria San Calogero?"

"Anna . . . of course I remember," and then he dropped the subject. "But where did Mrs Sciarabba go?"

"She couldn't stand on her own two feet any more and had to go and lie down," said Anna, disheartened by Montalbano's coldness. "Mr Puleo is with her. Could you tell me what you had to tell her?"

"Yes. Tell her I apologize for not calling her sooner, but that Luigino's help has been extremely valuable to me. We're now having some lunch, and I'll bring him home in a little while."

"All right," said Anna, cold as ice.

"Goodbye," said Montalbano, though he realized she'd already hung up.

"Iss ready!" shouted Adelina, appearing in the doorway holding a big pot of spaghetti with tomato and baby squid sauce.

Montalbano and Luigino came running.

After they'd eaten, Luigino, his clothes now dry and ironed, sat down with the inspector on the veranda.

Before leaving, Adelina cleaned up the kitchen and then came out to say goodbye and give the boy a hug.

After they'd been sitting there in silence for a spell, the inspector asked:

"Feel like telling me how it all happened?"

It was a bit like when a barrel blows its cork and the wine shoots out with such force that you're unable to plug it back up. Luigino started talking and never stopped, and so great was his desire to relieve himself of the burden he'd been carrying around alone for days and days that his words got all entangled with one another.

"No . . . I mean, yes . . . Actually . . . it didn't happen the way you said. I . . . I didn't ask the wolves for help. Actually, the whole thing started a few months ago. For no reason at all, three of my schoolmates started picking on me. At first it was just little stuff:

they'd steal my new T-shirts or my morning snack, or they'd take my homework and tear it up into a thousand pieces. That kind of thing. Then, when they saw that I wouldn't react — because I really didn't know what to do — they started aiming higher. They took my phone and ran it over with a scooter; another time they threw me into a fountain with all my clothes on. That day a couple of my friends stood up for me, but that probably made matters worse. They got really upset and just increased their abuse. They started waiting for me outside school, sometimes outside my front door; they broke the intercom system to our building; and they made off with my bicycle. Then they posted some videos on the internet, after which some of my other classmates started making fun of me and then . . . well . . . I just couldn't take it any more. I didn't know who to talk to about it . . . My parents . . . Papa is far away and doesn't even know if he'll be able to make it back for Christmas, and Mamma . . . well, Mamma is afraid of everything. One night I got so desperate that I exploded; I sat down at the computer and started telling everyone and no one in particular what was happening to me.

"So, that was how it all started.

"A few nights later I got a message, but I couldn't work out who'd sent it. It said: 'Would you like our protection?' Inspector, you have no idea what those words meant to me. I felt so . . . so defenceless, it seemed inconceivable to me that someone . . . that someone might want to, or be able to, help me . . . It didn't seem possible. So I replied, 'Yes, yes, absolutely.'

They asked me a whole lot of questions: where I lived, what school I went to, the names of the classmates who were bullying me, information on the teachers, the head teacher ... They even wanted to know my class schedule and the exact location of my classroom. I tried to answer all their questions. So ... I guess I should have suspected ... but, I swear, I had no idea and could never have imagined ...

"In the end they wrote back saying they would help me, but you've got to believe me, they never said anything about what they were planning to do.

"And so I started feeling less alone, and would go to school feeling more confident. I could face the abuse better now, knowing that it would all be over soon. But I never suspected ... The day they burst into our classroom with those masks ... I recognized the Anonymous masks right away and felt terrified. My blood ran cold. And then they fired their guns ... And they fired again, and again, when Salvuzzo's dad ... Inspector, do you really think they needed to fire their guns to protect me? ...

"When it was all over I went home ... I don't really know how I managed ... I vomited out everything inside me and went to bed with a fever. Mamma thought it was from the scare I'd had. Then we heard on TV that Anonymous denied any involvement, which got me really worried. So who were those people? What did they want? Why did they do it? I didn't have the courage to turn on the computer, and when I did, it made things even worse, if that was possible. I found a message from a certain Montarella, who I don't know, who told me that they'd discovered that I was the one behind the attack on the class and that if I didn't do what they asked, they would report me to the police. I'm sure it was the same people, and they were going to do everything possible to blackmail me and get money out of my dad. After thinking things over for a very long time I realized that the only possible course of action was to turn myself in, to come to you and tell you the whole truth. So this morning I didn't go to school, because I wanted to enjoy a bit of freedom. That was why you found me out there on the rocks. I wanted to breathe some of that air, because soon I wouldn't be able to any more. And when I was out there, I kept telling myself: 'Just five more minutes. Stay just five more minutes.' And then you showed up . . . So, what's going to happen now? I know I made a mistake, and I'm ready to pay for it. Just do me one favour: please help me protect my mother. She'll die when she hears I'm going to gaol. You have to help me."

He stopped talking, his voice breaking up, and was about to start crying but managed to control himself. So Montalbano got up, went into the kitchen, and came back out to the veranda with a jug of water and a glass, but when he got there Luigino had gone down to the beach and was heading towards the water's edge. The inspector stood there watching him, and at that moment an icy dagger pierced his heart. He felt as if he were rolling backwards in time, sucked back into the past. And he saw himself on the same veranda watching a boy running and hopping over the breaking waves . . . François! François, now gone. His inability to protect the youth and somehow prevent his horrible death weighed heavily on him now. At that moment he swore to himself that he would do everything in his power, whatever the cost, to keep Luigino out of the present case. He drank the water he'd intended for the boy, jumped down onto the beach, and caught up to him, and when he was beside him, he put an arm around his shoulders. Then he decided to speak.

"Luigi, about that blackmail email. I wrote it myself."

Luigino broke away from his embrace, took two steps backwards, and looked at him wide-eyed.

"You? The police? And why would you do such a horrible thing to me?"

"Because I realized you were behind the whole thing, and I wanted to make you come out into the open."

Luigino said nothing, turned his back, and started walking towards the house. Montalbano followed him. During the thirty-two steps it took him to reach the veranda, his brain very quickly mapped out the path he would have to take to get Luigino out of trouble.

"Wait for me here," he said, refilling the glass for the boy. He went into his bedroom, picked up his jacket, took out his mobile phone, and called the Postal Police officer, Laura Infantino.

"Inspector, I still haven't been able to —"

"Luigino's with me, at my house," said Montalbano, cutting her off. "Do you think you could come and join us right away? I'll explain how to get here."

CHAPTER
EIGHTEEN

Montalbano went back onto the veranda, but Luigino barely even noticed, so absorbed was he in reading something on his computer. He took advantage of the situation to get the whisky bottle and cigarettes. Then he returned and sat down beside the boy.

Some twenty minutes went by. The doorbell rang.

Montalbano went to the door. It was Officer Infantino.

How could this woman go about trailing a red sunset behind her at all hours of the day?

He sat her down in the dining room, sat himself down in front of her, and said:

"Please listen to me carefully."

And he told her everything. When he'd finished, he asked her a precise question.

"Do you think there's any way that you, personally, could take the credit for having resolved the case, keeping me and, most important, Luigino out of the whole thing?"

The young woman gave him a confused look.

"I think I understand what you're asking of me. But first I'd like to talk to the boy."

270

Montalbano stood up, and she followed him. Could it be that a red flash from the woman reflected off Luigino's computer screen? Because, for the first time in almost an hour, the boy looked up and returned to the world of the living.

"This is a friend of mine, Officer Infantino," said Montalbano, introducing her. "And this young man is Luigino Sciarabba, also a friend of mine."

The young woman sat down and placed her computer beside Luigino's.

"Thank you, Salvo. And now the two of us need to talk."

The inspector went down onto the beach, determined to go for a very long stroll.

Forty-five minutes later, as he was returning home, he unexpectedly saw Fazio coming towards him on the beach.

"Sorry to bother you, Chief, but I just couldn't wait any longer. You said you'd call me, but . . . But what's Laura Infantino doing here?"

"I'll explain everything later."

"She said they've finished and she wants to talk to you before she leaves."

They went back to the house.

Before going inside, Montalbano said to Fazio:

"You go into the dining room with Luigino now. Laura and I need to talk in private."

He stayed out on the veranda, and moments later, preceded by a bright red aura tending to orange, the young police officer arrived. They sat down, and Laura asked with her eyes if it was all right to take one of his cigarettes. Having earned his silent consent, she lit one, took two long drags, and began.

"Inspector, from what I've learned from Luigi's account, and from what I was able to verify on his computer, I think I can keep you and the boy out of this and track down the attackers on my own. They seem to be three hotheads, and I think they already have police records. But before making up my mind, I'd like to speak to Counterterrorism. I don't think they'll create any trouble for me, but first tell me something. Why? Why don't you want to be involved? I realize that the boy's a minor and all, but why don't you want to be part of it? Why do you want to make it so that I get all the credit, which I don't deserve?"

"There's a wonderful French play," Montalbano replied, "in which Ulysses, speaking to Hector, tries to prevent the start of the Trojan War. And when Hector, in shock, asks him why, Ulysses replies, 'Because Andromache, your wife, bats her eyelashes exactly the same way as Penelope.'"

"And what does that mean?" she asked, bewildered.

"I'm certain that if you read the play, you'll understand," said Montalbano.

Laura Infantino took a few seconds to reply, then said: "All right. I'll talk to Marchica. If you don't mind, I'll take Luigi home to his mother. That way I'll be able to reassure her. He's OK with it. We're friends now."

"Thank you," said Montalbano.

They both went back inside and found Fazio and Luigino playing a computer game of cops and robbers, and it was clear from the look on Fazio's face and the curses he was muttering that he was losing. Then Laura said to Luigino:

"Get your things ready and let's go."

Luigino strapped his backpack onto his shoulders, picked up his computer, and looked at the inspector, who held out his hand to him. Luigino shook it.

"You were great," said Montalbano.

Luigino opened his arms and hugged the inspector.

Then he turned his back and led the way to the door.

Telling the whole story of the morning in minute detail took up a good hour of the inspector's and Fazio's time.

"What are you going to do now, Chief? Come with me to the office? I can bring you back afterwards, if you like."

"No," said the inspector. "I really don't feel like it."

"Want me to tell Inspector Augello the whole story?"

"Yes, but tell him that my orders are that he make no mention of it to his son, Salvuzzo."

"OK," said Fazio, waving goodbye. "See you in the morning."

Left to himself, he sat down and heaved a long sigh of satisfaction.

Then his body reacted in its usual fashion. Without warning, a wolflike hunger assailed him. He went into the kitchen and found a platter of *sarde a beccafico* in the oven. He laid the table on the veranda, poured himself a glass of white wine, and ate so slowly that when he was finished it was already dark outside.

He cleared the table and went down to the beach to take a long walk, to lessen the effects of the dangerous sardines. But his walk itself proved dangerous, as his left foot suddenly got caught in something on the surface of the sand that nearly made him fall. He bent down and felt around, and finally pulled out a piece of plastic. What was this? He flicked on his lighter and saw a red-and-yellow net. Then he remembered. The net had been put there to protect the set when they were filming at Marinella, but the safety it provided was purely theoretical, since the people working on the shoot could easily have knocked it down. A symbolic protection, therefore.

But how many different kinds of protection there were in this world! There was a widespread desire to feel safe from everything: from what is known, what is unknown, from what might be but is not necessarily certain to be, from those who arrive from the sea, from those who worship a different God, or from those who worship the same God but pray in a different way. And so it was always best to play it safe. And the forms of protection proliferated. Hadn't he himself done everything possible to protect Luigino? And didn't Luigino want to protect his mother? And yet he didn't know whom to turn to protect himself. Hadn't the kid said: "Inspector, do you really think they needed to fire their guns to protect me? . . ."

274

In a flash, the thought of firing a gun brought back the image of the wall.

The wall that had been filmed repeatedly for years.

Maybe it was true that Emanuele had felt so worried about losing his brother's protection that he had shot himself.

He suddenly felt an overwhelming need to race home and call up Engineer Sabatello.

"Hello, Montalbano here."

"What a delight to hear from you, Inspector. What is it?"

"Could you come into the station tomorrow morning and bring those things you found?"

"I'm sorry, but I have to leave for Palermo tomorrow and will be staying there for a few weeks."

Montalbano would never manage to wait that long. "I'm sorry, but . . . do you think I could come to your place right now?"

"Well, I certainly wouldn't mind driving out to Marinella. Shall I come to you?"

"Perfect. I'll be waiting."

He'd just ended a long phone call with Livia, in which he'd told her the story of Luigino, when Sabatello arrived. Montalbano led him out onto the veranda. The engineer sat down, looked around, and heaved a long sigh.

"You chose a nice place to live," he said. "My compliments."

"Thank you," said the inspector. "Can I get you anything?"

"I'd rather not. I don't want to take up too much of your time."

As he was saying this, he set down on the table a small bag of rough canvas that must once have been white but was now tending towards a dirty yellow.

"This bag," said Sabatello, "when I found it, was tied up with string wrapped several times around and knotted repeatedly at the ends, and finally sealed with a lead medallion. Apparently Papa didn't want anyone to open it. Here's what I found inside."

He stuck a hand in the sack and pulled out a cartridge case, which he put down in front of Montalbano.

"This must be the empty case of the bullet with which Uncle Emanuele killed himself."

"Sidoti told me it had never been found," said the inspector. "How is he, by the way?"

"The poor guy's pretty far gone by now, I'm afraid. The doctors have given up hope. At any rate, I think Papa must have looked more carefully and finally found it . . . But it seems of no importance to me. It's just part of his obsession with memory."

He then extracted a sort of large, yellowish-brown ball from the sack, made of cloth.

"This is the kerchief with which, according to Sidoti, my father wiped away his brother's blood. Over time the fabric has become extremely fragile, so I haven't even tried to open it up. And the last thing is the weirdest of all."

He pulled out an envelope and handed it to Montalbano. On it was written: *My Last Will*. But the words were crossed out with a large X in blue pencil.

The inspector extracted a small sheet of paper from the envelope and started reading:

Vigàta, 12 February 1957
Since the last diagnosis of my illness has turned out to be dire and I've been given very little time to live, I will write my final wishes in my own hand.
Naturally all my personal possessions and property shall go to my wife, who will know how best to dispose of them. But I want the apartment I own on Via Vittorio Emanuele III, number 38, in which I have my surveyor's office, to go to my business partner, Gennaro Luparello, so that he may continue working.
In witness whereof,
Francesco Sabatello

"What's so weird about it?" asked Montalbano.

"What's weird is that he saved it together with the things connected to my uncle's suicide. Even stranger is the fact that he didn't destroy it, because he later wrote a second will that was then carried out. I brought that, too."

He took this out of his jacket pocket and handed it to Montalbano.

It was exactly the same as the one he'd just read, but for two things. The first was the date: *Vigàta, 16 May 1957*; the second was the addition of a codicil:

*I leave, moreover, the five hectares of land
belonging to me, located in the Vannutello
district, to my faithful farm manager, Gaspare
Sidoti, for the trust he has always inspired in
me . . .*

"Please leave these things with me," said Montalbano.

Without a word, Sabatello put the four items back into the little bag. He then said:

"I'll just smoke a cigarette and then leave you in peace. If you happen to make some sense of these things, please . . ."

"I'll let you know immediately," said the inspector.

Since a light wind had risen, he took the bag and moved into the dining room. After emptying it out, the first thing he did was to take the two wills and line them up one beside the other. He studied them long and hard, but what struck him most was the fact that, even in the first testament, Francesco made no mention of his brother, Emanuele. Which didn't really make any sense. Why would a man so attached to his brother not take the trouble to set down in black and white any instructions to assure that this invalid would be able to continue living in a manner one could call dignified? How was it possible that he hadn't bothered to name a caretaker or chosen an assisted residence where he would have been well looked after?

It was as if Francesco had never had a brother. Whereas, at that time, Emanuele was still alive and sleeping in the room next to his brother's.

278

And so? What was the explanation?

The answer occurred to him at once, but he pushed it away just as quickly as it had come into his head. No, that wasn't possible. And yet . . . why not? Why not indeed?

Perhaps the two brothers had even discussed it, and Emanuele, in all likelihood, had told Francesco he didn't think he could carry on without him. And that was the logical solution.

Montalbano's attention was suddenly drawn to the kerchief, rolled into a ball that Sabatello didn't have the courage to unravel. He touched it, running his fingers lightly over it. It was clear that the fabric, corroded by time and by the blood it had absorbed, would give way if one pulled on it. Holding the ball in his hands for a moment, however, Montalbano felt like a diviner. Maybe, just maybe, if he untangled that mass he would find the solution.

He got up, went into the kitchen, lit a gas ring, found a saucepan, half filled it with water, then put a sieve over the pan and, finally, the ball of fabric into the sieve. Surely the steam, in dampening the ball, would allow him to open it up gently. He went out on the veranda, sat down, smoked three cigarettes in a row, and, after half an hour had passed, went back into the kitchen. The ball had softened and expanded slightly. This was going to take a while. Arming himself with a bottle of whisky and another pack of cigarettes, he sat back down on the veranda. The wind had dropped, and he distracted himself by watching the lights of the fishing boats out at sea. After another half-hour had gone by, he went back into the kitchen. There'd been some progress; the ball was almost twice its original size. He touched it, but realized that it still wasn't time. He had to be patient. He added more water to the pan and left the kitchen. Turning on the TV, he sat down in front of it and watched a film, which he liked a lot, through to the end. Who knew why the TV folks only ever broadcast the good movies late at night. He then headed back for the kitchen, convinced he could now get down to work. After turning off the gas, he took the rolled-up kerchief, now as big as a football, and set it down on the table. It took him for ever to open it up, spreading it out ever so slowly with his fingertips until the ball became a perfect square. The first thing that jumped out at him was the presence of three holes that could not have been made over time because they were all identical, concentrated in only one part of the kerchief, and all in a diagonal row.

He got up to look for a magnifying glass. Finding one, he went back to the table, examined the holes through the glass, and saw that all three were darker around the edges, clearly burnt in some way. Now he understood everything. Then he started to fold the kerchief in such a way that the holes overlapped perfectly, one on top of the other. When this was done, the kerchief was now folded over itself three times and had become a blindfold. So he picked it up, put it over his eyes, and tied it gently behind his head. The three holes were now just one, which corresponded exactly with his temple. The bullet that had entered there had never come out the other side, proof that it had remained inside Emanuele's brain. Therefore all the blood had to have come out of his mouth and nose.

If that was the way it was, then it was utterly impossible that Emanuele, mentally disabled as he was, would have been capable, all by himself, of inserting the magazine, putting a round in the chamber, folding up the kerchief, blindfolding himself, and finally shooting himself. He could only have done all that, of course, if his suicide had been assisted. Assisted by, of course, his brother, Francesco. An assisted suicide, to protect him from life, through death. Yet another form of protection that hadn't yet occurred to Montalbano. And possibly Francesco had been assisted by a third party. Maybe the bequest to Sidoti, who hadn't been mentioned in the first will, could be explained by his presence during the suicide.

He tried very hard to remember what were the exact words the farm manager had used to describe the scene he'd found before him, after hearing the gunshot. Wait . . . He said that upon hearing the shot he'd started running along the boundary wall, gone through the gate, and raced up the path, and that already halfway down the side of the villa he'd spotted Francesco embracing his brother's lifeless body. Wait . . . There was something wrong in Sidoti's account. He'd made a mistake without realizing it, because, while from the side of the villa one could not see the window of the rear bathroom, one did, however, have a partial view of the wall of the shed. In short, the story the kerchief told was not the same as the story Sidoti had told him.

He absolutely had to go and talk to him.

281

He went back out on the veranda to wait for the first rays of dawn.

At eight o'clock, all dressed up, he was about to call the hospital when the telephone rang. It was Laura Infantino.

"Good morning, Inspector, sorry for calling so early. I worked all night with Marchica, and this morning we talked to the prosecutor. I can now promise you with assurance that the boy's name, and yours, will not appear in the report of the investigation. I can also tell you that we've located the three attackers and will soon make a move on them. Thank you so much for giving me this opportunity. It was a wonderful gift."

"Thank *you*," said Montalbano.

Hanging up, he immediately rang the San Giovanni Hospital.

He identified himself, and they granted him permission to visit.

Twenty minutes later, after being shown the way — so as not to get lost as he always did in hospitals — he found himself outside a door.

"Yesterday we put him in a single room," said the nurse, "because the chief physician feared he might not make it through the night."

Montalbano opened the door and went in. The combined smell of medication and death assailed his senses, and momentarily prevented him from stepping towards the bed. All he could see of Sidoti was his bandaged head and a yellowish hand lying on the bedsheet. His eyes were closed. The inspector pulled up a chair and sat down beside him.

"Mr Sidoti," he said softly.

The dying man seemed not to have heard. "Mr Sidoti, it's Montalbano."

Perhaps it was the name that stirred Sidoti, because he slowly opened his eyes, managed to bring the inspector's face into focus, and twisted his mouth into a grimace that might have been a smile. Montalbano laid his hand on his, gripped it, and held it tight.

"Thank you," Sidoti said in a faint voice.

"For what?" Montalbano asked, not understanding.

"I was really hoping you'd come and see me."

Montalbano said nothing, but only waited in silence.

"I'd promised, for love of Ernesto, to take the secret to the grave with me . . . But now that you're here, I can tell the truth. Like to a confessor."

"Did Emanuele shoot himself in front of the shed?" asked Montalbano.

Sidoti shook his head.

"He didn't shoot himself," he said.

Montalbano froze. Everything he'd imagined fell to pieces in his mind, and the fragments began to spin about in a kaleidoscopic vortex before coming back together in an image showing an even more horrifying reality.

"Did his brother, Francesco, shoot him?" he asked, noticing that his own voice was trembling, but not Sidoti's. The man had found the strength to speak in a clear, steady voice. "When Francesco was told he wasn't going to live much longer, he sort of went crazy.

Not for his own sake, but for his brother's. He kept on repeating to me, 'I can't leave him like this, I can't leave him like this,' and he started saying, 'You gotta help me, you gotta help me,' and he would say it all the time, like he was reciting the rosary, until one day I couldn't take it any more and I said, 'Help you how?' and he looked at me and said, 'If I can't do it, you can take over.' Every day, every minute, every hour of every day, morning noon and night, he would come over to me, always saying the same things. I started having trouble sleeping at night, and then one time, just to make him stop whining and talking, I said, OK.

"Then one morning he came to me and said it was time. He ordered me to wait for him at the bottom of the stairs, and a short while later he and Emanuele came down the stairs, holding hands. They went outside, and I followed behind. Francesco took him as far as the wall of the shed and asked him: 'Wanna play blind man's buff like we used to when we were kids?' And Emanuele said, 'Yeah, yeah,' and started laughing. So Francesco took a big kerchief out of his pocket, the kind the peasant women wear, folded it up on his knee, and covered his brother's eyes with it, knotting it behind his head. Then he took the pistol out of his pocket. And at that moment he looked at me in a way that made me understand that he could manage alone. I was just frozen, I couldn't even talk, but I felt my whole chest tighten like it was in a vice, and then he said to his brother, 'OK, I'm going to count to three, and then I'll let go of you and you're going to come and look for me.' And he started counting: one, two . . . He

284

was holding his brother tight with his left arm, and then he brought the pistol up to Emanuele's head. I was keeping my eyes closed. I couldn't stand it. And then I heard 'three', and the shot. What made me open my eyes again was a sound that didn't seem human. And I saw Francesco holding his brother in his arms, dead, and wailing like an animal so loud it seemed like he wanted his cry to reach the sun and turn it black. And then he became strong as a bull, and still wailing that desperate cry, he picked up Emanuele's body and hurled it as far away as he could, and then fell to his knees. Emanuele ended up almost right under the bathroom window. I still couldn't move. Then, crawling on all fours, Francesco made his way over to his brother, took him in his arms, removed the blindfold, and starting wiping the blood off him."

Sidoti stopped talking. His breath became a hiss. Montalbano feared those might be Sidoti's last words. But the man found the strength to say more.

"Go now . . . go . . ." he whispered. "Leave me alone." The inspector got up and was releasing his hand from Sidoti's, which had held his own tight the whole time he'd spoken, but the old farmer clutched it even harder.

"But first you must swear you won't say anything to Ernesto."

"I swear," said Montalbano.

Sidoti's hand, suddenly drained of strength, let him go.

"God keep you," said the inspector.

He turned his back and rushed out of the room.

Now he understood why Francesco, while still alive, had kept on filming that fragment of wall year after year, always at the same time of the same day of the same month: to preserve for ever in his mind, still present, that heartrending moment of pure horror, to let himself sink each time anew into that mire, weeping and despairing, almost as if castigating himself in expiation.

Two cases, he thought to himself while going out to his car. Both crimes had more or less the same motive: protection. And in both cases, it would be as if he himself had never been involved in them.

On his way back to Vigàta, he crossed paths with four trucks and one bus. The crews of the TV movie were leaving. The carnival was over. The everyday grind would now resume. But first he had to think up a big, whopping lie to tell Engineer Sabatello.

Sidoti had told him the truth.

In his youth, in 1968, he, too, had cried out that telling the truth was a revolutionary act, that the truth must always be told.

No, no . . . For some time now he'd known that the truth was sometimes better kept under wraps, in the darkest darkness, without so much as the glow of a lighted match.

Author's Note

As usual, the names and events appearing in my novels are the fruit of my imagination, at least as far as I know.

This book, drafted in 2015, was the very first I wrote by dictation. And therefore my infinite thanks go to Valentina, for all her precious help.

A.C.

Notes

page *40* ***involtini*** *...* ***tinnirume***: *Involtini* are roulades, and *tinnirume* is a Sicilian word that roughly translates as "tender stuff", but refers specifically to preparations of young spring vegetables.

page *91* **"wit'a woman named Maj, an' alls I c'n say is my, my, my, oh my"**: In Italian, as in Swedish, the name Maj is pronounced the same as "my".

page *131* **"the Dicos"**: Catarella is mispronouncing the name Digos, an Italian law-enforcement agency (whose acronym stands for Divisione Investigazioni Generali e Operazioni Speciali), specializing in cases of terrorism, organized crime, and other sensitive areas.

page *147* **"4I bis"**: Article 41 bis of the Prison Administration Act is a clause allowing authorities to suspend certain prison regulations for persons convicted of Mafia crimes, terrorism, drug trafficking, kidnapping, and other serious offences. Fazio's mention of it here would seem to refer mostly to the Mafia connection. One of the purposes of the provision is to

288

isolate prisoners from other colleagues in crime who might allow them to continue their activities from prison.

page 157 **Lou Ravi in a nativity scene:** Lou Ravi ("the enraptured one"), called "Lo Spaventato" ("the awestruck one") in Italian, is the shepherd expressing astonishment in traditional Provençal and Neapolitan nativity scenes.

page 170 ***Pizza and Sfincione***: Sfincione, or sfinciuni, is a Sicilian kind of thick-crust pizza, served with a variety of different toppings.

page 171 **Maybe if he'd lived a little longer with François . . . :** François was a Franco-Tunisian boy, orphaned during an investigation by Montalbano and briefly brought into his home, whom Livia had wanted them to adopt in The Snack Thief (Picador, 2004). When Montalbano adamantly refused to adopt him, Mimì Augello's sister took him in and raised him, with her husband, on their farm. François later reappears, now fully grown, in Blade of Light (Picador, 2015) as a militant working to overthrow the government of Tunisia.

page 177 **Ucciardone prison:** An old high-security prison in Palermo, famous for holding convicted Mafiosi.

page 184 **"I wasn't even born!":** Montalbano is lying to the boy. He was born in 1950.

page 239 **the poet Trilussa's "La vispa Teresa":** Trilussa, the anagrammatic pseudonym of Carlo Alberto Camillo Mariano Salustri (1871–1950), was a Roman poet who wrote predominantly in the *romanesco* dialect of that city, often with a humoristic and satirical bent. "La vispa Teresa" ("Precocious Teresa"), written in Italian, not Roman dialect, is a continuation of a poem of the same title (also known by the alternative title "La farfalletta", or "The Little Butterfly") by the Italian poet Luigi Sailer (1825–85).

page 264 ***ova a pisciteddru***: A kind of omelette with onions, with the option of folding in a little cheese (caciocavallo, pecorino, Parmesan, etc.). (With thanks to Mary Ann Manzella Vitale.)

page 273 ***sarde a beccafico***: Sarde a beccafico is a Sicilian speciality named after a small bird, the *beccafico* (*Sylvia borin*, "garden warbler" in English), which is particularly fond of figs (*beccafico* means "figpecker"). The headless, cleaned sardines are stuffed with sautéed breadcrumbs, pine nuts, raisins, and anchovies, then rolled up in such a way that they resemble the bird when they come out of the oven.

Notes by Stephen Sartarelli